LONELY
LIES

LONELY
LIES

The Sequel to Secret Lives

S.J. BROWN

Rev. date: 01/13/2015

To order additional copies of this book, contact:
Xlibris
800-056-3182
www.Xlibrispublishing.co.uk
Orders@Xlibrispublishing.co.uk
702866

ACKNOWLEDGEMENTS

First and foremost I would like to thank all of those that have supported my 'budding' author status by purchasing and indulging in 'Secret Lives,' my first ever novel. Thank you for your patience as you awaited the arrival of 'Lonely Lies,' the sequel. The expressive joy, excitement and exhilaration conveyed by you all was pure inspiration for me to journey on and create this perplexing, incomprehensible, mystifying sequel with which, I aimed to maintain your level of anxiety and satisfy your thirst and wonderment, keeping you all captivated in the trials and tribulations that the two 'best friends' invite you to engage in. I hope I have succeeded.

Secondly I would like to thank Hanifah Miah, an AS level, Creative writing student from Joseph Chamberlain college, Birmingham who rescued me by suggesting this sequel title during a group activity (and what a fantastic group they were) when I was stumped for an idea. Well done and a huge, great big thank you, my shining star!

Last but not least I would like to thank the many who truly have genuine faith in my ability to deliver, who respect my crazy, fanatical, foolish and ludicrous mind but still leave a seat for me in the 'normal' class to grow and develop even more... Lianna Bowers and Keety B for being my right and left crutch, holding me up straight so as not to fall, Missy Powelly for keeping me on track and encouraging me to pursue my dreams, Hannah Lewis one of the first to purchase Secret Lives and edit this sequel for me. Ann Powell, Pat Bennett, Dr Cox, Tillita St Juste, Mummy Morva, Mousy, Lexy, Sandra, Shanteela, Serena Craigie, Pearl Horrell, Sara, Stella, Natty, Val, Dianna, Tamarin Smith-Viret for taking it to SA, Fiona MacIntyre for taking it to Australia, Carina Carina for taking it to NY, Lisa Dickens, Terry, Phil, Klee-K, Janet Orton, Kurtis, Isabella, JCC....oh and the list goes on, just because your name may not be mentioned it doesn't mean I have forgotten you. Thank you all!!!

The same joy you all felt reading it is the same joy I possessed creating it.

CHAPTER 1

AARON.

Nina rolled over into Aarons arms. He welcomed her into his grasp and hugged her tightly to his chest. He was totally fulfilled to have his woman back right by his side. This time was going to be different. This time they were going to do it right.

Aaron listened to Nina gently breathing and reflected back to yesterday. He took the chance he was granted and made a race against time to expel all his love to her, she had made him understand. He no longer could contain the love he possessed for her and only her. Nina had given him a second chance and he wasn't going to let it pass. He knew that it would be hard but he was ready to rise to the occasion.

"Good Morning gorgeous," he said, kissing her eyelids as they fluttered open.

She looked up at him, "Good Morning," she smiled, shuffling herself upright and stretching. "Listen Aaron I am truly sorry for everything that I…"

"Ssshh," Aaron hushed her, pressing his forefinger against her lips, "Let's not talk about it again, we have a clean slate so let's make the most of it. No more secrets and lies ok?"

"OK," Nina replied and kissed Aaron passionately like it was her very first kiss with him, "No more secrets or lies"

NINA.

Nina patted her face dry with one of Aarons fluffy blue towels whilst staring at herself in the bathroom mirror. Noticing her engagement ring glinting brightly in the morning sunlight, she questioned herself. She was supposed to be feeling over the moon, ecstatic and full of joy and excitement that Aaron wanted them to share a life together, but instead she felt guilty. Guilty that she had stood Jordan up just as they were about to make new beginnings in Atlanta, guilty that things seemed to have worked out for her when Mark and Jordan's lives were a big, fat mess and they were torn apart, both having to start again from scratch, and guilty for keeping the 'secret life' she once endured a secret from her best friend.

"Are you OK in there?" Aaron asked knocking on the bathroom door.

Nina was now residing at Aarons. He had invited her to move in with him so that they could do it properly.

Nina could not relax totally. She knew deep down that despite Aaron's actions, he would never trust her one hundred percent. Was living with him his way of keeping her under his watchful eye?

Admiring her ring once more, Nina finished up in the bathroom and mentally prepared herself for the day ahead, she knew it was going to be a challenging one.

Mr Allen her 'ex-boss' was first on her agenda, he had told her that he would put in a good word for her regarding a job with one of his associates. Although welcomed back with open arms to work once again for Mr Allen, Nina had refused. A clean relationship slate and a clean work slate where no one was aware of her past and what it involved was her preferred and a safer option. Nina didn't really have to work for a good few months if she didn't want to, but that would be rubbing salt in Aarons freshly healed wounds. She didn't want to rock the boat, but not only that - she needed a daily distraction and to have a whereabouts that was real so Aaron would not become paranoid.

Second on her agenda was to catch up with Claire over a coffee or two to enlighten her on her staying in Birmingham and her engagement to Aaron. Nina chuckled to herself, Claire probably already knew. In fact when Nina really thought about it, if it wasn't for Claire telling her to make Aaron understand via a letter she would have been on that flight to Atlanta.

Nina decided to save the most tender piece until last…Jordan.

MARK.

Sitting in his car outside of his Mother's house Mark inhaled the deepest breath of air he could muster and exhaled slowly. A storm of emotions were brewing inside of him, he had never expected this. He switched the radio on, Tracy Chapmen's 'Fast Car' filled the speakers. He laughed at the convenient irony of the song.

He had witnessed the woman he had great feelings for gallop willingly into the arms of another man. Was it his fault? He had missed his opportunity, he had procrastinated and hesitated for too long, he wasn't quick enough off the mark.

"I did it to protect everybody," he justified out loud to the invisible passengers in his car, "I saved face and spared people's feelings, I did it because I am a good man, but when will good ever grace me?"

Now he was left with Jordan and the misery of their divorce proceedings and a house that they once called a home to sell. There was nothing left between them and Mark refused to sit and exhaust himself thinking about the 'shoulda, coulda, wouldas.'

JORDAN.

Jordan lay on her sofa wrapped up in her blanket seething with anger and frustration. How could Nina build up her hopes of starting a new life together to just drop her like a die for Aaron? Jordan had given up everything she had left to accompany Nina to Atlanta for good reason and once again she lay back on her mourning sofa wrapped up in pity. She was surprised that her sofa wasn't sopping wet from all the tears she had shed on it.

Jordan knew full well that her life was a mess and all the things she thought she could run away from would remain in her presence to haunt her making her life a battle field.

Alec would forever be lurking as long as Aaron and Nina were an item. She'd have to go through the intense task of divorcing Mark and selling the house, not to mention looking for another teaching job. Basically she had to start all over again.

Nina owed her an explanation and Jordan couldn't wait until later that evening to hear her out.

CHAPTER 2

NINA.

"Aaaaaahhhhhh!" Nina and Claire screamed, arms open wide, up in the air, running towards each other, dodging tables and chairs in their faithful coffee shop on the Bearwood high street. They embraced in the most heartfelt hug, squeezing the life out of each other.

"I am sooooo glad that you decided to stay," Claire beamed with pure delight.

"I'm not too sure yet if me staying is a good thing," Nina admitted. "There are a lot of things I still have to put right Claire, and I mean a lot of things, it's going to be hard work so I have to tread carefully. People's feelings are very fragile, very fragile indeed."

"Time is the greatest healer," Claire reassured her. "You sound like you know what you are doing."

The pair drank coffee and Nina informed Claire how the letter she had told her to write, in order to make Aaron understand, must have worked. She told her how they were literally just about to leave for Atlanta, when Aaron appeared through the morning mist and proposed to her in front of Mark and Jordan.

"Wow, how romantic," Claire giggled like a teenage girl, "It sounds like a scene from a movie!"

Nina couldn't help but laugh at Claire's exhilaration, but part of her questioned why she didn't feel that same stimulation. It must have been apparent in her eyes.

"OK," Claire said, lifting Nina's chin, "Spill."

"Spill what?" Nina shrugged.

"I'm not silly. Tell me what's going on and I mean tell me everything," Claire demanded.

For some strange reason Nina felt a closer bond towards Claire than to Jordan who was supposed to be her best friend and so that afternoon, at the little coffee shop on the Bearwood high street, Nina poured her heart and soul out to Claire truthfully.

The Masquerade Ball and Mark, how he met her at the airport and revealed that he knew it was her and how he declared his love for her.

"And is the feeling mutual?" Claire asked, noticing Nina shuffle uncomfortably in her seat.

"I can honestly say no," Nina replied with certainty.

"But...?" Claire dug a little deeper, sensing that there was more.

"But I know somebody who really does love him and it's a real shame," Nina sighed.

JORDAN.

Jordan pottered around her boxed up house retrieving only the essentials for daily use. After the effort it took to pack it all up she sure as hell wasn't going to unpack it all for no good reason.

Jordan caught sight of her phone flashing, it was Nina ringing her. She picked up but didn't utter a word.

"Hello?" Nina asked unsure if Jordan had realised she had answered her phone due to the silence on the other end.

"What time are you coming Nina I have things to do," Jordan lied trying her hardest to portray her anger and agitation.

"I'm on my way, I'll be ten minutes."

With that said Jordan hung up the phone without even saying goodbye.

Ten minutes later Jordan and Nina were sitting face to face at Jordan's kitchen table in total silence. It was so awkward that the fly that accidentally flew in through the open window, purposely flew back out right away.

With her impatient self, Jordan broke the silence and was the first to speak.

"So tell me Nina, why did you and Aaron split up in the first place and is he worth you staying? Have you really thought things through or are you going to string him along like you did to me just to drop him like a die? Do you even know what you really want from life?"

Nina knew that Jordan was angry with her and the situation she had left her in. After all it was her who had coaxed Jordan into being spontaneous and accompanying her to Atlanta, therefore to change her mind for Aaron with no regard for Jordan, the cold shoulder was only a small fraction of what she deserved.

Nina stared hard at Jordan pondering whether to tell her about her secret life as an escort.

"It's complicated Jordan and to be honest I don't really want to discuss it, that was the past and Aaron and I have decided to move on and start over afresh. We are holding an engagement party next month and we would both be very grateful if you would be a part of it."

"How?" Jordan grunted.

"I was hoping 'Miss Queen of all parties,' you would help to organise it?" Nina distracted Jordan and teased her.

Jordan cracked a smile, she loved organising events and she saw this as a great project to prove herself. "OK I will, but don't opt out at the last minute and tell me you and Aaron have split again," Jordan bitched.

"Listen Jordan, I am so sorry for what I put you through and whatever I can do to fix this please let me know, I made this mess and I need to clean it up."

Nina noticed a tear roll down Jordan's cheek. She could sense the hurt and distrust, the loneliness and heartache. She was clearly down in the dumps and Nina had to be a friend and try her hardest to lift her spirits. After all, she was a contributing factor as to why Jordan was feeling so low. She put her cup down and walked around the table to where Jordan was seated and hugged her tightly, squeezing her as if trying to free the pain from deep within.

"I know...I'm so sorry I truly am," Nina soothed her friend.

The rest of the evening the girls spent unpacking and rearranging Jordan's house to make it look as appealing as possible, in order to be sold quickly. Jordan wanted out and to start afresh ASAP.

Tired and hungry, the girls ordered a takeaway and sat in the living room munching and chomping away.

"So when you say I'm in charge of organising your engagement party, do you really mean it?" Jordan queried, scared to believe a word that came out of Nina's mouth.

"I said so, didn't I?" Nina laughed nervously becoming a little anxious as to what Jordan had up her sleeve. "I know you Jordan, what are you up to?"

"Nothing, I just needed to know. Does that mean I can pick the venue, the caterers, the décor...?"

"Yes."

"Ok, with that established, how many are on the guest list?"

Nina threw a cushion at Jordan and they both laughed, it felt good to be the terrible two again.

CHAPTER 3

JORDAN.

Although her evening with Nina didn't answer her questions she learnt that she had to get up and proceed with putting her life back together just like it seemed everyone else was doing. This time she was going to do it according to her complete satisfaction. She refused to be dependent on a man financially or emotionally. This time it was all about making herself happy and being content within herself even if it meant finding herself amongst a pile of self help books.

Things would have to get worse before they got better, that she knew and it all started with Mark - the divorce and selling the house.

MARK.

Mark sat on his Moms couch devouring some of his Moms homemade cooking which she had prepared, frozen and labelled for him before she had flown home to Jamaica for a month. Savouring each mouthful and smacking his lips his phone rang. Wiping his fingers on a piece of kitchen towel he read the caller display noticing it was Jordan. He had been anticipating this moment as she now was not going to Atlanta.

He cleared his throat before answering in his laid back tone. "Hello."

"Hi Mark it's me, Jordan."

"What's up?" He asked her looking at his plate of food hoping the call wouldn't last too long so he could get stuck right back into his grub.

"As I am not going away now I thought it would be best if we got straight on with the divorce proceedings and the selling of the house, it's what we both want so why prolong the necessary," Jordan stated without beating around the bush.

"I see you are still speaking and making all the decisions for the both of us, huh?" Mark remarked snidely.

Jordan adopted an attitude, "Are you serious?"

"Whatever. You speak to your Solicitor and I'll speak to mine, I'd rather complete this with as little to do with you as personally possible," he stated bluntly with no concern for Jordan's feelings.

"Ditto!" Jordan snapped back. She was going to treat him exactly how he treated her from now on.

Mark hung up and pushed his plate aside. He had suddenly lost his appetite. He hated the fact that she was staying, in fact he regretted the day that he decided to marry her and make a life together. Even back then he should have known from her selfish ways and bossy demeanour that she truly wasn't the one for him. Her moods, her attitude and regimented ways. He had witnessed how spiteful she could be especially if she felt threatened by someone else. The cons outweighed the pros in their relationship and the fact that she ended up being the unfaithful one astonished him to the brink. How could someone who pranced around so full of morals do such a thing? Still up to this day Mark was in total shock. Shocked at himself for not noticing the warning signs and ending up being taken for a fool. Well he was only going to play the fool once.

Placing his plate in the microwave in hope of finishing his food later, (hearing his Mothers voice in his head, 'Do not waste food, there are plenty of starving people in this world') he felt that he could do with going to the pub with a mate. Aaron. That was out of the question on his part really, knowing that he'd slept with Nina and also how he felt towards her and now the two were engaged to be married. He couldn't cope with that but he had to figure out some sort of control as he couldn't avoid Aaron forever, Aaron would surely catch on that something was wrong.

Nina and Jordan staying seemed to be more trouble than it was worth.

NINA.

"You got home late last night, did you have good day with your friends?" Aaron asked Nina.

Friends? Nina thought. He doesn't know I went to see Claire as well as Jordan yesterday. In fact he doesn't even know Claire exists, or does he? Nina instantly came to the conclusion that Aaron had followed her due to his paranoia concerning her whereabouts, checking to see if she was escorting again and then questioning her to see if she told the truth.

She knew this would happen.

"Jordan was ok. We set her house in order so it looks more appealing and ready to sell and then we had a takeaway. It was nice," Nina smiled at Aaron, not even entertaining the plural to his question, testing to see if he'd have the nerve to probe deeper.

"That's nice," he smiled.

Nina then remembered the promise they had made to each other, no more lies and secrets. She decided to tell him.

"Lunch time I went to meet a friend I used to work with for coffee and a catch up," Nina quickly slipped in.

Aaron smiled a little wider, "Are you going to miss working with her in the future?"

Nina wasn't sure if he'd asked because he really cared or if he was just relieved that she had told him what he wanted to hear.

Nina tried to warrant to herself that she had told the truth, after all she used to work with Claire.

Aaron surprised Nina with a candle lit, deep, hot, bubble bath that night. As Nina lay between Aarons legs, her head resting against his chest, he played with the bubbles placing them on top of her head, on her nose and her chin.

"So you want to play huh?" She laughed shaking the bubbles off of her giggling at his childish behaviour.

"Hell yeh!" Aaron said spinning her around to face him smoothing her wet hair out of her face and staring at her intensely.

"What?" She asked, holding his gaze, wondering what he was thinking.

"Nothing…" Aaron trailed off stroking her face.

"Tell me," Nina demanded biting on his bottom lip.

"It's just that I never thought I'd hold you in my arms again. I missed you so much when we were apart. I used to envision us showering together, I wished I would wake up to you in my arms, your scent still lingers on my t-shirt. I couldn't tell anyone that we had split, not even my eldest nephew Alec.

Nina was astonished, she didn't think that she had been a part of his thoughts so deeply and frequently.

"I thought about you too baby, every single moment of every single day." She kissed his chest, "I do love you."

Nina had never admitted those words or felt the way she did towards anyone ever in her life. She had no regrets telling him so because it was real. She remembered that gnawing pain of being without him and she didn't want to feel that way ever again. It was a pain that ate away at her mind every minute of every day. A pain there was no remedy for. The cause was the cure and so the cure was Aaron. Once he was back in her arms she felt whole once again.

"I love you too beautiful," Aaron said, kissing Nina's juicy lips.

Aaron wrapped Nina up in a large, towel and carried her to the bedroom. He gently placed her on to his bed and opened up the towel she lay on revealing her pristine body. He poured some baby oil into the palm of his hand. Rubbing his hands together he gently stroked Nina down from head to toe, her soft groans indicated pure satisfaction. As she lay on her front Aaron planted sweet, wet kisses down the length of her spine and then playfully he bit her bum cheeks. Nina giggled as he nibbled on her ear lobes before he entered her love box from behind. She gasped at the unexpected as she felt Aaron swell deep inside of her. He slowly thrust in and out of her with gentle strokes admiring how her body glistened in the darkness of his room. He pulled out and flipped her over on to her back passionately kissing and sucking on her breasts. He flicked and licked her nipples before entering her again, this time placing her legs upon his shoulders.

Their lovemaking session continued into the early hours of the morning, both of them shattered. They had exhausted themselves into a well earned sleep.

CHAPTER 4

JORDAN.

Jordan was back up on her 'high horse,' she was on a role and nothing could get in her way because she simply wasn't having it.

The house had had four viewings that week, two of which promised to get back to her. Her Solicitor was on her and Marks divorce case and she was in her element, steady organising Nina's engagement party.

Jordan had decided not to look for another teaching job as of yet, not until she had sold the house and got herself a nice little one bedroomed flat. She even thought about having a cat if she got a ground floor flat. It would keep her company, something to come home to. She was never very good at being lonesome.

Gathering together what she had titled her, 'engagement project,' she placed it in her Fossil bag, had a quick shower sprucing herself up for the day ahead.

As the days passed she slowly but surely began to feel herself once again but this time she was adopting a different attitude towards life. This time she came first. Mark had made it more than clear how he felt about her and that she had accepted.

Scooping her hair up into a neat ponytail, she put on her tweed blazer, grabbed her keys and phone and headed to Aarons to discuss the ideas and plans so far for Nina's engagement party.

Nina buzzed Jordan in greeting her at the door.

Kicking her KG's off on to the mat, Jordan wondered around Aarons flat. "That's a nice picture," she said, complimenting a picture of Aaron posing with someone beside him that looked a complete replica. "Who's that?" She asked nosily, picking the picture up and having a closer look.

"That's Aaron's brother," Nina said lowering her tone, "between us, he is in prison at the moment. That is Alec and Antoine's dad, it's quite a touchy subject, I see how it affects Aaron sometimes as he missed out on quite a bit of his nephews lives," Nina finished.

Jordan already knew from what she learnt from Alec when he was her well behaved, obedient student.

"Why are you speaking so quietly?" Jordan asked.

"Aaron's nephew is in the spare room asleep, the poor thing is exhausted, Aaron will be back to take him out in a little while."

"Oh I see," Jordan smiled reminiscing on the time Antoine stayed and the sight of him sleeping peacefully on Marks chest sucking his thumb. The two had become very fond of each other.

"Earth calling Jordan," Nina waved her hands in front of Jordan's face trying to release her from her trance like state.

Eventually the girls got around to the engagement party plans. Anyone would have thought it was Jordan's party the way she had to have everything perfect to the 'T'. It was all so classy and sophisticated. Nina more than adored the posh invitations which Jordan was ecstatic over as her next stop that day was to go and pick them up.

Nina lay on the sofa in her leggings and t-shirt stuffing her face with last nights pizza which Jordan had refused. Being the 'snob' she was, she didn't eat 'old food.' Nina paid her zero attention as she was used to her ways, some things you just couldn't change.

"That's your third slice, are you pregnant?" Jordan blurted out with no thought.

"Erm…no, I'm just peckish!" Nina scowled, throwing a cushion at Jordan.

"It's just that when I was pregnant, although not very far gone, I was constantly stuffing my gob and pizza was the one thing that satisfied my craving. Sometimes…"

"Sometimes what?" Nina asked, more interested in her food than Jordan having a moment.

"Sometimes I wonder what my life would have been like if I didn't have an abortion?"

Nina sat bolt upright choking on her pizza, "YOU WHAT?!" she said loud enough for the neighbours to hear. "You said you lost it, you friggin liar, and I felt sorry for you Jordan, why the lies? Why couldn't you have the child? What was so bad about the situation that you felt you had to do that?"

Jordan huffed it off and quickly started getting her stuff together totally embarrassed at the slip of her tongue, putting her KG's and jacket on out in the hallway with Nina following right behind. "I just had to," she simply stated, "it belonged to a menace, a menace to society and I refused to punish the child by bringing it into this world."

"But no one asks to be born Jordan and you could have tried your best, I'm sure you would have been fine. You have me," Nina tried to reassure her but it was too late.

"I don't have anybody but me and I knew I couldn't have done it alone!" Jordan grunted through gritted teeth.

Suddenly the bedroom door handle tweaked and both ladies jumped turning their heads as the door opened and Alec stepped out of the bedroom with a dark, menacing look in his eyes, only a look that Jordan noticed.

"Hey sleepy head," Nina ruffled his curly hair playfully trying to sway the situation, "Did you sleep ok? Did we wake you?" Nina tried to act like everything was cool.

Alec glanced past Jordan and turned to Nina ruffling her hair the same way she had ruffled his and laughed mocking her, "I'm cool thanks." He then turned back to face Jordan, "So Hi, how's it going?" he asked as cool as a cucumber.

Jordan's mouth suddenly became as dry as the 'Sandman's' at that precise moment. She tried sucking up enough saliva to respond without him sensing her panic and nervousness. "I'm fine thanks Alec," was all the small quantity of saliva would allow her to say.

Alec waved a goodbye before he passed them both and went into the kitchen.

"Typical male huh?" Nina said trying to justify Alec's submissive behaviour.

Jordan continued getting the last of her things together all the while avoiding eye contact with Nina. Nina opened the door for her, "Call me later ok?"

"OK," Jordan said, halfway down the communal corridor, she just had to get out of there, she felt hot and suffocated.

As soon as Jordan got inside of her car she wound the window right down and nestled her head in the steering wheel, 'Did he hear me say I had an abortion?' She started to fret, she had told him she had a miscarriage, infact she had told everybody she had a miscarriage. 'Oh my gosh what if he'd heard?' She muttered out loud to herself. 'I thought it was little Antoine asleep in there not him.' Jordan was on edge, Alec always made her feel this way by hardly doing or saying anything at all. Nobody knew who she was pregnant for except Aaron and Alec of course but she had a gut feeling that it wouldn't be a secret for much longer. Just when she thought she had gotten herself together.

NINA.

As Nina finished showering she heard the front door.

"Hello!" Aaron and Alec shouted as they entered the flat.

"Hiyah!" Nina greeted them from behind the bathroom door, "I'm just finishing up in here then I'll be in the bedroom preparing my stuff for my interview tomorrow!" She shouted as she wrapped herself up in her towel. She cleaned out the shower and then grabbed the baby oil before journeying across the hallway towards the bedroom. On her way she noticed that the living room door was closed. Never had she known Aaron to pull the door to, in fact he never pulled any of the doors to. Tip toeing a little closer, she stood against the door ready to move rapidly to the bedroom if they came out. She listened as to what conversation the two were so engrossed in.

"She told me she had a miscarriage," she heard Alec say.

"Does it matter now?" Aaron asked him, "it's done, let's move on."

"I thought I had uncle but hearing that she 'killed' my baby and then had the audacity to lie to me about it has made matters worse!"

"Lower your tone, Nina's in the other room," Aaron pleaded.

Nina couldn't believe her ears, she refused to listen to anymore. She fled as nifty as possible so as not to make a sound and escaped into the bedroom closing the door behind her. She sat on the edge of the bed frozen, she couldn't even begin to oil her skin she was so shocked. 'Oh Jordan, Jordan, Jordan,' she mumbled shaking her head. It all began to make sense now, it fit like a glove. Whenever Alec's name was mentioned Jordan would automatically try to change the subject, she would become uncomfortable and start fidgeting or disappear. Nina remembered her 'Birthday' dinner that Jordan had held for her and when the topic of bowling with Aarons nephews came up, she'd observed how pale Jordan had turned, the guilty look in her eyes.

Alec must have overheard the conversation between Jordan and herself earlier that afternoon, hence the tension in the atmosphere when he awoke from his slumber and made his presence known, she reflected.

"Hmmph!" Nina puffed eventually rubbing oil into her hands and along her legs. As she rubbed the excess oil through her hair she suddenly stopped. It just then occurred to her that Aaron knew all along what had happened with Jordan and Alec. But wasn't he pals with Mark? Did Mark know about Alec? Nina had a big bunch of unanswered questions. She wondered if she should let sleeping dogs lie or wake them. She then thought about her secret being poked. Would she like that?

Just as she was dressing into her pyjamas she heard the front door close and a knock on the bedroom door, "Baby, it's me," Aaron said, entering the room. "Mmmm, you smell sweet," he said sniffing and kissing her neck.

"Is everything ok? I heard the front door close," Nina asked with fake concern trying to push him off her trying not to laugh as his lips tickled her neck.

"Yeh, Alec has gone, he told me to tell you 'bye' as he didn't want to disturb you."

"Oh, ok," Nina smiled laying out her interview outfit.

Aaron sat on the edge of the bed admiring her organised and meticulous mannerisms, everything had to be matching and colour co-ordinated.

"Have you heard from Mark?" Nina asked Aaron randomly, curious as to what he'd say. She had her back to him as she continued hanging up her clothes.

"Why do you ask that?" Aaron screwed up his face and spun her around to face him.

"Because…you are both good friends and I want him to be at our party regardless of what is going on between him and Jordan. They'll have to learn to be civil to each other and act like the adults they're supposed to be," Nina preached.

Nina was still finding it difficult to shake off what she had just discovered. Part of her was desperate to know if Mark was aware that Alec was the one Jordan had had an affair with. She decided that after her job interview the next morning she was going to pay Jordan a visit as she still hadn't received the call that Jordan had promised her earlier that day.

CHAPTER 5

JORDAN.

Ding dong! Ding dong! Ding dong!

"OK, OK, OK!" Jordan shouted clambering down the stairs at full speed to answer her front door. Whoever it was had scared her out of her sleep. She wanted to stay in bed until at least noon but it didn't seem like that was going to happen. Fumbling through the keys for the correct one to open the door to the person on the other side who would not stop ringing the bell caused her to drop them in a frenzy. "Just stop ringing the bell, I'm opening the door god dammit!!!" She screamed becoming hot and angry.

No sooner had she opened the door, Alec barged his way into her house, pushing her aside and marching his way through into her hallway. Jordan stumbled but managed to catch herself from falling by grabbing onto the door frame. She slammed her front door shut and stared at Alec.

"What...?!"

Alec didn't give her a chance to speak, "You liar!" He shouted directly in her face, "You killed my baby and passed it off as a miscarriage like it was nothing. I never thought you could stoop so low!" He began clutching his curls and grinding his teeth.

Jordan began to feel frightened at witnessing Alec's rage, who knew what he was going to do next. His face was scarlet red with anger, sweat beads formed above his brow and his eyes glistened with tear film, he looked about ready to explode.

Ding dong! Ding dong!

MARK.

Mark hated to have to see Jordan but this visit was a must. She still possessed a box of stuff that belonged to him with his personal documents and papers, ones which his Solicitor had requested.

As he stood outside of her door ringing the bell he heard some commotion going on inside the house so he rang the bell a few more times. "Jordan it's me Mark!" He shouted becoming more and more impatient banging his fist on the front door.

The door swung open and Mark was greeted by a red faced Alec. He saw Jordan standing as still as a statue in the hallway looking timid and scared, in her pyjamas with tears in her eyes.

"What's going on?" Mark asked.

Jordan began to walk off but Alec refused to let her get away so easily, it was time she took responsibility for her actions like the rest of them had to. He grabbed her arm and pulled her back so she stood in the middle of himself and Mark, "Tell him!" Alec demanded.

Mark looked from Alec to Jordan and vice versa, "Tell me what?" He asked calmly. He knew something was wrong but he refused to react until he knew exactly what it was all about.

NINA.

Nina felt that her interview went well, she had answered all of the questions to the best of her ability and noticing accepting smiles from the panel she was confident that there was a good chance she had the job. Thanks to Mr Allen and his contacts she had applied for a part time position that funded a college course for her to expand her qualifications.

Feeling happy inside she drove towards Jordan's house, there were a few loose ends that needed tying up from yesterday. Nina was glad that she had had her interview that morning so she could devote her time and attention to Jordan for the remainder of the day.

Pulling up on Jordan's drive she noticed that Mark's car was also present. As she stepped out of her Audi A1 she heard shouting and nearing Jordan's front door she noticed that it was open. Mark was standing in the hallway with Alec surrounding Jordan. 'Oh no.' Nina thought to herself, if she was to guess then it was that something was about to go down and it had something to do with Jordan and the baby saga.

"Tell me what?!" Mark asked for a second time, his voice echoing off the hall walls.

Nina's heels clicked on the tiled floor causing all eyes to turn in her direction. "What's going on?" She asked noticing the intense and confused emotions scribed all over each and every one of their faces. "I can hear you from down the driveway so God knows what the neighbours can hear. Jordan?" She asked.

Jordan just simply looked at Nina through teary eyes, a pleading look that begged her to help her out of a sticky situation, a look that begged her to work a magic trick that she may have up her sleeve, a look that begged for comfort and protection from the two monsters that were sure to attack her as soon as she answered their questions.

With no reply Nina turned to Alec. "Alec, what are you doing here?" Again no reply but the heavy panting sounds exhaling from his nostrils.

"Mark?" He was her last hope of making some sort of sense out of the situation.

"That's the same thing I want to know," he said. "Well?" He asked Jordan yet again.

"I...I...I..." She began to cry.

"WHAT?!" Mark became frustrated, he couldn't take anymore.

"I didn't have a miscarriage I went and had an abortion."

"I wouldn't put it past you and your selfish ways but what has this whole ordeal got to do with me?" Mark hadn't yet caught on, "It wasn't my baby," he said without a care.

Nina remained quiet, she knew the storm was brewing and in a matter of seconds it was about to rain.

"She aborted MY child!" Alec confirmed.

Every muscle in Mark's body instantly tensed before their eyes, he clenched his fists tightly and punched Alec square in the face bursting his bottom lip. "After everything we did for you!" He cursed out watching as Alec wiped the blood from his mouth on his sleeve.

Nina noticed Alec clenching his fist also and thought it best to ring Aaron to get to Jordan's pronto, this was going to get messy and there was only so much she could do.

AARON.

Aaron was grateful for his lunch break, he had had such a busy morning at work, all he wanted to do was sit in his car and devour his 'Big Mac.' Just as he reached for his McDonalds from the drive through hatch his phone rang. He pressed the retriever on his car steering wheel to answer the call. "What's up baby?" He asked Nina.

"Baby it's me, you need to get to Jordan's house right away, there's a problem, please hurry!" Nina said in a panic.

"Calm down baby, what kind of problem? Talk to me."

"There's no time to talk Aaron just get here now!" She ordered him. With that the line went dead.

Aaron drove as quickly as he could to Jordan's to see for himself what all the fuss was about and just a Nina had said, there was trouble, big trouble. He could hear the goings on from inside his car as he pulled up on to Jordan's drive parking amongst the other numerous cars.

He couldn't believe what he saw. His nephew and Mark were engaged in a full on fist fight and it was spiralling out of control. Both Nina and Jordan stood helplessly afraid to intervene in case either one of them got hurt, therefore it was up to him to put a stop to this.

"Stoppit!" Aaron shouted using all his strength to drag Alec off of Mark.

Marks chest heaved up and down as he tried to calm himself down. He wanted to beat the living daylights out of Alec, student, boy, nephew, whatever he didn't give a damn at that exact moment.

"What's going on?" Aaron eventually asked restraining a trying Alec.

"Ask him!" Mark spat.

Aaron looked at Alec, "You didn't?" He questioned his nephew.

"I had to Uncle, I couldn't let her think that she could get away with it, like it meant nothing. Why should I always be the bad guy, the menace?!"

Marks eyes darted between Aaron and Alec. He began walking towards Aaron who moved in front of Alec acting as his armour.

"Wait a minute," Mark said pointing his finger as if he was about to poke out both Aarons eyes, "Are you telling me that you knew all along about him and Jordan? How long have you known? I know he's your nephew Aaron but damn man, I...I thought you were my friend."

Aaron saw the hurt in Marks eyes and he knew that there was nothing he could say to rectify the situation. He felt guilty as sin and sometimes hated that Alec had such a quick temper. Why did he never listen? Why was he so full of fire? Just like his dad. "Mark it wasn't like that," Aaron tried to explain.

"So what was it like then Aaron? Huh?" And before he knew what hit him Mark had thrown a flying punch straight to Aarons nose. Everyone heard the awful cracking sound and watched as blood spurted, flying through the air.

Aaron saw stars and became unsteady on his feet, Nina ran forward to steady him. Jordan tried to grab Mark and push him out the door but it was too late, before anyone could blink, Alec had picked up one of Jordan's stone ornamental pieces off the hallway table and clobbered Mark around the head. After one almighty blow Mark hit the floor with a loud 'thud!' and lay still, out cold.

Silence.

Blood trickled from the back of his head leaking a crimson pool. The pool slowly started creeping outwards.

Jordan screamed at the top of her lungs and bent down onto her knees her tears dripping all over Marks face. "What have you done?!"

"Quick!" Nina grabbed her phone and dialled 999.

CHAPTER 6

JORDAN.

Jordan stroked Marks face, inspecting all of the tubes and wires that trailed from his lifeless body and stemmed to the great beeping machines that were keeping him alive. It had been a week and he still was showing no signs of awakening from his coma.

Jordan couldn't function. Every day she would make her way to the QE hospital to spend time by his bedside pleading him to wake up, talking to him and touching him in hope of him gracing her with his presence back into her world. She would then go home and toss and turn, hardly boosting her energy levels before doing it all over again. She had lost weight from just pecking at bits of food here and there like a baby bird, her eyes were puffy and swollen from the constant crying and her head ached as if a marching band were playing the drums right there inside of her head.

Dragging her chair closer to Marks bedside, she gripped his hand firmly and lay her head on his arm and wept.

"Please come back to me so we can put this right. I know I am to blame for all of this, I know it's my fault but I promise you I never thought it would come to this. I don't care about the house or the divorce, all I care about is you. Please come back to me I need you Mark…" Tears cascaded down her cheeks following in the ready made trails from the previous days of constant crying..

NINA.

Nina arrived at the hospital, considering she had just started her new job, her boss had been very sympathetic towards her and had granted her an extended lunch break if she made up the time. She had made trips every other day for the past week to be by Marks side. He was her friend and regardless of anything he was of great importance to her.

Someone had once told her that although one was in a coma, talking to them and touching them could encourage them to wake up. She had nothing to lose so that is what she did each time she made her visit.

She marched up the corridor stopping right outside Marks room. Through the glass window on the door she saw Jordan weeping over Marks body, her head buried in the crevice of his arm. Nina's heart ached for her, especially when it came to Mark. Even though she had had an affair with Alec and the whole baby episode, there was no need for this drama it was all uncalled for, look at what had become of everybody. The consequences were dire.

Alec was nowhere to be found, no one had heard from him since the day he had clobbered Mark to the ground. He had fled the scene just before the ambulance and the police had arrived. No one had uttered a word concerning him, instead it was passed off as a fight between Aaron and Mark, Mark falling and banging his head.

Nina was getting it from all angles. Not only did she have to console Jordan she also had to return home to Aaron who was still very much upset at the way Mark had handled things. In his eyes Mark was the adult in comparison to Alec but the way he threw punches left right and centre you wouldn't have thought so. "If he had talked things through instead of attacking people at every opportunity maybe none of this would have happened," he repeated over and over like a broken record.

The way Nina saw it was they were all as bad as each other, Aaron and Jordan included.

Nina gently opened the door and creeped in. Jordan didn't even hear or notice her enter. Lightly touching Jordan's shoulder Nina pulled her off of Mark and into her arms. Holding her tightly she gently rubbed her back.

"I just wish he would wake up."

Handing her a tissue Nina told Jordan to go home. "You are in no fit state to be here. What if he wakes up, do you want him to see you like this? A wreck? I know it's hard but you have to be strong for him, we all have to be strong together. Go home babes and get some sleep, if not, at least get some rest and I'll bring you something to eat later on after I have finished work ok? Now wipe those tears from your eyes, you need to see clearly in order to get home safely."

Jordan did as she was told, picked up her bag and jacket and squeezed Nina's hand before she left.

"Right Mr Man," Nina said manoeuvring the chair that Jordan had sat on in a position to suit herself, "I have had such a busy morning at work and I'm starving. If you would just wake up now, you and I could indulge in something delicious together, I would even let you pick what you fancy, what do you say huh?" She asked him, tapping his hand. "We all need you with us over here Mark, all of us, what happened no longer matters," she told him trying to hold back the tears that involuntarily welled up in her eyes. "If I didn't know any better I'd say you are just waiting to make your usual grand entrance, all eyes on you eh?" She sat staring at him as if waiting for a reply. She kissed his hand and let a tear free itself. "If you love me the way you told me you do then come back to me," she threatened him wholeheartedly. It had been a week and Nina was beginning to lose faith.

Nina was unaware that Aaron was watching and listening through the glass window on the other side of the door.

AARON.

After what he had heard from the other side of the door at the hospital Aaron decided to make an appearance later that evening instead. From what he gathered the 'love' that Nina was talking about was not a 'friendship' kind of love.

Aaron was woken up from his nap by Nina's key in the front door. "Hellooooo," she sang out, kicking her shoes off in the hallway and making her way into the living room where Aaron lay on the sofa. She placed her handbag on the floor and knelt down beside him stroking his face careful of his nose, planting a kiss on his forehead. The hospital had secured it the best way they could, it was just going to take some time to heal. "Can I get you anything?" She asked him.

"I'm fine thanks." He didn't want to let her know what he had heard at the hospital, not for now anyway.

"I saw Jordan at the hospital today and she's in a terrible state, she's not coping well at all so I said I would take her some food around and I think I will stay there for a night or two until she picks up, you know, give her some company and support," Nina told Aaron.

Aaron sat himself up and cocked his head to one side and looked up at Nina as if she was crazy, "Support?" He asked. "If it wasn't for her lying and cheating ways none of us would be in this predicament," he said raising his voice.

"You're a fine one to speak," Nina stabbed back. "At what point were you going to tell me or Mark about the whole ordeal? Then this could have been prevented."

"I was protecting him!" Aaron defended Alec.

Nina got up and left the room making her way to the bedroom but not before firing back at him, "Well he never gave a damn about you or anyone else for that matter when he decided to clobber Mark around the head did he?" With that said she rapidly started packing an overnight bag for Jordan's, she hated confrontation so the quicker she got out of there the better.

Aaron got up off the sofa and followed her into the bedroom, "Maybe you should consider staying at Jordan's until you decide where you want to be."

Nina came to a halt with her packing and placed her arm akimbo. "What's that supposed to mean?" She asked astonished at the words that had just escaped his mouth.

"Nothing," he said and turned to walk away.

Nina couldn't believe that the one time she disagreed with him he didn't hesitate to push her away. "Well just to let you know, there will be no engagement party until Mark wakes up," Nina stated firmly before leaving the flat and getting into her car.

She hated arguments and rowing, she especially hated having to live with someone in their home. She missed her own abode, her own space, her haven. She was never that woman to be put out by her ear. Maybe Aaron was right, maybe she needed to decide where she wanted to be, was she ready for commitment?

Aaron decided to shower and go and sit by Marks bedside. He wanted him to wake up for a majority of reasons. Everything was shaky and unstable. Things needed some normalcy, he needed his friend back and he wanted to marry Nina but he had to be sure where her heart lay before he made that commitment.

Aaron approached Marks room and stopped. Looking through the glass he saw both of his nephews by Marks bedside, Antoine was nestled in Alec's lap.

Aaron stood admiring them both, it didn't matter what they did he would always try to understand and be there for them both.

"Hey big man," Alec said, "little man here was asking for you, he said he hadn't seen you in while and he misses you. I told him you were having a little sleep and that you would wake up soon. He wants you to take him to the cinema to watch the new Superman film in 3D. He's made you a goody bag."

"Yeh so hurry up and wake up sleepy head," Antoine added.

Aaron watched as Antoine jumped out of Alec's lap and placed Mark's 'goody bag' on his bedside cabinet and then gently kissed his forehead.

"Why are you crying?" Antoine asked Alec, noticing a tear slide down his cheek.

Wiping the tear away as quickly as he could he smiled at his brother, "I'm not crying cheeky," he said tickling his little brother. "You know I love you right?" He grabbed Antoine's face and kissed it all over.

"I love you to, cry baby," Antoine teased him kissing him back.

Aaron moved from the door and leaned with his back against the wall crouching to his knees. He rubbed his hands over his face, he had to get out of there yet again.

CHAPTER 7

JORDAN

With Nina stopping over at her house for the past couple of days, Jordan had no other choice but to get herself together, after all, Nina was right, the last thing she wanted was for Mark to wake up and see her a total mess.

"I've decided to continue with the 'engagement party' planning," Jordan told Nina at breakfast that morning. "It'll be a great distraction as well as something nice for Mark when he wakes up."

Nina didn't really know what to say, the way Jordan said it all nonchalantly as if she knew when Mark was going to rise and shine ready to attend the party. Not only that but Nina hadn't let on to Jordan that her and Aaron were going through a rough patch already.

If Mark did wake up who even knew what the repercussions of the ordeal would be. After all it was his head, skull…brain!

Trying to put all the negative thoughts to the back of her mind she believed it was better for her friend to be in a stronger position than she had been and if it meant her planning the engagement party then so be it. Thinking about it all she decided to make things up with Aaron…life's too short.

"Sounds like a plan to me, proceed indeed!" Nina said acting out a saluting action to Jordan making her laugh for the first time in a long time.

Kissing Jordan on the cheek and wishing her a good day, Nina left for work.

After brekkie with Nina, Jordan put her Beyonce album on and took a nice long shower. She had a power shower so after lathering her body wash all over her body and scrubbing from head to toe, she stood against the tiles and let the water droplets beat heavily against her body. Stepping out of the shower she wrapped herself up snugly in a fresh, towel and fell on to her bed, closing her eyes she whispered into the air, "Wake up Mark, wake up please."

Town was on her agenda that day to do some 'party planning,' so she made sure she dressed comfortably. She wore her skinny Levi's and her Zara t-shirt and Zara slippers. She slipped on her blue Mango blazer and grabbed her Miu Miu shades to hide her still puffy eyes. Before stepping out the door she inhaled a deep breath and instructed herself that with a positive attitude, positive things would prevail.

After accomplishing her tick list and feeling all proud of herself she thought she'd earned a jacket potato for lunch. Heading for Sainsbury's, rushing up the cobbled alley way by the Britannia hotel, BUMP!

"Sorry!" Jordan gasped looking at a sophisticated, classy, dressed blonde lady to see if she had caused her any harm.

"No, no, it was my fault I wasn't watching where I was going, don't worry," she said a little flustered.

As Jordan tried to help her pick up the contents of her bag (she could tell that the lady didn't really want the help) she realised that she knew her.

"Claire?" She queried.

The woman looked up and stared at Jordan, "Jordan?"

"Yes!" Jordan smiled full of excitement. The first and last time they had met was the night her and Nina were celebrating leaving for America. "Long time, how are you?" Jordan asked Claire.

"I'm doing fine, infact I'm even better knowing that the both of you chose to stay. You know I would have really missed Nina a lot, she is such a good friend."

"Things happen for a reason," Jordan told her. "Listen Claire I don't mean to be rude but I am starving and I was on my way to get a jacket potato from Sainsbury's..."

"No worries," Claire cut in, "I'm in a bit of a hurry myself so you go and get some lunch and we'll meet up soon."

"Oh, Claire," Jordan called her back quickly, "before you go, just to let you know that as Nina said 'yes' to marry Aaron, they are having an engagement party and I'm in charge of organising it," Jordan bragged,

"Therefore I was wondering if I could have your contact details so I can sort out an invitation for you?"

"No problem," Claire said as she began rummaging through her handbag.

Jordan noticed that she had not one, but two phones.

They exchanged numbers and went their separate ways.

As Claire walked away Jordan spotted a little silver case shining on the floor. She picked it up thinking that Claire must have dropped it. "I'll give it to Nina later to give to pass it back to her." All that was on Jordan's mind was food as she briskly walked to her destination.

After finishing her potato, Jordan made her way to the car park, digging into the depths of her bag for her car keys she came across the silver case that belonged to Claire. Getting into her car she sat down and curiosity got the better of her. She opened it up and came across a set of business cards. Jordan put her hand over her mouth dumbfounded. In that one moment a million things came together to make one.

She had bumped into Claire coming out of the Britannia hotel. She wore very sexy, expensive, classy attire. She looked a little flustered, she had two mobile phones...she worked with Nina.

Claire was an escort.

Jordan's mind went into overdrive, she began reminiscing about Nina. The time Mark and her went shopping and saw Nina on their way home going into the Radisson hotel all dressed up in a LBD. Then there was the time when Jordan had spent the day playing 'Colombo' to find out what Nina was up to because her new found confidence and sexiness, not to mention the money . It was unexplainable back then but not anymore if what Jordan suspected was correct.

Was Nina an escort? She had told the truth, she did work with Claire?

CHAPTER 8

AARON

Aaron had left work a little earlier than usual to visit Mark. He sat by his bedside observing the surroundings. He disliked hospitals. The smell, the noises from all of the different machines and the beds with the bars and the pastel coloured blankets. He hated it all.

He cupped his head in his hands and reflected back to the day it all happened, the day that placed Mark in his hospital bed, the day that blew everyone away. Now they were all scattered but all feeling more or less the same pain, hurt, resentment and doubt.

Aaron spotted the 'goody bag' on Marks bedside table from Antoine. Little, sweet innocent Antoine, unspoilt and naive, pure and simple. Aaron remembered yesterday when he watched from behind the door and saw Antoine sitting comfortably in Alec's lap. He hoped and prayed that Alec's fiery temper and selfish ways didn't rub off onto him. Antoine was so gentle, kind and caring and Aarons concern was that the pair spent most of their time together and Alec being much older was supposed to set an example. An example he was nervous might be contagious.

Feeling awkward and not quite knowing how to place himself he turned the chair around to face Mark. His eyes were closed as he lay, living in another world.

Looking around to ensure he was totally alone and no one was peaking or listening at the door Aaron spoke out loud to Mark.

"So are you going to wake up for Nina? She's waiting for you to, that's if you love her like you said you do."

Aaron got up and began pacing the room. "What am I doing?" He scolded himself, "Why am I being like this? The poor man's in a coma because of my nephew and I am getting all jealous over something I don't even know for sure. Grow up Aaron, get it together, you are better than this!" He told himself.

Sitting down again he grabbed Marks hand, his friends hand, "Wake up Mark, please wake up. There's life to enjoy. The Angels are not ready to take you home yet, I feel it, you haven't finished walking your path so get up and put on your shoes." At that moment Aaron felt Marks hand squeeze his. Immediately Aaron looked at Marks face and noticed his eyelids fluttering. With his heart in his mouth Aaron instantly rang the nurses buzzer.

The nurse ran into the room and before she could even enquire Aaron blurted out full of excitement, "His eyes fluttered and he squeezed my hand!"

The nurse checked Mark over and made him comfortable and then turned to face Aaron, "Calm down Sir, this happens sometimes, you just have to be patient."

"But there is hope right? He is going to wake up sometime soon?" Aaron asked her.

"There's always hope," she reassured him before disappearing.

Aaron sat in his car and inhaled a long, hard, deep breath before exhaling downwards into his lap. Everything was crazy, he really thought Mark was going to wake up right there and then. Aarons thoughts were interrupted by Jordan ringing his phone. He gathered his emotions before answering her call.

JORDAN.

Sitting on her sofa, still trying to come to terms with her latest discoveries concerning Claire and more than likely Nina's role, Jordan decided to get to the bottom of it and find out for certain what Nina had been up to and had been hiding for so long. There were so many things that floated in the mist. Why Nina and Aaron split up in the first place, why Nina was drastically going to set up a life in Atlanta and her fabulous lifestyle. All of this whilst her life was a glum shambles. She had a plan. Grabbing her phone off the coffee table she dialled Aarons number.

"Hi Jordan," Aaron answered.

"Hey Aaron, are you ok?" She sensed something was wrong by the tone in his voice.

"I just went to see Mark Jordan and he squeezed my hand and his eyes fluttered..."

"Open? Is he awake? What did he say? Has he asked for me? Aaron tell me!" Jordan rambled on at high speed.

"No Jordan, no..." he tried to explain but still Jordan continued.

"Where are you? I'm on my way!"

"No Jordan!!! Calm down, it's not like that, it was just little movements, apparently it happens sometimes so the nurse told me."

Jordan moved the phone away from her face and folded her lips tightly together to stop her cries escaping but she failed to stifle it and let loose. Aaron could hear her and his heart ached for her, she had a lot going on.

"Jordan are you there? Can you hear me? I know it's hard but we all have to be strong together, he'll pull through ok? This was sign...a good sign." Getting no response he tried again, "Jordan are you there?"

"Yes," she just about managed to say. "I'm going to go now Aaron," she said before hanging up.

She had forgotten why she had originally called Aaron, the news she had just heard had knocked her off track. She was ready for Mark to wake up, she was going to bring him home. His Mom was away in Jamaica visiting relatives, she had no idea what was going on and Jordan just hoped that Mark woke up and she got him home before her return. She wanted her husband back and she was going to do all she could to have him.

NINA.

Nina put her key in Aarons front door and entered into the hallway. She kicked off her Dune shoes and placed her handbag down before walking into the living room to find Aaron sitting on the sofa watching the TV. "Hello," she greeted him.

Aaron sat up and patted the seat next to him for her to sit down.

"Are you ok?" She asked him trying to figure out what was wrong. She started to silently panic. Had Mark woken up and told them all about them sleeping together at the Masquerade Ball?

"Listen Nina," he began, "I went to see Mark today and…"

"Is he awake?" Nina gasped, covering her mouth with her hand.

"No, no, but I thought he was going to wake up. His eyes fluttered and he squeezed my hand."

"Oh my gosh! That's brilliant isn't it?" Nina said full of excitement.

"Yes it's hopeful," he told her, "but listen, it got me thinking about us and how rocky things have been between us of late over silly little things and I don't like it. I hate when we argue, I just…"

"Sorry to butt in but I don't want you to speak just yet. I've been thinking too and it seems like we are rushing our relationship. As far as us living together goes I don't want my living situation to be threatened every time we have a disagreement. We weren't living together before so why the rush to now? Convenience isn't an excuse. I think it would be better for us to pick up where we left off and I get a small place of my own and we work it like we did before until we are certain we are ready to take the next step. What do you think?" Nina held his hand and looked into his eyes. "I love you and I want us to work that's why I am suggesting this," she assured him.

Aaron stared at her and kissed her hand. He could only agree, especially after everything they had been through. There were a few weak areas that required strengthening in order for them to work, although he hated to admit she was right. "That's ok, I understand, as long as we are happy that's all that matters."

"Thank you," Nina whispered, kissing him gently on the lips.

"No problem."

"Have you spoken to Jordan about what happened today?" Nina asked Aaron as she went into the bathroom and ran the shower.

"Yes, I spoke to her earlier, she was really upset, I told her to ring us if she wants or needs anything."

"Ok I'll ring her later then," Nina told him before getting undressed and stepping into the shower. After her long day at work the water beating against her skin felt so nice. She closed her eyes and willed Mark to wake up. Her thoughts were soon interrupted as Aaron stepped into the shower behind her and caressed her sweetly underneath the raining water. He planted wet kisses on her shoulders before spinning her around and gently loving her thoughts away.

CHAPTER 9

AARON.

Aaron freed Nina from his clutch as her alarm went off causing her to suddenly awake, groaning and moaning out of her peaceful slumber.

"You're going to miss this," Aaron whispered into her ear as she rolled over, struggling to will herself up to get ready for work.

"Miss what?" She asked, her mind still fuzzy as she yearned desperately for more sleep.

Aaron sat up observing her fight the morning fight and laughed at her before elaborating. "Waking up together," he stated, crawling over to her and dragging her back into the bed and wrapping her up in the duvet for kisses and cuddles.

Nina giggled as he tickled her, "You just get on with moving my stuff to my new flat today whilst I go and work my ass off," she laughed.

"Are you insinuating that moving heavy loads of stuff that does not even belong to me might I add, is not commendable work?" Aaron asked tickling her even more. "Huh? I can't hear you."

"Ok, ok, ok…!!!" Nina screamed, trying to scramble herself free as the tickling started to become unbearable.

Aaron gave into her and pushed her into the bathroom as he continued on into the kitchen to make them both some breakfast. He had a long, hard day ahead of him, not just physically but emotionally as Jordan was his buddy for the day.

Really he was a bit nervous about Nina moving out although he knew it was for the best. The points she had made were valid, they made sense and she reasoned them well. He agreed so that their relationship wouldn't fall apart. All great things required hard work. His main concern was his paranoia eating him up. He knew he would be tempted to spy on her. Who knew, he could be blowing it all out of proportion and they could end up being happy go lucky. All he could do was wait and see, go with the flow. He loved Nina and that was all that mattered.

He heard the bathroom door open and adored how his lady sexily wiggled down the hall into the bedroom. Her cute little figure swayed side to side, the dimples in her lower back so prominent, her thick strong legs, her smooth skin scattered with water droplets from her wet hair. He smiled as the droplets fell from her hair to her shoulders and swam down the curve of her spine nestling in the dimples just before her bum.

Aaron could not forget what she had done but nothing compared to how he made her feel. He tried to understand how the past was 'just' sex, a duty, a job and that when he lay down with her they made sweet, sensual love to not just each others bodies but minds and souls. When she breathed he felt her heartbeat and he listened to its beat every time. She was his woman, he loved her.

All dressed and ready to head off, Nina grabbed a piece of toast, kissed Aaron on his lips and handed him the spare key to her new abode. "Have fun and tread carefully around Jordan," she warned him and with that she left for work leaving Aaron with his head and his hands full.

JORDAN.

Ding dong, ding dong, ding dong. Jordan leaped out of her bed in sheer panic at the sound of her doorbell ringing. The way it rang was a fresh reminder of the day the incident occurred with Mark. She gulped down her emotion knowing she would be visiting him that evening.

Peering through her bedroom window she noticed Aarons car and suddenly remembered that today she was supposed to help Aaron move Nina's stuff into her new flat.

"I am so sorry Aaron," Jordan apologised greeting him at her front door as she tied up her fleecy dressing gown. "I must have overslept, what time is it?" She asked yawning and ruffling her 'bed head.'

"It's 10am Jordan but don't worry about it," he assured her. "I'll tell you what," he began, handing her a set of keys folded up in a piece of paper, "here are the keys to Nina's storage unit, you collect the boxes on her list and bring them over in your car when you are ready, I shall be at the flat by then with all of her stuff from my flat, ok?"

Jordan agreed relieved that Aaron wasn't disappointed with her late awakening. He was very calm and collected, that she admired. "That will be fine Aaron, thanks I'll do that." She smiled at him as he made his way down her path to his car. As she watched him drive off she couldn't help but think back to the day when Nina met him and how he had become such a positive part of her life, Nina's birthday dinner, who his nephews were and all the rest, but she couldn't understand what had happened for him and Nina to split and if it was what she assumed it to be, how could he want her back?

Shutting the front door Jordan went into her kitchen and clicked the kettle on. She rolled the set of keys out of the list and read what Nina had requested. "Easy enough," she said out loud to herself.

Her attire for the day was to be a jogging suit and her Keds, function and fashion in one.

As she laced up her Keds on the bottom step she grinned to herself as a certain thought crossed her mind. "Opportunity knocks," she sniggered before grabbing her bag and car keys and skipping out of the house to her car.

CHAPTER 10

NINA.

Work was extremely busy for Nina that morning but she daren't complain, after everything that had happened she was grateful and lucky to even have a job. Grateful to Mr Allen and his contacts Nina ploughed through her last set of files.

Lunch time couldn't come quick enough as an eager Nina jumped into her car and made her way to her and Claire's favourite pub for a catch up and some good old 'pub grub.'

As she parked up her car she noticed Claire enter the car park and do the same. As fast as she could she gathered her bag and jacket off the passenger seat and leaped out of the car again noticing that Claire was doing the exact same thing. The pair then raced each other to the pubs entrance shouting; "Early is on time, on time is late!" Leaning against the wall, laughing and heaving breathlessly, they both entertained each other on what seemed to be their little ritual.

"You crazy woman!" Nina spluttered, coughing and laughing at the same time.

"You're the crazy one," Claire clarified, "and unfit," she added.

"Tell me something I don't know," Nina agreed, "now let's go and eat some unhealthy food," she laughed even more trying to stand up straight to give Claire a hug.

"Oh how I've missed you," Claire admitted, "I really have."

The women ordered large plates of food, Nina having worked up an appetite that morning at work and Claire obviously from all of her sexercise.

"I saw Jordan the other day in town," Claire informed Nina. "We accidentally bumped into each other".

"Oh yeah," Nina replied intrigued as what was to follow being unaware of them meeting.

"Yes, she took my contact details so she could send me an invite for your engagement party. I am telling you this just incase you don't want me there. After everything I would totally understand. I won't be hurt if..."

"I want you there Claire, it wouldn't be right if you didn't attend. No ifs or buts ok?"

"Ok," Claire simply smiled.

After lunch the girls said their goodbyes before going their separate ways. Nina decided to send Aaron a quick text message to see how him and Jordan were getting on before heading back to work.

AARON.

Aaron lazily unloaded the last of Nina's boxes from the boot of his car. It had poured down with rain constantly all morning and it seemed as though it had no intention of easing up.

"At last," Aaron gasped setting down the last couple of boxes in Nina's hallway whilst removing his wet jacket. He glanced at his watch wondering how Jordan was getting on at the storage centre. He suddenly remembered that Jordan was in her own time zone having overslept that morning causing her to be behind schedule.

Looking around for something to do to bide his time whilst he waited for Jordan, he wondered around Nina's new, empty flat. He began to reminisce and forced himself to stop. This was a little bit too much for him to handle, honestly he didn't understand why they couldn't just remain as they were.

To distract himself Aaron dialled Jordan's number and waited patiently for her to answer. He had tried earlier on but she didn't pick up therefore he presumed she might have been driving.

"H-hello," Jordan answered.

Aaron sensed that something wasn't right, "Jordan, are you ok?" He asked. "What's happened? Where are you?" He questioned her hoping nothing major was wrong.

"I...I...I'll see you shortly, I'm just packing the last set of boxes into my car, I shouldn't be much longer. I'll see you in a bit," she babbled hurriedly, hanging up the phone.

"Ok," Aaron said. Waving at the thin air Aaron dismissed it, he'd discover what the problem was when Jordan made an appearance no doubt.

Standing in what was to be Nina's bedroom, Aaron walked over to the window and gazed out at the rain. The raindrops beat heavily against the window pane, outside was scarce, no one wanted to be out in this weather. The odd person rushed down the road, hood up and head down. He noticed a cat seeking shelter under a small tree in the garden opposite. "Come on Jordan," he whispered into the empty room becoming impatient.

Refusing to nosey around Nina's new flat Aaron maintained his stance at the window. His place would no longer be a home without her in it, his bed would be cold and he would no longer have the comfort of her legs wrapped around his during the night. He was going to miss chatting in bed on weekends, their lazy Sundays together, he was going to miss her. He didn't understand what he had done wrong. Didn't she want him? Was she still escorting? His head was spinning and after what he heard Nina say at Marks bedside he was beginning to doubt taking her back, had he made a mistake? They were supposed to be engaged, why did it feel like they were growing apart? The whole situation was torturing his soul and he was trying his hardest not to let it surface. Would any other man have taken her back after what she had done?

JORDAN.

Jordan's wipers were going so fast she was frightened that they'd fly off the car. The rain had no intention of stopping. "Trust this to be the weather today when I have to move stuff," she moaned.

Pulling into a car parking space outside of the storage centre as close to the entrance as possible, she fumbled inside of her bag trying to find the note with Nina's storage reference number and password. After a frantic search she finally found it with the list of boxes Nina wanted to be taken out stapled to it. "Phew!" She sighed, "Panic over."

After signing in and sorting out the paperwork, one of the workers directed her to where Nina's storage cell was and gave her a four digit extension number to ring from the phone located in the cell on the wall by the entrance door to ask for a worker to come and help her transport the required boxes to her car. "Thank you," Jordan said and with that made her way as fast as she could to Nina's storage cell. She felt guilty that she had overslept putting Aaron out and she didn't want to keep him waiting much longer, she had to pick up her pace.

Scanning the numbers above each cell door Jordan finally found cell number thirty. She laughed to herself wondering if Nina had picked that cell for her stuff deliberately or if it was just pure coincidence. Jordan opened the cell door and stepped into a cold, dark, echoing room the size of an average garage. She flipped the switch on brightening up the space enabling her to see. There were boxes neatly stacked and labelled in rows in front of her, a few tied black sacks also labelled and some of Nina's furniture. Her bed was dismantled and leaning against a wall and her electronics were bubble wrapped and set down next to her plastic covered sofa. It was all too quiet and so Jordan played some music through her phone as she looked down at the list Nina had given her.

Crockery and cutlery, cookware, microwave, towels and linen, three boxes of shoes…

As Jordan separated the things that Nina required and placed them by the door ready for one of the workers to help her carry them to her car, she noticed that all the boxes and bags were labelled bar one. The box had not been sealed like the rest had and it was placed on the top as if Nina had dropped it off there recently. Trying to ignore it and respect Nina's privacy, Jordan proceeded to dial the number on the telephone in the cell. She pressed the first two numbers and then hung up replacing the receiver. She gave in and walked over to the box.

Kneeling down Jordan slowly opened the box and carefully removed the layer of tissue paper on the top. Suddenly losing her balance she fell flat on her bottom and pulled the box in between her legs delving eagerly into what the depths contained.

Nina's Prada heels lay on top. "Well worn, not surprised," Jordan muttered noticing the worn out sole, setting them beside her. Next she nosed inside a posh bag that held an array of sexy underwear from crotch less panties, fish net stockings, bras and Victoria Secrets. Jordan then stumbled upon a mask that covered the eye area but had a fish net to cover the mouth. "Sexy like something one would wear to a Masquerade. What's all of this about Nina?" Jordan yearned to understand. Journeying on through the label less box Jordan became shocked and surprised by each and every item she retrieved. Expensive crystal jewellery, from Swarovski, a mobile phone, pepper spray, a toiletry bag full of condoms, a book as to what seemed like a diary. Jordan flicked through it and recognised it as Nina's diary from the day she snooped in her room and through her stuff. It had her birthday meal date, her Ireland trip, the 'part time work' thing that remained unexplained and the numerous male names scattered throughout.

Slamming it shut frustrated that she still was left sitting grey, Jordan spied another book, Turning the pages Jordan began to read what seemed to be Nina's journal.

> '...I can't believe that I had the guts to go through with it and I am officially my own woman. Thanks to Claire I can wave bye bye to the boring, simple Nina and say hello to a world filled with sunshine.

Jordan didn't quite grasp what Nina had meant and so she read on.

> '...although my highest paying customer, Frank is now getting out of hand and I'm finding it hard to cope. It's very early days and he's already catching feelings that are beyond that of a client. I should have guessed from the gifts he's showering me with... he's becoming a pest, I better stop putting it off and seek Claire's advice. Meeting 999 emergency!'

Pulling Claire's business card out from her purse, Jordan had reached a conclusion but to make sure it wasn't an assumption she read some more.

> '...why did I have to meet Aaron now, he's perfect in every way, he fits the criteria, he's all I've ever wanted. Why now when I have just found my way? Why did he show his face now? Why? Why? Why?'

Jordan hungrily flipped back and forth through the wad of inked pages grabbing snippets trying to piece all the information together, far too impatient to follow the chronological order.

> '...Jordan is catching a scent, I have to be extra careful, I don't want her to know about my secret life, I just want something to call my own. Knowing her, because she can't be a part of it she'd destroy it for me! According to her I'm a boring sod and I want her to continue believing that. I know she is unhappy in her

*marriage if not with her life and she won't confide in me because
she thought she always was the better one and knew best...'*

Jordan paused and swallowed her emotions. She was stunned that her
'best friend' thought so low of her. She was in awe that Nina had been
escorting but she was reassured that her instincts were confirmed. She
knew she wasn't going crazy when she noticed the designer clothes and
shoes that Nina was sporting, her attire change, her splashing the cash
and sudden social demands, it all made sense.

Just about to close the journal and refuse to read anymore, feeling
hurt, betrayed and disgusted, Jordan glimpsed Marks name on the
displayed page.

*'...OMG!!!!!!!!!! All I want to do is cry, why today? Why Mark?
Why Aaron?'*

"Why what?" Jordan flipped to the next page furiously.

*"...I know I'm selfish I would rather sleep with my best friends
husband than to reveal my identity...'*

Jordan slammed the book face down on the floor and shook her head.
She knew she had to read on to get the full picture but she felt unable to.
Had she read it right? Nina slept with Mark? Mark didn't know it was
Nina?

Jordan refused to get upset just yet and returned to the journal.

*'...telling me about Jordan and the baby as he sexed me and
groped me. I felt awful as he sucked and chewed on my nipples,
purring into my skin whilst explaining his wife's deceit, my best
friends husband. Crazy thoughts raced through my mind faster
than the waltzers at a fairground. I sat on top of him full of
regrets. Aaron must never find out about us, this I'll have to take
with me to my grave.'*

Numbly, Jordan fingered on to the next page.

*'...waving at Claire I exited the sex Masquerade and decided
there and then to call it quits. The whole situation with Mark
had removed the rose tint from my glasses and reality slapped me
so hard I shivered. Shivered out into the cold night air only to be
greeted by an outraged*

Aaron. What else could have gone wrong that night. I will never forget his eyes, the warm, hazel glow turned into an ice cold, grey stare that was enough to slice me into two pieces. That was the day he left my heart exposed or should I say I shattered his heart into a million pieces.'

Jordan calmly and collectively put everything back into the box in the order she had found it and closed the flaps together. She pushed it from in between her legs and slowly stood up wiping tears from her eyes. At a loss for words and in too much disgust and distress to fathom what she had just read, she robotically dialled the four digit extension number for the worker to come and help her move the selected boxes.

One thing she knew was that she wasn't going to let this dog sleep on, she had woke it and it needed feeding before being put back to rest. She added the unlabelled box to the pile to be taken to her car making sure she picked up a flat packed box for later use on exiting the building.

CHAPTER 11

NINA.

N ina sat in the comfort of her car tapping her fingers away on the steering wheel to the 'Police' whilst wailing at the top of her lungs secure in knowing that no one could hear her in the confinement of her vehicle.

It was pouring down with rain outside but regardless of the dark, grey, miserable sky, Nina felt full of sunshine and joy. Finally reaching her destination, the Queen Elizabeth hospital, she began the game of, 'hunt for a parking space.'

Mark was her priority that early evening especially after hearing from Aaron that he had shown signs of waking up. Trotting down the hospital corridor towards Marks room, as fast as her heels allowed her to, Nina instantly stopped as she caught sight of who was sitting at Marks bedside.

Unsure of whether to interrupt or not she lingered at the door. It seemed only fair that his Mother had time with her son and so Nina turned her back and began to walk away.

With her tear filmed eyes Nina had barely taken a couple of steps down the corridor when she heard her name, "Nina." Slowly turning around she faced Irene, Marks mother, beckoning her to come into her open arms. Irene was like a 'second mum' to Nina, she had practically raised her from a young age as herself and Mark grew up together as close friends.

As Nina made her way towards Irene the disturbance and pain was apparent in her eyes. Nina embraced her tightly and rubbed her back then kissed her on the forehead. Nina had to hold her with all of her strength as Irene's knees buckled as she wept and bawled from deep within repeating, "My son, my son, my only son!" All Nina could do was hold her up as she released the pent up emotions. "I'm so sorry Irene, I really am," were the only words Nina could find to say.

Irene eventually had calmed down as Nina led her back into Marks room observing how Mark still lay there the same way he had done so at all her previous visits. "I'm just going to get us a cup of tea and then we'll have a chat when I get back," Nina told Irene, helping her to adjust herself comfortably in the chair before leaving the room.

"Ok my darling," she whimpered, wiping her bloodshot eyes with an overused, crumpled tissue.

Nina stood in the queue at the coffee shop in disbelief, this was the last thing she had expected to happen today.

'Ring ring, ring, ring…' hurriedly digging through the contents of her bag trying to find her phone, Nina suddenly realised the situation between Jordan and Irene. On top of that she was trying to figure out how to relay the news to Irene knowing that her first and foremost question was going to be, "What happened to my son?"

"Hello," Nina answered all flustered.

It was Jordan, "Where the hell are you?" She asked angrily. "I've been waiting here for you by your new…"

"JORDAN!" Nina raised her voice stopping her mid sentence.

"Where are you? What are you doing?" Jordan grilled her suspiciously.

"For goodness sakes Jordan will you just listen to me!" Nina shouted down her mobile phone causing heads to turn in her direction. "Marks mother is here at the hospital…" she began.

"What?!" Jordan gasped.

"I saw her and I thought it would be for the best if I left her to spend some time with her son but it was too late, as I attempted to …"

"How was she? What happened then? What did she say?" Jordan panicked, firing question after question like bullets from a gun.

"She's in a terrible state," Nina carried on, "I mean, wouldn't you be if you were called back from Jamaica when you not long left to this? I could hardly walk away from her Jordan, she's like family to me and so I'm standing here in the coffee shop queue…"

"Mmmmm, like family huh? Jordan muttered, "It's ok."

"It's not ok Jordan!" Nina said through gritted teeth, "She is going to enquire as to how her son ended up in that hospital bed. A coma."

Silence.

Nina guessed as much because if the whole situation was to be dissected and stripped down to the bare bones, Jordan was the culprit, Jordan was to blame. She cheated on Mark with Alec, she became pregnant and tried to pretend it belonged to Mark, possessive Alec lashed out at Mark all due to Jordan's lonely lies and deceit and the repercussions resulted in Mark tangled up in hospital wires.

"Nothing? I thought so," were Nina's last words before she hung up on Jordan and tried to figure the best way to enlighten Irene of how poor Mark had ended up in a coma.

CHAPTER 12

JORDAN.

"I'm so sorry I took so long," Jordan apologised repeatedly to Aaron as he helped her take the boxes out of the boot of her car and place them in the communal area of Nina's new apartment.

"It's ok, don't worry, you're here now," he panted, moving quick trying to avoid getting soaked in the rain.

Jordan took the boxes out of her car and passed them to Aaron and he would run and set them down and then return for another. Within ten minutes or so due to methodical team work they were just about finished.

"And what about this one?" Aaron asked Jordan ready to lift the remaining box form her car.

"…erm, no …no, that one is mine," Jordan replied brushing her hair out of her face with her fingers and then grabbing the box out of Aarons hands, placing it in her boot and slamming it shut. "Now come on, let's get Nina's stuff inside of her flat, I'm knackered."

Whilst sorting Nina's boxes out following her strict instructions of NOT to unpack as that was her favourite part, Jordan noticed Aaron frequently glancing in her direction.

"What's on your mind?" Jordan asked unable to understand why Nina was moving into her own space when her and Aaron had re-united ten minutes ago.

Aaron brushed his face roughly with his hands and sighed, "A lot of things…"

"Such as?" Jordan probed a little further.

"What do you think?" Aaron said getting up and putting his jacket on. "We are all done here Jordan so you get hold of Nina, I'm heading back to mine to sleep. Here's the keys, lock up and drop them back to me later." With that said Aaron picked up his car keys and shut the door behind himself.

Jordan was left totally alone with herself and her thoughts, in Nina's new home with Nina's belongings. She sat on the floor with the many boxes (her favourite place it seemed) and took a deep breath. After the greatest discovery that day she assumed Aaron was crazy for wanting Nina. What was it that made her so special? A tear slid down Jordan's cheek and crawled into her mouth. Swallowing the salty tear Jordan sat and then stood thinking and thinking. She then sat and then stood and then thought a little more driving herself insane fighting to diminish the thoughts that were terrorising her, intimidating her and haunting her. 'Nina was an escort and slept with my husband and has the audacity to be all nice to my face. She deserves an Oscar.'

Getting up and stretching Jordan paced the flat, her mind still buzzing and lively, she began getting overwhelmed and knew that she had to calm down. "I wonder where she is now?" Jordan got her phone and touched Nina's name waiting for her to answer, it rang a while before eventually she picked up.

Sitting in her car feeling numb, biting her lip and rubbing the back of her neck, Jordan breathed quick breaths and then closed her eyes taking a longer, deeper breath and resting her head back on the head rest. So Marks mother was back, what did this mean for her now? Leaning forward and resting on her steering wheel Jordan watched as the raindrops fell and beat against her windscreen. Nothing seemed to be changing for the better concerning herself and she couldn't help but beat herself up. If she hadn't slept with Alec all would have remained well. She would be at work in a job that she loved, she would be going home to her husband and they'd be trying for a baby, oblivious to who was or was not to blame for not being able to conceive.

Wiping her eyes Jordan suddenly remembered the box in the boot of her car, Nina's version of Pandora's box. Her eyes sparkled as a plan entered her mind. Why should she be frowned upon and blamed? Be deemed as the 'baddy',' be the one responsible for all the madness that was occurring amidst herself, Aaron. Nina and Mark? They were all just as bad as each other with their secrets and lies and she was going to make sure they were all going to get their share of grief and pain.

Assembling the empty box she had picked up from the storage unit, she filled it with a wad of empty papers, magazines for weight and plastic bags, Jordan placed the original tissue paper on the top. She had a pair of heels at home that looked similar to Nina's Prada's, she would place them on top as well as another layer of tissue paper to make it look as it was and then return the box to storage. It was time to rock the boat. On her way home she got a copy of Nina's apartment key cut before returning the original one back to Aaron.

NINA.

"Thank you for dropping me home," Irene hugged Nina gratefully.

"Do you want me to come in?" Nina asked.

"I'd rather be alone if you don't mind Nina, I'm sorry, it's just that…"

"No need to explain, I understand…just call me if you need me for anything and I mean it," Nina kissed her cheek before leaving.

Getting into her car and driving off her heart thudded against her chest, it felt as if it was about to burst. Feeling nauseous she pulled up into the nearest petrol station and took a sip of water from the bottle she carried in her bag. "I'm sorry Mark," she cried, tears streaming down her face, "I'm so sorry."

Retrieving her phone from her bag she composed a blanket text message to Aaron and Jordan: 'Mark's mother is back and the story is that he was attacked by a gang of guys.'

Wiping her eyes Nina sat staring at her phone and shivered. She had protected Jordan and Alec and she couldn't help but ask herself why?

CHAPTER 13

AARON.

Aaron was startled awake at the sound of Nina's key in his front door. He glanced at the huge analogue clock situated above the fireplace that Nina had bought for him. It read nine o' clock. He hadn't heard from his fiancé all day and just now at 9pm she was gracing him with her presence after he had spent the entire day moving her things into her new home. Aaron was not impressed. She hadn't answered any of his calls or even had the decency to return a call. He tried not to think the worst and assumed that she had opted for a 'girly' sleep over with Jordan in the new flat, but he was wrong.

Aaron stretched and rose up from the couch as Nina's shadow appeared in the door frame, flickering with the light from the television.

"Hey Mr sleepy head," she cooed at him making her way towards him. "How is my baby?"

Aaron gently pushed her aside and made his way into the kitchen to get a glass of water.

"Excuse you," Nina said with an attitude.

"You're excused," Aaron replied sarcastically.

"So, what is it that I am supposed to have done this time Aaron?" Nina asked annoyed and fed up of Aaron blowing hot and cold.

Aaron gulped down his water and gasped, refreshed, shaking his head. "Ok Nina, where have you been from eight o' clock this morning until now? And why didn't you answer any of my calls?"

"I have been at work!" Nina raised her voice in frustration.

"Until now?" Aaron laughed brushing past her again before re-entering the living room.

"Will you stop that!" Nina shouted pushing him back. "If you have something to say just say it! I am sick and tired of this Aaron, if only you knew what my day entailed you wouldn't be treating me this way," Nina whimpered, exhausted. "I came home to you because I thought you would comfort me and make it better like you usually do but instead I get the cold shoulder and I have no clue what it is I have done." Nina walked down the hallway and slipped her feet into her heels and grabbed her bag, she refused to let Aaron see her cry.

Aaron caught her by her arm and pulled her close to him, he could see her struggling to fight back her tears. He pushed her against the wall and kissed the tears that fell from her eyes. "Kiss me back baby," he told her. Nina moved her head, she wasn't in the mood for games. "Kiss me baby, kiss me," Aaron whispered hungrily, sucking on Nina's lips and down to her neck. "Come on baby, let's make love and make it better."

"Get off, I just wanted to have a cup of tea and tell you what happened at the hospital today, I don't want this Aaron," Nina snapped, pushing him away. She felt his arousal instantly disappear but she couldn't care less. He always wanted sex lately anytime anywhere and it was getting on her nerves.

Although feeling total rejection, Aaron swallowed his pride and grabbed Nina's hand and lead her to the living room. He went to put the kettle on whilst Nina kicked her heels off for the second time that evening. "I'm sorry, you can talk to me, I just miss you that's all."

Over a cup of tea Nina informed Aaron about Irene turning up at the hospital and Jordan's reaction when she told her over the phone. She then admitted how much it hurt her to see Irene in such a state and so she took her home to an empty house. "It broke my heart leaving her all alone like that," Nina quickly sipped her tea so as not to get emotional.

As Aaron sat back and listened attentively he couldn't help but feel a little jealous of the bond that Nina and Marks mother shared. It indicated that Mark and Nina also shared a strong bond.

Nina finished speaking and noticed Aarons silence. "What are you thinking about?"

"Nothing Nina…it's just that…"

"It's just what Aaron?"

"I understand now what a crazy day you've endured but when you don't answer my calls I can't help but think…"

"That I'm escorting?" Nina completed his thoughts for him knowing full well that that would always be lurking in the back of his mind.

"Do you blame me?"

Nina held Aarons gaze, she had had enough, she couldn't cope with this for much longer. "I actually do not blame you Aaron but if there is no trust there is no love. I have enough on my plate right about now, my job, Mark laying half dead in a hospital bed due to your nephew and Jordan, his emotional wreck of a mother and trying to move into my new home. I thought you were the one constant, stable thing in my life but I guess I was wrong huh? You just remember one thing Aaron," Nina stated sincerely as she yet again slipped her feet into her heels and grabbed her bag, "You asked me to stay and I stayed for you. Everything I do is for you," she pointed her finger at him, "If you didn't want me you should have let me go!" With that Nina slammed the front door and made her way to her car.

Aaron brushed his hands over his head and grunted. He felt like his head was about to explode. How did they get to this place?

NINA.

As Nina approached her car she noticed a piece of paper on her windscreen hooked beneath the wiper. 'That wasn't there earlier,' she thought to herself. Picking it out and unfolding it Nina read the note.

HOW ARE YOU DOING SUNSHINE?
I MISS YOU XXX

Nina furiously screwed the note up and got into her car. Feeling a little spooked she locked her doors and tried to calm her breathing. Ready to hastily go back up to Aarons place and curse him out she realised that it couldn't have been him that placed the note on her car as she was busy arguing with him the whole time. Mark wasn't the culprit as he was in a coma. It then dawned upon her that the list of suspects was endless due to her escorting past and her client list. She fobbed it off as just one of her clients wishing she was back in the game. With that she reluctantly made her way to her new abode.

Turning her key in the lock of her new home Nina felt pure emptiness surround her. All of her homely goods were boxed up and placed in one room, the room that was eventually going to be her bedroom. 'What have I done?' She asked herself. She felt as if she had made rash decisions which had led her to nowhere. 'Maybe I should have gone to America.' It was too late for that now, everything had been rearranged to accommodate her stay, not only that but there was no way she could leave when Mark was lying in a coma.

"Shit! The milk!" Nina suddenly remembered the milk and other essential items she had purchased after dropping Irene home. Opening the fridge to put the shopping away she noticed a small, familiar looking card taped to the front of the fridge. She ripped it off to have a closer look. It was one of her client cards from when she used to escort. "What the hell?!" She screamed tearing it up and letting the small pieces flutter to the floor, "Who is doing this?"

Yet again Aaron was first in the firing line as he was the only one who had a key to her new flat apart from herself. 'Why would he do this?' She wondered beginning to feel nervous.

Nina was exhausted from her strenuous day. She had aimed to stay the night at Aarons, eat some food and share a nice, deep, hot bubble bath with him then wrap up together all cosy and comfy in his arms. All of that went to pot the moment he threw her past in her face. 'Stupid me, I should have known we wouldn't be able to work.'

Grateful for her OCD trait Nina easily found exactly what she needed due to effective labelling. Her furniture was to be delivered over the weekend so until then Nina stubbornly decided to make do with what belongings she had. No way was she going back to Aarons and Jordan wasn't attractive company to her either at that moment due to their phone conversation earlier concerning Irene. Nina's misery didn't love company. Instead, bed less, Nina used her mountains of cushions to make up a cosy corner and she threw her favourite blanket that her aunt had made for her on top. She lit a scented candle and undressed hanging her clothes on the door.

Stepping into the shower Nina turned it up as hot as she could tolerate it and lathered her Nivea body wash all over herself. Closing her eyes Nina wished her hands were Aarons hands rubbing and touching her and making her feel good. She stood directly beneath the showerhead and let the water rinse off the soap suds. She began rubbing her skin hard and rough leaving red marks and patches all over her body. Tears rained from her eyes mingling in with the water that the shower spat out. If only she could wash away her dirty past so easily.

What did she have to do in order to prove to Aaron that she no longer meddled in the escorting world?

CHAPTER 14

JORDAN.

Sitting alone at her kitchen table eating her scrambled eggs on toast that Saturday morning Jordan felt quite pleased with herself. She hoped that now Nina was fretting a little trying to figure out who was haunting her. Like a crazy woman Jordan sat talking to herself at the table as if she had an audience, "How could she? She slept with my husband and was escorting. Aaron knew and he still took her back, how could he?"

Cursing and eating simultaneously, brimming with hurt and fury, upset and confusion, Jordan reflected not too far back to how everybody ganged up on her regarding the 'baby' situation and for Mark ending up in a coma. She wasn't the one who threw the punches. "I'm going to teach each and every one of you a lesson," she spat, bits of egg flying from her mouth. She wanted to inflict a hurting upon those who had done unto her.

Ring! Ring!...her phone sang and the caller ID read Nina. "Hello Nina are you ok?" She answered with a smile.

NINA.

"Just through here please," Nina directed the delivery men into the lounge to place her new furniture.

She had decided on a simple, minimalist look. Something quick and easy to leave if necessary. The way things seemed to be going she didn't intend on staying long, she had a weird feeling, negative vibes rotated around her, the ground felt unstable beneath her feet, she was just waiting on Mark to wake up from his slumber.

"All done my love," one of the workmen interrupted her depth of thought by handing her a device to scribble (as best as she possibly could) her name and signature. "Just sign and print love and we'll be out of your way," he instructed her. Nina did so and thanked them before shutting her front door.

Sighing, Nina admired all of her new stuff and decided to give Jordan a call to see what she was up to.

Jordan answered right away, "Hello Nina are you ok?" She asked, sounding chirpy.

"Hey Jordan, yes thanks I'm doing ok. What are you up to today?" She enquired wondering why she sounded so happy and praying the answer was going to be, nothing.

"Not much, why what's up?"

"Well…erm…I know you have already done a lot for me by moving my stuff into my new flat but how do you feel about coming over to help me make my house a home? The furniture has just arrived and I thought it needs that 'classy' touch, what do you say?"

"Sure," Jordan easily agreed, "I'll make my way now, have you got food to eat over there?" She asked trying to do her 'best friend' duties.

"Awww, bless you" Nina grinned, "Yes I have the basics, don't worry, just bring your cheerful self, I need some of those beans you have in your belly, we will talk when you get here."

Buzz! Buzz!

Nina let Jordan into the building and waited at her door to greet her. To her surprise, Jordan held out a beautiful bunch of flowers and a box of her favourite chocolates. Nina kissed Jordan's cheeks and hugged her. "What's this in aid of?"

"Just a little house warming stroke cheering up gift," Jordan laughed entering Nina's apartment. "Come on let's find a vase to put these pretty babies in and get cracking with the task in hand."

"You are so good to me, already you have lifted my spirits, thank you," Nina commended her.

"You were there for me when I was down and with the current situation we have to keep each other afloat, don't you agree?"

"I sure do," Nina replied becoming suspicious as to why Jordan was acting like everything was rosy. The last time she checked Mark was still in a coma.

Nina showed Jordan her new goodies hurriedly opening the boxes like a little kid at Christmas. Nina being the lazy kind ordered the furniture already assembled, she wasn't into that following instructions business if she could help it.

Sitting on Nina's 'make do' bed of cushions and cackling at the fact that Nina had actually slept on it, the girls stuffed their faces with Nina's box of chocolates and discussed decorating. "At least I had my faithful cushions!" Nina squealed as Jordan threw one at her head teasing her.

"Indeed you did," Jordan giggled as a cushion bounced off her head. "So why didn't you call me and sleep over at mine?" Jordan queried. "There's plenty of room and you know that."

"To be honest with you Jordan, yesterday was hellish," Nina said picking at the cushion on her lap. "Work is stressful at the moment, then I was worrying about Aaron and yourself moving all my stuff in the atrocious weather conditions, not to mention my visit to Mark and Irene being there. It was all so unexpected. I couldn't leave her Jordan, I just couldn't and so I ended up taking her home. I then intended to spend the night with Aaron, I knew it was late but I still went to see him but that resulted in a falling out so I dragged myself here in no mood for any company."

Jordan rubbed Nina's back and kissed her forehead.

Nina continued, "I didn't even get the opportunity to thank you both for all of your hard work," Nina muttered full of guilt. "You know I feel so useless lately Jordan."

"What did you tell Irene?" Jordan asked abruptly changing the subject.

Typical of her to make sure her back was covered, Nina thought before responding, "Exactly what I text you and Aaron. Hopefully we will get to Mark before Irene to get our stories straight," Was Nina's plan.

"And what if it doesn't work out that way?" Jordan panicked.

Ring! Ring! Nina read the caller ID on her phone. "It's Irene," she glared at Jordan

"Hello Irene," Nina frowned putting her on loudspeaker following Jordan's signal for her to do so.

"Nina darling, he's awake, my baby is awake!" She sobbed down the phone.

"Really?" Nina screamed full of joy and excitement.

"Yes, I prayed and I prayed and God is good, he answered my prayers," she hollered down the line.

"I am so happy Irene, are you at the hospital?"

"Not yet I just received the call from the hospital, I have rang for a taxi, I will make my way."

"Ok, I will tell the others and we will meet you there. Irene just to let you know..." Nina began believing it only respectful to let her know, "... Jordan will be with me."

All the while Jordan's eyes were glued to Nina's as the call proceeded. She listened carefully to the words exchanged and tears rolled down her cheeks. Nina hung up and wiped Jordan's eyes, she knew this was tuff on her. "Come on now we've waited for this moment long enough. Now let us get ourselves together and looking presentable so Mark has nice things to look at," Nina said without even thinking.

AARON.

Aaron slowly crawled through Saturday afternoon traffic en route to the hospital to see 'main man' Mark after Nina had called him to tell him the good news. 'Good for who eh?' He expelled his thoughts loudly.

Aaron didn't know what to feel at that precise moment, unfortunately he wasn't elated as he had a feeling something was or had gone on between Mark and his woman.

His plan was to fade into the background and observe. He was thankful that his 'friend' had woken up so the air could be cleared and everybody could get on with their lives.

Although he was still pissed off at Nina from yesterday he couldn't ignore her and planned on making it right after the hospital visit.

CHAPTER 15

JORDAN.

Sitting in the hospital toilet cubicle Jordan bawled her eyes out. It didn't matter that she looked a mess because Mark had no recollection of her whatsoever. He didn't recall who she was or the fact that they were married, she felt transparent.

Nina came bounding into the toilets calling for her, "Jordan, Jordan where are you?" Jordan's whimpers enabled Nina to locate her. "Jordan it's ok, he has lost his memory, he doesn't remember any of us," she tried to reassure her, "in time it will come back we just have to try and encourage him to remember."

Jordan stopped crying and looked up at Nina, "When he looked at you and Irene his eyes changed slightly as if he remembered you both a little. I thought I was of great importance to him Nina so how come he looked at me like I was dust?"

"Stoppit!" Nina said angrily. She had had enough of Jordan and her selfish attitude. "The impact of his injuries has resulted in this, you heard the doctor, in time, slowly but surely it should come back." Nina stood up from the crouching position she was in, "I am going to leave you to get yourself together and I will see you back in Marks room." Nina rustled in her bag and found her packet of Kleenex tissues, she handed a couple to Jordan and walked away.

Watching as Nina hooked her Marc Jacobs hand bag over her shoulder and ruffled her curly hair Jordan felt sick in the pit of her stomach. She hated having to be all nice and fake but it was essential she maintained her game face. She wanted to break Nina down just like she had done to her with a basket full of smiles. She saw Marks eyes glint as he looked at her and so did everybody else. Wiping her tears, powdering her face and applying her Mac lip gloss, Jordan grabbed her Radley bag. She was going to show them, she was going to make Mark remember.

The words from Nina's journal circulated through her mind causing her blood to boil, '...*I would rather sleep with my best friends husband than to reveal my identity...*'

"Bitch!" Jordan yelled, the sound echoed off the bathroom walls. '...*I felt awful as he sucked and chewed my nipples...*' The words spun faster and faster in her mind. "I bet you did," Jordan shook trying to contain her emotions and trying not to cry. A lady entered the bathroom at that moment gawping at Jordan. She forced a plastic smile and took a deep breath before leaving the bathroom.

AARON.

Aaron stood helpless with his hands in his pockets as Jordan fled Marks room upon hearing the news that he was experiencing memory loss. She refused to come to terms with the fact that he didn't recall who she was. "Mark it's me your Wife," she tried to explain to him over and over again, but it didn't matter what she said or how hard she tried he just couldn't remember her.

Irene took her turn and sat next to him holding his hand, "Mark baby, it's me, your Mother," she said soothingly. Again Mark stared at her blankly for a while before he touched her face. Using his hand he wiped the tear that fell from her eye.

Nina took a step forward and smiled at him. "You're just playing with us all aren't you Mr man?" She softly joked attempting to break the ice. He sat up and gazed into her eyes.

"It's me, Nina, do you remember when we broke your Moms expensive lamp playing ball in the house and we were so afraid we tried to blame your pet hamster?" Irene chuckled and Mark smiled. He grabbed her hand and held it tightly shaking his head.

Jordan pushed her chair back and made a quick exit, she couldn't handle anymore.

Aaron stood still in the corner as Nina coaxed him to try and speak to Mark. "You heard what the doctor said Nina," he reminded her, "I don't want to confuse the poor guy any further, don't you think that

Jordan needs you right now?" He asked her taking Jordan's empty seat. He checked out her attire, again always on point. He loathed how she shoved her past in his face with her designer gear but he loved how she looked sexy all the time. Over time he had learnt to be stern with her and not let her sweetness win him over. She was so loving and caring to everyone, she was the girl you loved to hate and he loved her.

"You heard him Nina," Irene agreed, "go and check on the brat! I am going to go home now and prepare Marks room for him ready for when he comes home tomorrow." She gathered her stuff together.

"Would you like me to take you home Irene?" Aaron offered.

"No sweetie, I'll be ok, the fresh air will do me good and Lord knows I could do with the exercise," she kindly refused laughing.

Aaron kissed her hand full of guilt. It was his nephew that had put Mark in this place, if ever she knew. Mark was a good friend to him and his mother was such a beautiful, kind hearted lady. Even amongst the heartache and pain she still had her charm and wit.

Nina watched as Irene kissed Aaron on the cheek, "You have a good man here Nina, treat him well," she warned her.

Nina walked Irene halfway down the corridor before parting as she reached the bathroom where Jordan was weeping.

Aaron and Mark sat staring at each other until Aaron broke the silence. "How is your head feeling?"

"Sore," was Mark's brief but truthful response.

"Do you remember how you got here?" Aaron tried his luck.

"Who are you? The Police?"

Aaron smirked, "No Mark, my name is Aaron and I am your friend. You have been asleep for a long time and you have not long woken up and so you are not thinking straight."

Mark gave Aaron a puzzled look, "Was that really my Mom?"

"Yes Mark and she's going to take you home tomorrow and look after you."

"But if that other woman is my wife shouldn't I be going home with her?" He queried, sipping some of his water whilst looking around the room.

Aaron was at a loss for words and decided to change the subject. "Do you remember Nina?"

Mark put his cup down and fidgeted a little, "I...I..."

Waiting anxiously for his reply Aaron fidgeted a little to.

"I don't."

"It's ok mate," Aaron said getting up and handing him the 'goody bag' that Antoine had made for him. "Here, although you may not remember him, my little nephew Antoine made this up for you. You introduced him to 'goody bags' not long ago," Aaron grinned watching Mark open the bag with a smile on his face.

NINA.

Hating every last minute of the time spent in the hospital, Nina sat on the wall outside and gratefully inhaled a breath of fresh air. She had agreed to catch a lift home with Aaron as Jordan had made it perfectly clear that she needed to be alone. Maybe this would be a good opportunity for her and Aaron to have some alone time too, she thought as she watched the goings on outside. It always amazed her that the sick could muster up plenty of energy to climb out of their hospital bed and drag themselves miles down the hospital corridor, drip and all, for a ten minute puff on a fag.

"Did you speak to Mark?" Nina asked Aaron trying to find a nice CD to put on for their journey home.

"I did," he replied, eyes on the road.

Nina checked out her surroundings as they drove through Selly Oak. It had changed and improved but it still obtained that student feel. The cheap bars and coffee lounges, the grand houses that had been manipulated into student accommodation, the tall trees that lined the road sides barely letting any sunlight through.

Stopping at a set of traffic lights Aaron turned to face Nina, "Did you notice how Mark looked at you in comparison to Jordan?" He asked, searching her eyes deeply.

Nina looked away and carried on flipping through CD after CD. She didn't understand what he was getting at and she refused to entertain him.

The lights turned green and Aaron drove on without another word. Nina slid Chris Brown into the CD player and they both sat in their own silent worlds listening to the words of the song.

'I don't wanna go there, please don't make me go there...they're spreading rumours about me...'

"Are you coming in? It would be nice to spend some time together, don't you think?" She begged subtly, unclipping her seat belt and leaning toward Aaron kissing him gently on his lips.

Aaron unclipped his belt also and returned Nina's kiss, passionately caressing her face and sucking on her bottom lip. "Mmmmmm. I miss this," he moaned.

They both got out of the vehicle and made their way to Nina's flat. "I cant wait to show you how Jordan helped me to arrange and dress it all," she enticed him, turning her key in the lock happy that Aaron was willing to come in and make it better. She hated stress in relationships especially over trivial matters.

He kissed the back of Nina's neck and chewed on her earlobe ushering her to hurry up and open the door. He wanted to give her something special. "How about we christen a few rooms baby," he cheekily suggested feeling on her ass.

As Nina pushed her front door open they both rushed in hurriedly removing their coats longing for each other. Aaron suddenly stopped in his tracks and grabbed Nina's head and turned it forcefully to view the shoe mat. "Is this a joke?" He asked.

There on the shoe mat lay Nina's (ex) Prada heels. Aaron stood rigid and glared at Nina hoping and praying that she could justify them lying there blatantly in front of his face. He slowly walked over to the shoes and spied a piece of white paper sticking out of one of the shoes. He tipped the shoe up and the paper fell to the floor. Picking it up he read what was written on it;

Remember when you used to do it to me in just these heels?

I miss you Sunshine xxx

"What? What does it say?" Nina's heart beat increased, guessing it was similar to the note she found on her car. Aarons face displayed outright anger and rage, his whole body trembled as he threw the paper to the floor. His eyes changed from the usual soft, glinting hazel colour to a grim grey. He clenched his jaw, "You promised me," he just about managed to say before grabbing his coat forcefully nearly breaking the coat peg and storming off.

Nina bent down, stunned and picked up the slip of paper. A giant tear dripped down her cheek and landed heavily on the paper causing it to fall limp in her hand. "What the hell?!" She yelled, "Who is doing this to me?!" She fell into a crumpled heap on the floor kicking the Prada heels causing them to fly down the hall and bang off the wall. It seemed as if her world was spinning out of control. Her head pounded, she was horrified.

CHAPTER 16

MARK.

Opening his eyes Mark took in his surroundings. The smell, the beeping noises coming from the machines to the left of his bed, the trail of wires connecting parts of his body to the machines. The piercing bright lights caused him to squint. He felt hung over, right over.

Within seconds a nurse was standing over his bedside adjusting his pillows and blankets, setting him out a water jug and cup and recording his obs. "The doctor will be here right away. Do you know where you are Mark? Are you ok?" She sang at him like he was a child.

Through the drought in his mouth he croaked, "The hospital?"

"Yes, that's correct," she began but before she could sing anymore a doctor appeared at his bedside and stood next to her.

"Hello there Mark, how are you feeling?"

Mark looked at the Doctor, she was young and tall with really long brown hair, tied back in a neat pony tail. She had a precision cut fringe, the most precise cut fringe he'd ever seen in his life. Her face was pleasant with rosy red cheeks. "Like I've been clobbered around the head with a rock," he replied seriously.

The Doctor then asked him some more questions, "Do you know how you ended up in hospital?"

Taking his sweet time to try and piece everything together in his mind and remember rightly, he overheard the doctor muttering to the nurse. "...he may experience some memory loss due to the extent of the injury to his head so we need to tell his family and friends to encourage him to try and remember the important things. The bang to his head was very severe, infact he is very lucky to be alive."

Before Mark could answer the original question the Doctor spoke, "It's ok Mark, do not worry, in time little things will remind you of your life and slowly but surely you'll become updated." She patted his shoulder and walked away after giving the nurse instructions.

The Nurse was still standing by his bed, messing with the wires and writing things down on the clipboard. "I've informed your mother that you are now awake and she's on her way. Until then you just relax and try and drink some water. Try and take things at your own pace. I have ordered you some food as well, you must be hungry," she sang at him before leaving him alone with his own thoughts.

Mark lay still staring at the ceiling tiles, "Memory loss, hey?" He remembered exactly what happened as if it was the same morning. All of the people he put his trust into seemed to have let him down and betrayed him. All he had ever done was be nice, complacent, easy going, laid back Mark and look where that had gotten him. His kindness seemed to have been his weakness. Jordan had an affair with Alec and Aaron knew. The only person he felt comfortable with was Nina, even though they had their ups and downs and the whole Masquerade saga, they always ironed out the creases right away so they both knew where they stood. No lies. Yes he did harbour deeper feelings for Nina but he was respectful and because of her relationship with Aaron expanding he took a step back. All of their secrets and lies would soon be revealed, what goes on in the dark comes out in the light.

Right there and then as he lay in the hospital bed with all the madness sprinting through his mind, Mark conjured up a plan. 'Memory loss it shall be then,' he smirked wickedly. 'Time for me to step into the game', he cackled to himself closing his eyes thinking of all fun he was going to have. Rolling over he glanced at the 'goody bag' from Antoine and a tear rolled down his cheek, it caused a wave of memories to burst the flood gates in his mind. He began having flashbacks to when he lived happily with Jordan, the married couple they were. But unbeknownst to him she was unhappy. He thought about Nina's birthday meal when he first met Aaron and was chuffed to have gained a new mate.

'That girl over there is beautiful' he remembered whispering to Clive breathlessly as he floated across the hall, his feet hardly touching the ground, carrying him to the sexy lady in the mask with the net covering her succulent lips. He remembered how good she smelt and felt, how sweet she tasted and how strong her legs were as she straddled him. It seemed as if a sweet nectar flowed from her nipples as he sucked them hard tugging them gently with his teeth, he just couldn't get enough.

"Wake up baby," he heard. As he opened his eyes his mother stood before him with a hanky wiping the saliva off of his chin. As she kissed his forehead he closed his eyes and privately apologised to her for what he was about to put her through.

CHAPTER 17

NINA.

Sleepily swiping her hand beneath her pillow, Nina searched for her phone to stop it vibrating. It was Sunday and she sure would not have set an alarm. Through half closed eyes Nina peaked at the screen and saw that the caller ID read Irene. Rolling over she glimpsed the clock face and it showed 11am. "Hello," she answered groggily.

"Oh Nina darling, did I wake you?"

"Yes but it's ok Irene I have to get up anyway. Are you ok?"

"I am so sorry baby girl, I didn't know who to call or what to do."

"About what?" Nina asked curious as to what the matter was. She was having Mark home today so everything should be all good.

"Oh Nina, I got up early, very early adding the last minute touches to Marks room all ready for him, happy that my boy is coming home. I even booked the taxi for a certain time and everything and when I arrived at the hospital his bed was empty and all neatly prepared for the next poor patient," she story told.

"Well where is he?" Nina asked confused.

"They told me that he has gone home with his wife. That dreaded woman never ceases to amaze me," she cursed after Jordan. "I tried to be civil to her although I know she is no good for my son and it has gotten me nowhere. I really hate to bother you Nina darling and put more pressure on to you but you better go and speak to her and find out what she is up to before I do or else I will not be responsible for my actions!"

"Ok, Ok Irene, not to worry, I'm getting up now and I shall go around to hers once I have had a shower and I'll check what is going on."

Nina was mentally and physically drained and any little bit of sleep she grabbed still wasn't enough.

"Thank you Nina, oh how I wish he had married you…but Aaron seems a nice guy." she said in the next breath. "Please ring me once you have been around to Jordan's."

"Sure," Nina ended the call.

Just as Nina was about to drag herself into the shower her phone rang again. "Hi Nina, it's me Dave, I think I am outside if my sat nav is correct."

Nina scrambled to her window and peeped through the blinds. "Yes you are, I can see you," she confirmed, "press number twelve and I'll buzz you in."

Dave was one of Nina's brothers friends. He was always around their house growing up and even now he made a visit once a year to go and see Nina's brother in Atlanta. A loyal friend and also a locksmith which was the reason Nina had called him.

After Aaron had stormed out leaving her to wallow in her own self pity, all cried out Nina racked her brains as to who could be tormenting her. Assessing the situation simply, whoever it was had a key to her flat as there was never any signs of breaking and entering. The person knew her car and the person also knew the password and reference number to her storage unit where her 'secret life' box was stashed hidden amongst her other belongings in order to scatter her belongings around to remind her of her past.

Aaron was the only one with a key to her place, he had sorted out her car for her and she had given him the password and reference number to her storage cell the morning he was to go with Jordan and move her stuff into her new place. He was responsible as there was only one key. It all made sense. Why was he doing this? Was he that paranoid that she might be escorting again and trying to frighten her? Or was it payback?

Getting Dave to change the locks would help her narrow things down and find the miscreant. She hated to admit it but she had a terrible feeling that the person was close to home, too close for comfort and all she wanted to know was what their intentions were? She was no longer afraid, if they wanted to play, she was ready. She was going to catch Aaron red handed and then he'd have a lot of explaining to do.

Nina opened her front door greeting Dave with a kiss on his cheek, "Thank you for coming Dave, especially on a Sunday."

"Not a problem. So what's this all about then? Didn't you just move in here a couple of days ago? He asked.

Nina couldn't tell him the full story because she knew he would tell her brother and then he'd have twenty questions for her telling her she should have just hopped on that flight to him and left all the rubbish behind.

"I just don't feel secure here with these petty locks Dave and yesterday there was a break in in one of the other flats," she lied, "and as I live alone and I am out most of the time I just wanted to be safe." Nina showed him the locks. "I'm going to take a shower whilst you get on with that Dave. I have somewhere to be once you've finished. Go ahead and help yourself to a drink," she welcomed him, before getting all that she required and closing the bathroom door.

Oiling her wet skin, Nina sat on the edge of the bath trying to figure out what Aarons reasons were for tormenting her. Did she honestly deserve this? Refusing to let another tear escape her eyes she pulled on her GAP jeans and her Bob Marley fitted t-shirt. She spritzed her curly hair and applied some Vaseline to her lips and unruly eyebrows.

"All done Bab," Dave showed her what he had done and how he had fitted a Yale lock for extra security. He handed her two sets of keys.

Thanking him, Nina handed him an envelope with some money inside.

"No, no, no Nina, it's ok," he protested, putting his hands up in the air so as not to take the envelope.

"But you came out of your way and it's Sunday too," she tried to convince him with all her might to take the money.

"You are my little Sister so not to worry," he said, winking at her before leaving.

Satisfied and feeling automatically safe at the sight of the locks on her door Nina twiddled the two sets of keys between her fingers. "Now we'll see," she mumbled, lacing up her Allstars and laughing. "I am the only key holder to this casa!"

It was Autumn but it wasn't cold, just a bit nippy. As she drove to Jordan's house Nina adored the golden and red leaves as they floated softly off the trees and fell to the ground littering the pavements, some remaining crunchy and crisp and the unfortunate ones sopping wet and mushy. She loved this time of year, everything was so tranquil and calm before the crazy festivities of Halloween, Bonfire night and the mad Christmas rush. Feeling in her glove compartment for her 'sunnies' Nina slid them on to dim the bright sunshine that disrupted her driving vision. She pressed play on her CD player and Disclosure filled her car speakers. Bouncing in her seat to the rhythm of the beat she smiled for what seemed like the first time in ages. Wasn't it amazing how a couple of locks could make her feel so much better.

'No For Sale sign and new curtains?' Nina removed her sunglasses to have a second look just incase she hadn't observed right the first time. 'What's going on Jordan?' Stepping out of her car Nina walked up Jordan's garden path and rang the doorbell, locking her car as she waited for her to answer.

JORDAN.

After witnessing the way Mark responded to Nina at the hospital and the way Nina shrugged it off nonchalantly, making out that Jordan's behaviour was 'over the top' had caused Jordan to burst with resentment. She deliberately left the hospital before Nina and Aaron knowing she had just enough time to plant the Prada heels in the hallway. She aimed to keep Nina on her toes and what was even better was she knew that Aaron would more than likely go in with her if he was taking her home. Nina needed bringing down a peg or two.

Irene was second on her list. Jordan knew full well how Irene felt towards her and she was just acting at the hospital due to the audience. As soon as Jordan had got home that evening after her spiteful move at Nina's, she unpacked her house to make it back to the home it was when her and Mark lived together, happily married. She took down the 'For Sale' sign planning on calling the agent on Monday morning to take her house off the market. She even went as far as doing a late night supermarket run, stocking up on all Mark's favourite foods.

Sunday morning she intended to reach that hospital before Irene and bring her husband home where he belonged. She would help his memory, most certainly.

Ding dong, ding dong!' Jordan's doorbell rang out disturbing her train of thought. Preparing herself to open her front door and come face to face with Irene, Jordan took a deep breath and reminded herself that no matter what, she was to remain calm and collective, after all, technically, Mark was still her husband.

Swinging the door open, to Jordan's surprise Nina stood on the opposite side, "Oh," Jordan frowned, "I thought that..."

"That I was Irene?" Nina stated and questioned at the same time. "Jordan, what are you playing at?" Nina pushed passed her welcoming herself into Jordan's home, "I've had Irene on the phone to me early this morning way before I was ready to rise and shine going out of her mind over her missing son!" Nina scolded Jordan whilst bending down and removing her shoes at the hall mat. "You knew she was taking Mark home today and.."

"And nothing Nina," Jordan heaved getting defensive, "He is my husband and I am more than capable of taking care of him, simple."

Nina followed her through to the lounge where Mark sat comfortably on the sofa with a blanket watching the television. Ignoring Jordan and her 'Queen of Sheba' status, Nina sat down next to Mark. "How are you doing?" She rubbed his shoulder.

Jordan leaned against the doorframe watching how Nina soothed her husband. Flashbacks from the pages of Nina's journal attacked her memory at full force as she observed her behaviour.

"I'm ok, just watching this programme that is supposed to be funny but to me it isn't," he chirped, throwing a handful of peanuts into his mouth and flinging his head back at the same time.

"Don't you want to be at home with your Mother?" Nina asked, remembering the reason as to why she made the visit in the first place.

"Nina!" Jordan barked, "Stop it!"

"No Jordan I won't, you knew her plans and still you carried on with your selfish ways, I'm sorry but as far as I can see you are causing trouble," Nina protested with honesty.

"Fine then," Jordan said noticing how Mark hadn't flinched or reacted in the slightest to their raised voices, "ask him where he wants to be?"

Nina couldn't believe what Jordan was doing but she turned to face Mark, "Mark?"

He stared at her like a lost puppy dog and she silently willed him to choose his Mothers home. His eyes glowed for a brief moment and she smiled subtly, "I'm...I'm fine here Nina, I don't understand the fuss,

Jordan's my wife isn't she? Mom is more than welcome to come here whenever she likes so I don't see the problem really."

Jordan grinned from ear to ear.

Nina got up and made her way to the hallway to put on her shoes but not before kissing Mark on his forehead goodbye. She turned to face Jordan at her front door, "Why are doing this Jordan?"

"Doing what Nina?" She held her gaze until Nina looked away.

Nina didn't reply, she just walked down the drive and got into her car.

NINA.

"I'm so sorry Irene, Mark has made up his mind and is happy to stay with Jordan," Nina explained to Mark's mother as she sat in her car on the in car calling system. "I wouldn't take it personally Irene, he knows not what he's saying or truly doing," she continued trying to excuse his decision hearing the effect it was having upon his poor Mother. Nina then switched off, she was no longer listening to a word Irene was saying. She couldn't help but think that something was wrong. Why was Jordan behaving like this and Mark, well Mark that was something different altogether, she felt something was wrong but she couldn't put her finger on it, not just yet anyway.

JORDAN.

Glad that Nina had finally left and chuffed with Marks decision to stay safe in her arms, Jordan smiled to herself. Now all she had to do was re-create their perfect past and convince Mark that all still remained the same and everything he required was right there with her and once everybody saw it for themselves and believed it, they could be left alone to get on.

She aimed to show Nina that he who laughs last laughs longest. She was going to expose her filthy past and take home the winning trophy - Mark.

CHAPTER 18

AARON.

Slowly dragging himself to his car after clocking out of work, Aaron slumped into his car seat. How had life taken such a drastic turn in what seemed like a split second? He was finding it difficult to jump the many hurdles storming in his direction, one minute his relationship with Nina was fine and the next it was a fat mess. He had tried to convince himself that someone else could have her, he was done with her, he didn't want her anymore, but then he clung to her beauty, not just superficial beauty but her character, her personality, how she carried herself, worked hard, went out of her way to help any and everybody, and no matter how hard he tried he just couldn't shake her off.

Seeing her Prada heels sitting in her hallway confirmed his worst fears but what he couldn't understand was the pretence she portrayed as if she was clueless as to how they had ended up right there on the mat in plain sight. She was caught red handed and he knew he had to let her go. The last time he had seen her was that same night and he knew their next meeting would be saying hello to goodbye, he couldn't handle anymore, it was time to call it a day but first he had to speak to Alec.

"Where are you?" Alec questioned his uncle down the phone, "I'm here at Nando's waiting on you, hurry up uncle"

"Get a table and I'll be there in five minutes," Aaron told him.

NINA.

How she made it through her working day Nina had no idea. Her mind was re-playing the night that her (ex) Prada heels somehow made a surprise appearance into her new home. Itching to find the soul destroying prankster had left her concentration span at zero percent. Clock watching intently, Nina edged off of her chair eager to get the hell out of work and do what she had to do. She had to stop off at Aarons on her way home before he reached there. Impatience had gotten the better of her and she went to see her manager and conjured up a pitiful excuse so as to leave half an hour earlier.

She had changed the locks on her door at home but for her own self satisfaction, to confirm her accusations were correct that Aaron was the culprit, she had to check his place for her 'secret life' box, the box that was hidden in the storage unit to which he had the keys to. She kept trying to figure out why he would do this to her. She didn't understand as she had already conveyed the details of her past to him in as much detail as he wanted.

After permission had been granted, refusing to hang around a moment longer, Nina made her way to her car. "Not again?" She quickened her pace and as she neared her vehicle her eyes widened with doom as the sight of the white envelope hooked beneath her wiper came into clear view. As she lifted it up she felt the weight and realised there was more than just a letter inside. Looking around to see if she was being spied on she jumped into her car and locked herself in. Breathing rapidly trying her hardest to lower her distress levels, she fumbled with the envelope dreading what was inside. Eventually she opened it and a pile of different flavoured condoms fell into her lap followed by a note:

HELLO SUNSHINE, DO YOU REMEMBER
WHICH ONE WAS MY FAVOURITE FLAVOUR?
I REMEMBER WHICH ONE WAS YOURS.
I MISS YOU XX

Nina sat stiff as a board and stared at the contents that sat in her lap. This was the last straw she had had enough, it was time to confront Aaron, who else could it possibly be? Stuffing the condoms back into the envelope with the letter, trying her hardest not to cry, biting on her bottom lip and sucking it up, she composed herself and headed in the direction of Aarons flat.

AARON.

Aaron spotted Alec sitting at a table by the window in his favourite Nando's on Broad Street. He was drumming his hands on the table top scanning his surroundings probably looking for him. Taking a seat opposite his nephew he cracked a smile, "So what have you ordered for us then?"

"You never told me to order food," Alec scowled, "You just told me to get us a table."

"Ok," Aaron laughed, "I was just joking with you, why do you always have to be so serious and fiery?" he asked grabbing a menu out of the holder on the table and rubbing his hands together salivating.

"Uncle, I'm not really hungry."

"What have you eaten today?" Aaron wanted to know if he was eating well and looking after himself properly.

Alec looked up at his uncle, eyes only, "I'll just have some chips and a drink then," he compromised avoiding a lecture.

Aaron smiled, "That's cool."

It wasn't long before their food arrived and they were tucking in. (Well Aaron was tucking in) In between mouthfuls he began to tell Alec how Mark had woken up and decided to join them again. He informed him concisely of Marks current state due to the repercussions of his injury.

Alec stopped eating and slowly took a sip of his drink. He didn't utter a word or make a sound, he just listened to his uncle go on about how the hospital visit went and how hard it was on them all including Irene, Marks mother.

Aaron wrapped up what he had to say and looked at Alec searching for a sign, anything of a responsive nature, but all he received was a blank expression. "Alec you are my nephew and I will love and protect you no matter what. I wanted to tell you about the situation with Mark because I don't want any more trouble. It's time for you to calm down and take a step back and a deep breath whenever you find yourself in a fiery predicament, think with you head not your fists. Marks memory loss is unfortunate for him and those close to him but although I hate to say it, lucky for you," Aaron finished.

Alec turned his head and watched the people passing by outside. Aarons heart went out to him. "I didn't mean to Uncle...I didn't mean to..."

"Come on," Aaron said standing up, "let's go to the car," he offered, leading the way out of the restaurant. Alec followed close behind desperate for some fresh air and to save embarrassment.

Once they were both in the car Alec let his emotions flow freely. "He was attacking you uncle, he was attacking everyone, throwing his weight around, even before you arrived. He wouldn't stop Uncle and I'm so sorry but it was either him or me!" Alec raised his voice with fury.

"It's ok, calm down, I understand, what's done is done," he reassured his nephew spotting his eyes changing colour slightly, afraid he might lose his temper. "Listen, nothing has changed between us and I want you to know that you are still welcome anytime to chill with me whenever or whatever ok?"

"What about Nina? She's close to Mark isn't she?"

"What about her?" Aaron asked with an attitude, upset that her relationship with Mark was so obvious.

Alec sensed that something wasn't right with them and probed a little deeper, "Is everything alright between the two of you?"

Aaron was a private person and didn't really want his nephew caught up in his affairs.

"Well?" Alec provoked, curious at his uncles hesitation to reply.

"I think I made a mistake by taking her back," Aaron began.

"Hold on, you broke up once before?" Alec asked confused, trying to understand what his uncle was going on about.

"Yes," Aaron decided to be honest with his nephew, after all he was now a young adult so he gave his maturity the benefit of the doubt and proceeded to explain. "She did something that a majority of men would not forgive full stop, but I did because I love her and what she did is rearing it's ugly head back in my direction and it's evident and yet she denies it."

Totally clueless at his uncles riddles and rhymes Alec felt honoured somewhat that he had confided in him, even partially, "I have no idea what she has done and you don't have to tell me, but if you took her back the first time it must have been for a good reason and therefore I'm quite sure you can work through this together, whatever it is," he smiled, "plus," he added, "I like her, I like her a lot, she's fun, she's fair, bubbly and full of joy and not to mention…"

Aaron ruffled Alec's hair and got him in a pretend headlock, "And what?" He teased.

"…and she's pretty!" Alec gagged laughing.

"Come on let's go back to mine," Aaron laughed starting the car.

As they drove a sense of relief washed over Aaron, he had finally got through to Alec and he could see that he was sorry for his input towards the incident with Mark and was willing to make a change. His thoughts switched to Nina and how Alec complimented and commended her. He had noticed personally how everyone seemed to adore her but he had to be strong and set that aside, he refused to be fool twice over. The evidence was as clear as day and he aimed to get to the bottom of it.

NINA.

Nina wondered around Aarons flat disappointed at how untidy it was. Clothes were just thrown on the floor and the bowl in the kitchen sink was full up of dirty dishes. Trying her hardest to ignore the mess she switched her mind back to the task in hand, searching for her 'secret life' box. She was convinced he had it otherwise who else would be placing her own objects around her flat and tormenting her? He was the only one with access.

Looking under the bed, in the wardrobe, behind doors and everywhere else she could possible think of, she gave up and slumped on the sofa. "I just don't understand." Leaning forward and placing her chin in the palm of her hands she racked her brains for another explanation. As she did so she saw some of Aarons mail sitting on the coffee table. It was open so it must have been yesterdays as he usually checked his mailbox after work and he hadn't been home yet. "Paternity test results?" She twisted up her face in confusion, "Parent of whom?" Before she could read any further she heard the jingling sound of keys in the front door. Startled and alarmed, not knowing what to do with herself, she stuffed the letter back into it's envelope as best and as fast as she could and tried not to panic. A team of excuses ran through the tracks of her brain begging for first prize, how was she going to explain her presence to Aaron but further more who was his child?

AARON.

Aaron and Alec stumbled into Aarons flat still laughing at a joke that they had shared in the car but stopped abruptly at the sight of Nina trying to get past them to leave.

"Nina," Aaron gawped at her, "What are you doing here?"

Feeling a little awkward Alec excused himself and went into the spare bedroom.

"I er...er..." Nina stuttered with sheer embarrassment.

"You what?" Aaron rudely asked still thinking about their last encounter with the Prada heels. "You are not leaving here without talking to me, we are a mess and I want this sorted out today," he said signalling for her to go back through to the lounge, "So please don't leave just yet."

Nina was at a loss for words, Aaron was always so nice and reasonable, that's why she loved him but that opinion soon vanished as she remembered the paternity letter she had just clapped her eyes upon. 'Everybody is living a lie,' she thought to herself wondering how long it would be before he decided to tell her about it. "No, I can't do this now, not with Alec here, I have to leave, come to mine tomorrow evening and I'll talk to you then," she told him heading towards the front door.

"No Nina!" Aaron raised his voice, "We need to sort this out now!" He said grabbing her arm and gently pulling her towards him.

Alec heard the noise and came out of his room. Just as he did so Nina tugged her arm back causing the contents of her handbag to spill out and scatter all over the place. The envelope containing the condoms flew everywhere followed by her lip gloss, phone, keys and diary,

Time stood still and the silence was deafening as each of them paused as still as statues.

It seemed like forever before anybody moved. Aaron glared at Nina, his eyes bulging, his heart pounding and as he scanned the floor concentrating on the condoms waving at him, his expression turned from a frown, to outrage and as he turned to look at Nina it turned into dismay. Standing and staring deep into Nina's eyes he searched for her, the Nina he once knew. He couldn't believe what she had turned into to. The woman he had loved so much and thought so highly of had let him down. As much as he wanted to continue loving her he couldn't, not anymore. This was the straw that broke the camel's back.

"I can explain..." Nina muttered as her eyes filled with hot, salty tears, burning her lower lids as they escaped slowly down her cheeks.

"How? Just leave Nina, I can't tell your truth from your lies anymore."

Dismissing the fact that Alec was witnessing the whole thing and fed up of dealing with it all alone and in the 'correct' way she turned around and let Aaron have it, "No, you're right, I can't explain this, but you can!"

Shocked Aaron questioned her, "Me? How?"

"Because it's you who has been doing this to me!" She screamed, "It's you who has been planting objects from my past in my flat and on my car, these condoms, the heels, the business card, as well as leaving notes with them making references to my past then playing like you know nothing about it and blaming me. Why are you doing this to me Aaron, is this why you took me back, to punish me?" She broke down crying in a heap on the floor, "I can't take it anymore, I'm sorry ok? I'm sorry for what I did, what else do I have to do to prove that I no longer meddle in that life anymore?"

Alec hovered astonished at what he was witnessing and retreated back into the spare room and shut the door giving them their privacy.

Helping her up unable to stand the sight of her so upset he asked, "How do you come to that conclusion Nina?"

"Because only you have keys to my flat, you know my car and I gave you my password, reference number and keys to my storage cell the day you moved my stuff, and it was from that day that all of this started", she brushed his hands off her.

Noticing her hands shaking Aaron told her to go and sit down whilst he went to get her a glass of water. As water gushed out of the cold tap Aaron became lost thinking back to the day Jordan and him moved Nina's belongings. Suddenly it clicked. As quick as he could he filled her a glass of water and carried it straight in to her. He watched as she drank it down in one gulp. Sitting down next to her he began to relay his thoughts. "Look at me Nina," he started, grabbing her face and turning it to face him, "I would never do anything so low," he began, wiping the tears from her cheeks, "I can't believe you even thought I would, but I think I have an idea who is behind all of this, as to the reasons why I'm not sure."

Nina put her empty glass down on the coffee table spotting the letters again itching to bring up the paternity test results but Aaron had captured her attention, "Who?"

Aaron confessed to Nina what happened the day her stuff was moved, "Jordan woke up late and therefore wasn't ready when I went to pick her up so I told her to go to the storage unit when she was dressed and pick up the boxes that you had listed. I gave her the list along with the reference number, the password and the keys wrapped up inside."

Nina was horrified, she hadn't told Jordan about her 'secret life,' she had no idea. Trying to hold it all inside and maintain her expression she asked, "But what about being able to enter my flat?"

"Well," Aaron recommenced, "I was extremely tired after moving all the stuff and helping Jordan move the boxes from the car to the flat, so I left her at yours to finish off and told her to lock up and drop the keys off to me later."

Nina was lost for words, she sat still, swaying slightly in shock. This meant that Jordan knew about her past. "Did she drop them off to you?"

"Yeh, that same evening."

"So how did..." before she even finished she answered her own question, "She must have made a copy."

Aaron never said a word, he just watched Nina sitting and thinking. It all began to make sense if their facts were correct regarding Jordan. Aaron immediately felt guilty. Each and every time an incident occurred he had just walked off and left Nina alone wallowing in upset and fright. He had let her down. "Nina I'm so sorry."

Nina didn't hear his apology, her mind was elsewhere. If Jordan had found her 'secret life' box then she would have gone through it and found her journal. "Oh no!" Nina stood up and grabbed her bag and darted out of the door.

"Nina wait!" Aaron called. But Nina was gone.

NINA.

Nina sat in her car and rustled through her glove compartment in search of something sweet, she needed a 999 sugar fix to calm her nerves. She sat cuddling a bag of Haribo sours, gnawing rapidly, her eyes transfixed on nothing. She had ten tonne trucks carrying heavy cargo driving through the many roads of her mind heading to destination unknown. She was lost.

'So it wasn't Aaron,' she thought, relieved but disturbed at his prediction. The clock read 7:45 pm and Nina decided to settle her mind and go to the storage unit to see if her 'secret life' box was still sitting there safely. "I can make it," she told herself knowing it closed at 8pm.

"Sorry love, we are closing now," one of the storage unit workers notified her.

Trying not to panic, desperately needing and wanting to make sure her box was there she tried to come up with a pitiful excuse. "I'm so sorry but I think I have lost a couple of boxes and I just wanted to quickly check that they were here," she pleaded.

"I'm sorry darling but the shutters are going down in five minutes.

"I'll be two minutes!" She begged, clasping her hands together. "I just need to have a quick glance in my storage cell to check that they are safe and then I shall come back another day at a reasonable time. I really need to know they are safe," she pouted, poking out her bottom lip.

"What number is your cell?" He asked giving in to her sad, puppy dog expression.

"Thirty!" She jumped up with glee verifying her reference number and password.

"Go on then, run!" He ushered her.

Nina grabbed the keys gratefully from his hand and ran down the long corridor to her cell as fast as her tired legs could carry her. She opened her cell and flicked the light switch on. As light graced the room her eyes scanned it for her unlabelled box, her 'secret life box.' The box that contained enough material to ruin lives. 'Aunty always told me never to keep a journal, write and destroy, why didn't I listen?'

"Come on darling!" She heard the echo of the workers voice call to her.

"Bingo!" She ran up to it and opened the flaps to reveal a layer of tissue paper. Removing the tissue paper she saw her Pradas. "But how? I have them at my place."

"One minute to go lady!"

Pushed for time she put the tissue paper back and shut the flaps. She pushed it into a corner feeling that it was weighty and turned off the light. She locked her cell and once again ran as fast as could back down the long corridor.

"Is everything ok?" The worker asked politely.

Nina smiled, "yes thank you," she said handing back the keys and bending down beneath the half closed shutter to exit and got into her car. Now she was totally confused. If her box was there how was it that the contents got to her flat and her car but the box was full? Drumming her fingers on the steering wheel Nina decided another trip to the unit was due with ample time to actually go through the box to see what it actually held because it just didn't make sense.

CHAPTER 19

NINA.

I t was mid-week and Nina was drained. She had tossed and turned all night and the lack of sleep was catching up with her. She had no clue how she had managed to drive to work safely that morning. Not only was she trying to work out how the contents of her box got around if her box was safe in storage, but she was trying to figure out why Aaron had a paternity test letter. Although the least of her problems she couldn't help but feel hurt. Aaron never once stopped to listen to her when she tried to tell him that she wasn't escorting anymore, he had accused her plenty of times and it had taken a lot of grief and disruption before he even began to listen to her and now he had a secret.

Thud! Kate her co-worker dropped a set of files on her desk waking her up out of her daydream. Nina scowled, "When for?"

"By the end of the day," Kate laughed, "Sorry."

"I better get on with it then," Nina caught sight of the clock, it read 11:42am.

Trying to focus and concentrate was difficult as she still remained puzzled. She intended to get to the bottom of it and it started with a visit to Jordan's after work. Feeling so alone with lies and deceit spiralling around her, Nina tried to get stuck into her work but failed miserably.

AARON.

Feeling a little comfort now knowing the situation with Nina, Aaron aimed to fix things. He felt guilty as he ploughed through his working day. Guilty for not believing in her and for breaking her down, walking away from her and not listening to her when she tried to explain, guilty for not being there for her when she needed him the most. Having learnt what she had been facing all alone he understood why she had behaved how she had done.

He had arrived at the conclusion of it being Jordan from observing her behaviour towards Nina. The way she looked at her with 'green eyes,' how she silently competed with her, trying to dress similar to her or do one better. How she rolled her eyes at Nina when she spoke or if people paid her attention as if she wondered what was so special about her. What was special about her was she took great pride in everything she did, how she presented herself, impressions, especially first impressions, they meant a lot to Nina. She was naturally a jolly, bubbly person who was nice to everyone, even when people weren't that nice back. Jordan seemed like a woman scorned but for what reason Aaron wasn't too sure. There may be more to what he knew about their friendship, something that remained locked away and unspoken about.

Whilst on the subject of Jordan, Aarons mind reverted back to the day at the hospital when he overheard Nina telling Mark to wake up if he loved her like he said he did. Trying to stray his thoughts and failing he yearned for peace of mind and decided to take an early lunch and get some fresh air.

Sorting things out with Nina was a 'must' as well as being a father to Antoine. What a sticky situation, he still had to break that news to Nina, he couldn't lose her, she was his life, he prayed she didn't fly off the handle when he told her the situation.

MARK.

Although he found it tough and taxing playing the game of amnesia, Mark had to maintain it as precisely as he could so as not to get caught out. His strategy was to say and do the minimal. Still in pain due to his head injury he enjoyed his days at Jordan's being waited on hand and foot and being pampered. It was restful and relaxing. He watched her and how she dressed to impress him and treated him like a king. She had tried to seduce him and get intimate with him a few times but he had fiddled his way out of it. No way could he forget that she had slept with Alec and had been pregnant by him.

For days he had listened to her telling him the facts about how they were as a couple, how they lived before the incident and more. He would just listen intently to her version and vision of their 'perfect' life. As he listened he pitied her. She knew she had done him wrong and now she was bending over backwards, working her fingers to the bones in order to straighten things out. Her efforts were plausible but the game she was playing wasn't.

Having to pick her over his own mother ripped through his soul but he had to expose Jordan for who she really was, malicious, selfish and spiteful.

JORDAN.

Satisfied how things were going at home and how Mark had settled in nicely got her thinking about her next steps. She'd successfully got him all to herself and everyday she had reminded him constantly about how their lives used to be, she wanted him to get it into his head that he belonged with her.

She knew that it wouldn't be long before she would have to return to work and so she'd have to find a new job. Her funds were running low having to look after them both and taking the house back off the market. But she had to move fast with Mark, she needed him to be and feel stable for her to do so.

Admiring how Mark lay comfortably on the bed watching television she snuggled up close to him and began stroking his face. He never flinched or moved a muscle as she carried on, stroke after stroke, caressing him. She wanted him to stroke her back, she quietly suffered, aching and craving his love, affection and attention. She wanted to be the only thing on his mind. She climbed on top of him and stared deep into his eyes, "Kiss me," she whispered, her lips touching his as she spoke, "Kiss your wife."

Mark pecked her on her lips and gently rolled her off of him, "I can't see the TV."

Feeling totally rejected and empty Jordan made her way downstairs into the kitchen to make herself a drink. She was going to jog his memory alright.

CHAPTER 20

NINA.

Ding dong! Nina stood at Jordan's front door but nobody answered. She knew that someone was at home because she could hear the TV and Jordan's car was sitting on the drive.

"I know you are home Jordan," she shouted through the letter box, "I need to talk to you!"

Immediately the door swung open and Mark stood in front of her. Standing and fixing herself up she greeted him, "Oh Mark, I didn't expect you to answer the door, are you ok? Where's Jordan?" She babbled.

Mark opened the door a little bit wider inviting her in and shutting the door. "She's gone to the estate agents to sort out something to do with the house, she wanted to walk, said she needed the exercise," he told her, as he lead her through to the lounge where he had been watching TV and munching junk food with his blanket, the same as all the other days.

"How are you and Jordan getting along?" Nina asked trying to be tactful but nosey at the same time. She was disgusted at what Jordan was doing by stealing him from the hospital and playing make believe with Marks head and heart.

Mark stopped and stared at Nina for a while before attempting to speak. He then stopped and shook his head.

"What it is Mark?" Nina asked full of concern as she watched him rubbing and shaking his head.

"It doesn't matter," he said breaking eye contact with her.

Nina grabbed his hand, "What is it Mark, you know you can talk to me," she encouraged him, "Look at what we have been through."

"She's doing my head in Nina," he confessed, "She keeps going on about how we used to be, the things we used to do together..."

"She would do, she's trying to exercise your memory, freshen it up," Nina butted in seeing the confusion in his mannerisms.

"My memory doesn't need jogging, Nina, it's fine," he stated loudly.

"But..." Nina began.

"But nothing Nina, my memory is fine and dandy."

Nina edged away from him slightly creating a gap between them on the sofa, she was the one who was now confused. "I don't understand Mark."

Mark shuffled himself closer to her closing the gap between them both and grabbed Nina's hands, "Nina what I am about to tell you has to remain between the two of us, do you hear me?"

Nina could barely speak from trying to figure out what Mark was doing. The cogs were cranking in her head. "I hear you."

"Nina I don't have amnesia, nothing is wrong with my memory, I remember everything rightly. I know that Alec clobbered me over the head and put me in hospital and yes I am very lucky to be alive and have survived with minor repercussions. I know Jordan cheated on me with Alec and he was fuming because she aborted his child, I know that Aaron knew all along and kept it from me..."

"Stop! Stop!" Nina barked shaking her head in disbelief.

Mark refused, he had to tell her and so he carried on, "I know everything Nina, I remember it all, every last bit."

"Then why are you staying here with her then?" Nina asked puzzled. She sat twiddling her thumbs, as if she didn't already have enough to think about and now this.

"I want her to see that she cannot go around ruining peoples lives and think that she can get away with it."

"But what about Alec, he was the one who clobbered you?"

"He was angry because of her. It all stems down to her."

"I had a pleasant life Nina. Call me a fool for believing life was good with her but I did sincerely believe we were a strong couple. We rarely argued, we both had good jobs, our own home, we were married and trying for a baby and then she decides to branch out on me and throw it all away. Did she really think nothing was going to come of it?" Mark didn't wait for Nina to answer, "How is it that I then went from living in my own home to lodging in my Mothers spare room with my life piled up around me in boxes and black bags? Feeling worthless because I'm firing blanks. Isn't it funny how life goes?" He confided in her.

Nina had never stopped to think about everything that Mark had been through. She had only ever understood more from Jordan's aspect from spending time around her more so than Mark. She understood his need for her attention over that period of time and she kept knocking him back believing he wanted her to be with him when really he was seeking an ear to listen and a shoulder to cry on. She felt ashamed, he was a good friend to her, why didn't she see it, why didn't she know better. She was being bias because Jordan was her 'bestie' but right about now her feelings were swaying.

Listening to Mark got her thinking and she decided to make a team out of him. She had a problem that he could help her with. He was the one dwelling behind the 'closed door' therefore he would know all. "I understand Mark, I really do, but what are you going to achieve by pretending you can't remember?"

"Satisfaction," Mark replied sternly, "I'm going to tear her world apart and see how she copes, I'm going to leave her at rock bottom to start all over again and I'm going to make her fully aware of how her actions have continuous consequences on not just my life, but everybody else's. Look at Alec and what he did, I would have been outraged if she had aborted my child and then lied that she had a miscarriage, she messed with his young mind. Look at the predicament she put Aaron in. I'm not mad at him, he was protecting his nephew, I probably would have done the same if I were in his shoes. Having time to think things over has made me realise these things Nina."

Nina dived in sneakily and manipulated the conversation towards her suspicions, "What does she fill her days with if she's not working at the moment?"

"I don't know Nina but she's up to something."

"What do you mean?" Nina sat up straight giving Mark her full attention.

"I see her in her office most times typing up what looks like phrases in bold letters and when I walk in she switches the screen to the saver. One time I caught her stuffing an envelope with something but again she covered it up so I couldn't see what it was. Sometimes she will spontaneously up and disappear for half hour or so but because I don't have a car and am not supposed to drive for now I can't follow her." Mark stopped as he noticed Nina's eyes widen with fright, "What is it Nina?"

Nina told Mark the same as she had told Aaron about her findings in her flat and on her car, she told him what Aaron had said happened on the day that they moved Nina's belongings. She told him about her 'secret life' box being in storage and after the appearances of the random objects she went and checked that it was still there and it was. "She doesn't know about 'Sunshine' Mark, only you and Aaron do, that's why we split up in the first place," she told Mark as if he didn't know, hanging her head in shame.

"Forget about that," he told her lifting her chin up, "So what if she finds out that you were 'Sunshine' what would she gain from it? Anyway look at what she's done."

"You don't understand Mark, I kept a journal whilst I was 'Sunshine' and I documented my thoughts and feelings of the night…you know… with you at the Masquerade ball as well as Aaron finding out about 'Sunshine'".

Mark stood up and began rubbing the back of his head again. "Mark sit down and calm down please! This is not good for you, I shouldn't have thrown this at you, you need to rest," Nina patted the sofa inviting him to sit down.

"Look at me Nina, this is a mess. Here I am playing the fool to get her back for what she did to me and I'm just as bad. She's out there probably with the same intentions as me, bitter and wanting to get back at somebody, anybody. We have to stop this Nina."

Panic and distress were written all over Marks face. Destruction was what Nina felt blowing in the wind. She was in too deep, if Jordan had read her journal she was sure to tell Aaron that she had slept with Mark if all of the predictions from Mark and Aaron and even herself were true. Then it would all be over.

Silence enveloped them both hugging them tightly. Both of their minds baffled, bewildered expressions sitting on their faces taken aback by their discoveries.

Nina was the first to speak, "What are we going to do? What if Aaron finds out that we slept together?" Nina felt disorientated, she had too much to deal with. "I need to find out if it is her who is leaving the notes and stuff. I actually came here to openly confront her," Nina admitted.

Mark leaped out of his seat, "I know, check her car, I haven't noticed her bring anything into the house," he said reaching for Jordan's car keys from the glass bowl on the table.

Grabbing the keys from Marks hand Nina strode out of the house and down the drive towards Jordan's car. Releasing the locks she lifted the boot open. Sitting comfortably, tucked in the corner sat an unlabelled box. Nina reached to open the flaps, her stomach twitched with nerves. Pulling them open one by one Nina saw a layer of tissue paper covering the contents.

"What are you doing?"

Nina nearly jumped out of her skin butting her head on the boot open above her. She turned around to face Jordan who didn't look amused at all. "I er...erm..."

JORDAN.

"I'm going to the estate agents to tie up a few lose ends, do you want to come? Get a bit of fresh air?" Jordan tried to coax Mark up off the settee to do a bit of exercise. She'd noticed how he had become a little chubby from lazing around with the blanket and junk food day in day out.

"No, my head is hurting, I'm going to stay home and have a nap," he refused and handed her the car keys.

"No," she waved his hand away, "I'm going to walk," she said dragging on her knee high riding boots and buttoning up her coat. "I could do with the fresh air, I need to clear my head," she mumbled as she left the house.

Thankful her appointment was finally over Jordan slowly walked home deliberately taking the long route through the park. She was becoming impatient with Mark. Her plan wasn't working. Having Mark back wasn't what she thought it would be. He wasn't showing her any signs of love or affection or even an ounce of attention, it was as if she didn't exist. All he did was eat her out of house and home and lounge around all day everyday.

Then there was Nina. Scaring her seemed to be easy but discovering her key to get into her flat didn't work left her stuck and having to re-assess her tactics so as not to get caught.

Jordan sat on the park bench beneath a tree and watched the autumn leaves fall to the ground. Shoving her hands in her pockets she closed her eyes and breathed in a deep breath as the wind whirled gently around her. Refreshing her thoughts she decided that if Mark continued to reject her she would have no choice but to let it accidentally on purpose slip to Aaron the encounter at the Masquerade ball.

Checking the time on her watch Jordan pulled herself up off the bench and slowly wondered the remainder of the way home thinking about what to cook for dinner. As she neared her house she saw that the boot of her car was open. "What's Mark doing now?" She thought and picked up her pace. As she got even closer she realised who was scouring the boot of her car and started running as fast as she could picturing the 'secret life' box tucked in the corner. Her heart was beating rapidly, she was out of breath and her neck was clammy. Slowing right down she tried to calm her breathing and unbuttoned her collar, "What are you doing?" She caught Nina just in time before her hands removed the layer of tissue paper.

Nina turned to face her, her face was pale and her hands were trembling.

Jordan shoved her hands into her pockets trying to hide her to trembling hands and portray a cool, calm, demeanour.

Stuttering and stammering, Nina eventually told Jordan that Mark had asked her to go and check if his 'hoody' was in the car.

"Couldn't he come out and get it himself?" Jordan asked irritated.

"He said it was too cold, I didn't mind, I was just leaving anyway," Nina tried to break the ice with a warm smile. "You can tell him it's not in here," she said shutting the boot and handing Jordan her car keys.

Jordan snatched the keys from Nina's hands and began making her way inside.

"Are you ok?" Nina asked caught off guard by Jordan's weird behaviour.

"What did you want?" Jordan wanted to know stopping in her tracks and slowly turning around.

"I just came to check that you were ok and to see if there were any improvements with Mark."

"We are doing just fine," Jordan sated, "Perfectly fine so I'll see you then."

Feeling as if she were being forced off the premises Nina made her way to her car. She saw Mark lurking at the front door.

Jordan stormed inside of the house, "How long was she here?" She prodded Mark.

"About five minutes, why? What's wrong with you?" Mark asked playing the fool.

"Nothing, I'm just tired that's all," she apologised before wondering into the kitchen alone to prepare some dinner. She couldn't let Nina mess up her plans and the more Mark ignored her needs and wants the more he ignited her fuel to burn, burn the biggest fire ever.

CHAPTER 21

NINA.

It was Friday night as Nina strutted around her bedroom admiring herself in her vintage, full length mirror. It had been a while since she had had a night out and even longer since she had 'hooked up' with Claire.

Applying her last layer of nude lip gloss and spraying some perfume in the air, she twirled beneath it and let the delightful smelling mist kiss her hair and skin as it slowly floated downwards. Left with a massive choice of shoes to pick from, Nina became distracted by her phone beeping. It was a Whatsapp message from Aaron.

> *'Hey beautiful what you doing tonight? I would like for us to spend some time and tie up the loose ends, I want to make it better. Xxx'*

Not really wanting to reply, unsure of how she felt about him at that moment after seeing the paternity test letter, she kept it simple.

> *'Sorry but I'm going out for a drink with the girls, I need some time out, maybe tomorrow?'*

She felt confused, everything was misty and had no clarity. Aaron was such a gentle, reasonable soul and maybe he was going to tell her about the paternity test but right about now she wasn't ready to hear about it.

"Taxi time!" She said picking up her house phone off her bedside table and dialling whilst slipping her feet into her Fendi heels. Dropping the essentials into her snakeskin, envelope style clutch she smiled to herself, she aimed to have a fantastic night and get stupidly drunk. She felt sexy, she felt like 'Sunshine.' A tingling, excitable feeling flooded through her veins, a feeling that she missed. After everything that was going on lately she was tempted to say, "Screw what people think, I am an escort, I enjoy it and so what if you don't like it!" She remembered not being 'attached' and pleasing only herself, but then she remembered yearning for 'attachment.' She could never be satisfied it seemed.

The taxi beeped his horn outside and Nina locked up her flat leaving the hall light on and headed out into the cold night air. As she got into the taxi her phone beeped again.

> *'Please let me make it right with you. Come home to me after your night out, I do love you.'*

'Sunshine' instantly vanished from her thoughts.

Three cocktails later and Nina had updated Claire of the shenanigans that the past couple of weeks had thrown at her. "I feel drained Claire. It's been crazy, scary, messy and most of all eye-opening. Claire we all have secrets and I've had whiffs of theirs but what frightens me is Aaron and Jordan getting a whiff of mine."

Claire fiddled with her cocktail umbrella, "What secret? I thought they all knew?"

"No! Aaron and Jordan don't know that I slept with Mark and Jordan is completely in the dark about me escorting at all," Nina said defensively, panic wavering in her voice.

"I don't mean to be rude darling, but you are all as bad as each other," Claire giggled, tipsy. "Just go out there and live life, enjoy and do what makes you happy. If Aaron is the one then go ahead and make something of it honestly, if not then nip it in the bud and go your separate ways sooner rather than later." she advised her friend. "Things don't have to be complicated."

"How dare he lecture me and accuse me of escorting again when all along he has a paternity test result?"

"Well that's just it," Claire said with a glint in her eye and a cunning grin, "How dare he? Now come on let's have some fun and go and hit the dance floor." Claire dragged Nina off her bar stool shaking her hips to the music. It didn't take much to convince Nina when it came to dancing, she was already tipsy so why not get tipped right over the edge?

All eyes were glued to both girls as they made their way to the dance floor in rhythm to the beat.

AARON.

Buzzzzzz! Buzzzzzzz!

Aaron felt for the switch to his lamp light nearly knocking the glass of water off the bedside cabinet. He caught sight of the clock, 4am. Struggling to make his way to the intercom he grumbled a sleepy, "Hello?"

"It's me, Nina," she giggled.

He then remembered that he had invited her to come over after she had finished her night out but he didn't expect it to be so late or should he say so early. Buzzing her in regardless he left the door open for her and returned to his bed.

"Hello baby," she said as she entered his flat, kicking off her shoes and throwing her clutch on the chair in the corner of the bedroom. She swayed like a drunkard and tapped Aaron who was laying on the bed, his eyes half open from disturbed sleep. "Help me get out of this dress please," she asked him, twisting her arms behind her back trying to unzip her dress.

Aaron sat up and stood behind her carefully unzipping her dress. Nina let it fall to the floor and stepped out of it turning to face Aaron wearing just her CK underwear. She sloppily fell into his arms, heavy from alcohol consumption giggling and gurgling nonsense in his ear.

Aaron had slowly come around and became alert when he had laid eyes on Nina's luscious body. She looked so delicious and appealing, so sweet and vulnerable. She clasped her arms around his neck and he leaned forward and kissed her succulent, juicy lips. She kissed him back, biting gently on his bottom lip just like she always did causing him to feel powerless. He unclipped the clasp on her bra and freed her breasts sucking and rubbing each one equally as she gasped in sheer satisfaction.

A little unsteady on her feet Nina lost her balance and fell into Aaron causing him to fall on to the bed taking her with him. He rolled on top of her taking full control kissing her from her breasts down to her navel, twirling his tongue around and around on all her sensitive areas as she moaned and groaned. He removed her panties hastily and threw them on the floor and began scrumptiously devouring her lady garden. Nina's body jumped and squirmed as Aaron took her to higher heights with his tongue as his only tool. She was thirsty for more.

Even more horny from the alcohol present in her system Nina pushed Aaron over and commanded authority. Aaron stood up and Nina got down on her knees and began to treat him watching as his toes curled with pleasure. "Let me take you to ecstasy," she whispered, blowing her warm breath on his 'soldier,' "let Sunshine take you all the way."

Aaron pushed her away and went to the bathroom. When he returned to the bedroom he found Nina sleeping naked across the bed snoring. Hurt and aghast at what she had just said to him, he put her in the bed properly and pulled the duvet over her to cover up her exposed body before grabbing the blanket off the bottom of the bed and making his way into the living room. The sofa was to be his bed for the night. He couldn't stand the sight of her at that precise moment and her being drunk was no justification as far as he was concerned. "Goodnight Sunshine." he whispered into the empty room.

NINA.

Nina opened her eyes and slowly looked around at her surroundings. She registered where she was shortly after she spotted the picture of herself and Aaron from the bowling alley that they had taken together in the booth. The clock read 10:25am and Nina wondered where Aaron was as she rolled over to his empty side. She was all alone in her birthday suit. She climbed out of the bed and went through Aarons drawer to find a t-shirt to put on. She picked up the clothes from the night before that were strewn across the bedroom and stumbled. "Ouch my head," she groaned, pressing her hand on her forehead.

"There you are," she smiled as she wobbled into the living room to find Aaron comfortably watching TV and eating a bowl of cereal on the sofa. "You left me to sleep all alone, I missed you," she told him getting underneath the blanket with him.

Aaron stopped crunching his cereal and stared at her. She obviously had no memory of what happened last night and to excuse her because she was drunk was a 'no, no.' Therefore every time she had a little alcohol floating around her system he was to be reminded of her sordid past and play the role of one of her clients? He wasn't a job! Finding it hard to contain his thoughts and opinions he let it out, "Do you usually spend the entire night with your clients Sunshine?"

Nina jerked her head back and looked at him confused as to what that question was in aid of.

"I always assumed it was just, slam, bam, thank you ma'am," he snarled in utter disgust.

Nina flung the blanket off of herself and slapped Aaron across the face, "How dare you!" She screamed getting up and stomping towards the bedroom to gather her things together.

"That's it, run away as usual," Aaron shouted after her, slamming his bowl down on the coffee table.

"Why would you say such a thing?" Nina bawled, "Didn't we have a nice night together? I thought you wanted to make it right so why all of this?" Nina was shaking with vexation.

"I did want to make it right until you woke me up at stupid o' clock in your drunken state. Our lovemaking turned into a role play and according to you I was one of your clients who Sunshine was going to take to ecstasy."

"Huh?" Nina stood absolutely still, dumbfounded. "Did I?"

"Yes Nina you did and I felt like nothing, I felt irrelevant, I felt as if you didn't see me for Aaron and so I spent the night on the sofa. I couldn't bear to sleep beside you after such a fresh reminder that I was never your only one!"

Nina's eyes shifted around the room avoiding contact with Aarons. She felt so ashamed. "I must have been really drunk," she cried.

Aaron tried to fight feeling sorry for her. The saying, 'you make your bed you lie in it' came to his mind. He didn't want to be next to her. He didn't want to live with the mess, he couldn't do it anymore. "You know, I really wanted to make it right with you. I was irritated at being woken up at 4am but I set that aside when I saw your beautiful face and then we started to make it right. I feel as if I'm putting my heart on the line with you Nina, if it's not one thing it's another."

Nina was lost for words. She honestly couldn't remember what had happened. She tried to understand how she would feel if the tables were turned and then she remembered the paternity test. "Ok Mr Perfect," she knew it was a low blow but she was tired of going around in circles. Their relationship was like a broken record, "who are you Father to?" She had no idea what the results were but she took a chance insinuating that she knew.

A blank expression washed over Aarons face.

"Well?" Nina shot.

"Listen Nina, I was going to tell you but I was waiting for the right time."

Nina denied him an explanation just like all the times he had denied her of one and began getting herself ready to leave.

"Nina let me explain, please don't leave," Aaron begged.

"Like when you let me explain?" She said sarcastically.

Aaron couldn't fault her reason. He went to touch her but she pushed him away. "I'm Antoine's Father, Antoine is my Son."

Nina picked up her clutch, she didn't even bother to put on her shoes, she just grabbed them and left Aarons flat without a word and her shoes dangling from her hand.

Still in her clothes from the night before Nina lay with her blanket on her bed crying her eyes out. She wished she had gone to America instead of staying to be attacked by people from all angles, people who she thought meant something to her. All alone, lies circled her mind pecking at her.

She picked up her phone throwing it back down right away, she didn't even have anybody to talk to about it all, she certainly felt lonely at that point. Her phone beeped making her jump, it was a text message off Claire.

> *'I was going to ask you last night after what you had told me but I changed my mind when you told me you were going to stay at Aarons after we had finished partying. Basically I was wondering if you would see to a client of mine, he pays very well indeed and is very loyal to me, I don't want to let him down but unfortunately something has come up. It was just a thought, you can say no, I'd understand.'*

CHAPTER 22

AARON.

"Have you told her?"

"Yes," Aaron told Tressa, Alec and Antoine's mother over the phone. She'd been nagging him for days to tell Nina about him being Antoine's father and he didn't understand why.

"Well what did she have to say about it then?" Tressa pestered and pushed eager to know Nina's reaction.

"Nothing," Aaron sighed, "Nothing at all, she just walked away so I have no idea what she's thinking or feeling. Anyway, what does it have to do with you?" He said fed up of her harassing him.

"It matters to me because I am done Aaron, it's now your turn. I've raised those boys single handed so now you can take Antoine, Alec is grown and can look after himself."

"Wait just a second, hold on a minute," panic struck every nerve in Aaron's body, "What do you mean I can have Antoine?"

"Exactly what I just said," Tressa replied with attitude. "He loves being around you and Alec much more than with me and you have the space in your flat to accommodate him so I don't see the problem."

Aaron was fuming, Tressa was one sneaky, conniving woman, "It isn't that simple Tressa, does Antoine even know what is going on?"

"We'll just have to tell him, he'll find out sooner or later," she said matter-of-factly.

"Why are you being like this?" Aaron was curious to know, "What are you aching to do with your 'freedom' from him?"

"Well…" she began but Aaron didn't want to hear it.

"WELL, we need to sit down together as adults and discuss this properly, it's not a situation that can be resolved via a phone call and the changes you are requesting, or should I say demanding, will certainly not happen overnight," Aaron reasoned.

For the first time in a very long time Tressa became quiet, "Ok," she softly agreed, "What do you suggest?"

Aaron thought for a moment, "How about we meet at TGI Fridays, Antoine likes it there and we can talk to him and listen to what he wants."

"You're paying then," Tressa told him.

"Tressa!" Aaron tried to catch her before she hung up the phone.

"What now?!" She huffed.

"Just remember that he's only a child, he's six years old for goodness sakes."

"Meaning?" She asked, acting as if she had no clue why Aaron would say such a thing.

"Just try not to manipulate his mind, let him be."

"Would I do that?" She asked defensively.

"Erm...do you really want me to answer that?" Aaron laughed.

"Whatever!" Tressa dismissed his rude comment and hung up the phone.

"AAARGGHH!!! What a mess!" Aaron yelled kicking his work bag that sat at the front door. First thing Monday morning before he had even started work and Tressa had rang him to discuss him having Antoine permanently.

As he drove to work Antoine ran through his mind followed by Nina and Alec was close behind. Did he know? If so what did he think about the whole situation? He drove in silence, he wanted his ears clear and free from noise just in case his phone made any form of sound. He wanted to hear from Nina, it didn't matter what it was, a text, a Whatsapp, he didn't care, anything would do. He shook his head and thought how ironic it was that it was now his turn to try and make her understand.

NINA.

Not even her zesty, fruit burst shower gel had the power to invigorate her that Monday morning. The fantastic weekend she had planned had turned out to be disaster, a shambles. Nothing seemed to be working out for her lately, it was just one thing after another and it seemed never ending. She had stood at her closet doors for ages scanning the rails trying to decide what to wear to work that day. A little disappointed in herself because she hadn't organised it all the night before she settled on her plain, black day dress with a skinny, brown belt, plain black tights and her brown Mango shoe boots. Simple yet chic.

Sipping her tea in haste and dropping fruits and snack bars into her lunch bag she grabbed her bag and coat and made her way to her car.

She didn't know where she stood with Aaron, she was totally confused. One minute they were engaged and living together and the next minute she had moved out into her own place after constant accusations of her still escorting by him. She'd had to put up with idle threats and torments from someone, which interestingly enough had stopped since she had changed her locks and to top it all off she discovered that Antoine was Aaron's Son.

Out of the blue Nina burst out laughing hysterically and uncontrollably. It was either that or cry. The other drivers and passengers that sat in the lines of traffic stared at her blankly as if she was crazy but she refused to care. She didn't care about anything or anyone at that precise moment in time and it was such a great feeling, sitting all alone in her car in a line of traffic. She had missed that feeling. Not having a care in the world and she longed for some more of it.

Pulling up into her work car park she took her phone out of her bag and re-read Claire's text message. She wasn't bothered about money, she had money from past times, it was that feeling of being free and in control, happy and comfortable, sexy and smart, that's what she was yearning for. She had nothing to lose, her and Aaron seemed no longer an item. "One last time," she whispered to herself as she replied to Claire's message.

MARK.

Jordan had gone to a job interview that morning and Mark had decided to actually get up and get out. He put his gym bag together and ventured out on foot to the local community gym for a workout and a swim.

Mark clearly saw the signs surrounding the swimming pool, 'NO JUMPING INTO THE POOL.' but he didn't care and jumped in anyway making a loud splash.

"Oi!" The lifeguard shouted walking over to the edge of the pool trying to get as close to Mark as he could, "If you do that again you'll have to leave!" He said pointing at the signs as if Mark hadn't seen them.

"Ok, I'm sorry," Mark apologised trying not to laugh. He swam underneath the water drowning out all of the sounds. He then floated on his back glaring at the bright, white lights on the ceiling. The water felt so good, he felt light as a feather, he felt like nothing mattered. He thought about Jordan and wondered if pretending to have no memory was worth it. He figured it wasn't and decided to come clean and move back in with his mother and start again, brand new.

IRENE.

"Hello my darling boy," Irene greeted Mark at her front door, "What a lovely surprise, come on in. Are you hungry?" She asked, standing on her tip toes to reach his face to kiss it.

"Always hungry for your cooking," he said without thinking.

Irene stopped for a split second before asking, "What do you remember about your Mama's cooking?" She held on tightly to his hands with hope flickering in her eyes praying that he would tell her something to settle her soul, to reassure her that some things were coming back to him.

Mark could read her like a book and having thought after he had spoken as opposed to before he had to stylishly get out of it somehow. "I know that when my belly is hungry Mama will make it right," he smiled kissing her forehead.

Irene leaned against her Sons chest and inhaled his scent, "Boy you stink, go and wash yourself up before we eat," she slapped his arm and pushed him in the direction of the bathroom. She was so glad her son had come to see her.

Whilst Mark indulged in a long, hot shower, Irene stood smiling in the kitchen as she dished up a mountain of her good home cooking onto a plate for her son. Rice and peas, buttered cabbage and carrots, stew chicken and coleslaw. Joy swam through her veins grateful that although her son didn't remember much at least he remembered to come home for some food and love from his Mama, she felt honoured.

"I have been thinking," Irene began as she admired Mark wolfing down brimming spoonfuls of food, "How about you come to Jamaica with me for a bit?" She finished.

Mark stopped eating and placed his spoon to rest against the side of his plate, "When?" He asked wondering why she had suggested it.

"Soon baby, everybody was asking after you when I was there and when I actually thought about it, it has been a while since you showed your face back home," she looked at him. "It would probably do you some good," she smiled, "Good food, sunshine, catching up with the family..." she noticed sadness fill his eyes.

"Maybe," he picked up his spoon and carried on shovelling more food into his mouth smacking and licking his lips as he sucked the chicken off the bone.

Usually one for table manners Irene let it slide. That day the sound was music to her ears, it became a beauty rather than an irritation. "It was just a thought to help jog your memory and to escape from the goings on here, give you a chance to figure out what you want from life and where you want to be," Irene went on, "I just want what's best for you."

Mark winked at his mother, "I know."

JORDAN.

"Mark!" Jordan shouted as she entered her home, "Mark, I'm home!" She said searching each room but finding no sign of him. "Where is he?" She said, upset that he had disappeared without leaving a note so she knew whether he was safe or not. Jordan instantly became worried because of his head injury and the fact that he was walking about. She tapped her fingers on the kitchen counter top trying to work out where he could possibly be. She went upstairs and saw that the closet doors were open and his side was spilled out all over the place. His gym bag was missing. She chuckled to herself as she tidied up the clothes, 'About time you went to the gym,' she thought laughing to herself some more. At that moment she told herself to have a little bit more patience as it seemed Mark had noticed her getting on and wanted the same for himself. She knew him well and she knew for sure he wasn't a layabout. What she really wanted was some intimacy regardless of her past with Alec and his with Nina, she just wanted it all to be water under the bridge and for them to be whole again.

CHAPTER 23

NINA.

"I refuse to leave here without knowing for definite what is going on with my box," Nina told herself as she sat in her car outside of the storage centre. This time she had arrived at a decent hour allowing herself plenty of time to scout through the box thoroughly. She needed to establish what items were present and what items were absent, this mess needed wrapping up before it got out of hand. Nina had come to the point of realising that all the secrets needed to be revealed and if it meant people getting hurt so be it, she was sure their wounds would heal eventually.

Nina recited her reference number and her password to the worker which she had done so on numerous occasions but this time she was trembling quite obviously.

"Are you ok?" The worker asked remembering her face.

"I...I...am, yes thanks," Nina just about managed to say, signing the forms promptly in order to hurry up and get in so she could hurry up and get out.

Her focus took a sudden turn as she started up the corridor, she slowed right down, her legs turned to jelly and she became hot, her hands clammy with sweat. She yearned to know the truth behind the haunting of her 'secret life' and if Jordan was the culprit she longed to know why she would do such a thing. Thirsty to reveal the contents of her box Nina unlocked her cell door and flicked on the light switch. The familiar sight of what remained in her cell came into view along with her 'secret life box' sitting more or less alone away from the bulk of her other possessions.

"OK," she breathed, rubbing her hands together and walking towards her box. As she pulled back a flap at a time she had a flashback to when she stood at the boot of Jordan's car carrying out the exact same actions. Her heart thumped hard as she expected Jordan to suddenly appear from nowhere and stop her in her tracks, tell her not to look in there, tell her the truth.

"No it's my box and my life, I need to know," she coaxed herself to continue. Just like before a layer of tissue paper lay on the top. She removed it to reveal a pair of black heels that looked like her Prada's. "Hold on a minute," she squinted, picking them up and observing them from every angle possible, "These are not my Prada's, in fact, they're not Prada's at all." She threw them to one side and probed on through past the next layer of tissue paper stumbling upon a wad of plastic bags and old magazines. "To make it seem weighty and full, clever!" Nina laughed in anger frantically throwing the contents all over the room, left right and centre. It seemed that Aaron's and Mark's accusation was spot on. Jordan had set her up and clearly taken the time to play it right. "That sneaky little…"

Nina flopped on to the floor in a sorry state with tears running down her face. That was it then, Jordan had her box but most importantly her journal, she therefore knew what had happened with Mark at the Masquerade Ball. "It's my own fault!" She scolded herself, "I should have never kept a journal, I was just asking for this."

Nina shut off the lights and made her way to the reception desk to hand in her keys.

"Are you alright?" The worker asked her noticing her blotchy red cheeks and red, puffy eyes.

"Yes thanks," she barely responded dragging herself to her car.

Now what's going to happen? Nina contemplated. If Jordan knew why would she go to such great lengths to harbour Mark under her roof? Nina shuddered as a chill came over her. Something didn't feel right and the way that Jordan had been behaving lately enhanced her feeling. Knowing Jordan the way she did, Nina would say that Jordan had something up her sleeve, but what, she had no idea. "I have to speak to Mark," she said reversing out of her parking space.

JORDAN.

"Oh it's you," Jordan mumbled as she opened the door to Nina, "So what do I owe this pleasure?" she asked sarcastically.

Nina was confused with Jordan's attitude but if she was right about the 'box' then her attitude was explained. "Is Mark home?" Nina asked ignoring her sarcasm.

"No, he's gone to the gym," she simply stated.

"That's good," Nina smiled relieved that Mark was gaining his independence back.

"Yes it is and he'll soon be going back to work to at this rate," Jordan added proudly trying to make out that everything was fine and dandy at home. Little did she know, Nina knew better. "Is there something you wanted?" Jordan asked again blocking her doorway.

"No, it can wait," Nina said plastering a fake smile across her face, "It sounds as if you are both doing well and things are slowly getting back to normal so I'll leave you alone. I just wanted to see if Mark was alright from the other day but if he's out gallivanting I'm sure he's ok," Nina said before turning to walk back to her car.

"Nina!" Jordan called after her.

Nina turned around awaiting her reason for calling out her name, "Yes Jordan?"

"We are doing just fine, thank you for enquiring, I'll tell Mark that you passed by." With that said Jordan closed her front door and Nina got into her car.

CHAPTER 24

MARK.

Mark sat upstairs on the bus making his way home from his Mothers house with a full and satisfied belly. He wasn't allowed to drive as yet due to his head injury. As he neared 'home' he began feeling glum and down, he hated the life he was living and today he had decided that as soon as he reached Jordan's he was going to lay his cards on the table. Having listened to his Mother speak he was fooling nobody but himself let alone making it harder for nobody but himself.

He didn't like Jordan anymore, he hated what she had turned into, it was as if she was a stranger to him but they were living under the same roof. Why spend another day living an unhappy life when he could do something about it? He questioned himself knowing the answer.

As the bus drove on Mark gazed out of the window feeling like a school kid again, how times had changed. The last time he caught a bus he was probably seventeen years of age. The buses back then didn't have cameras with the screens and pushchair spaces. He had watched people get on and scan bus passes but trying not to make his awe obvious he escaped upstairs where it seemed quieter for a bit of peace. Reflecting back to his past made him realise that he was a man and although he had loved and lost it was time to move on and pick himself back up again. Maybe his mother was right and a break in sweet Jamaica would be the perfect remedy. He was going to tell Jordan the truth about his memory and how he felt about her, no more pussy footing around.

"Thanks driver," he slung his sports bag over his shoulder and got off the bus.

NINA.

Wrapped up all snug with her blanket that her aunty had made her with the TV on low, Nina wondered over and over why Jordan would go to such lengths instead of just confronting her but no excuse was valid enough to pluck. Nina was tired of thinking.

She was itching to ring Aaron and tell him what she had discovered at the storage unit being as she couldn't get a hold of Mark but she remembered how she felt about him and his fatherhood. He was a 'no go zone.' It would end up being her 'secret life' versus his 'secret fatherhood.'

Nina blinked away a few tears as she stared at the TV. Aaron was supposed to be her everything. She smiled to herself as she thought back to when they first met. How he kept up with her rhythm as they danced the night away. She giggled at his bank holiday surprise when he made a move and kissed her catching her off guard, capturing her feelings and wrapping them around his fingers. Going bowling with his nephews crept into her mind spoiling her flutter of happiness as she thought about Antoine. Nina loved those boys, it wasn't Antoine's fault, sweet, pure, innocent Antoine, her gem or should she say Aaron's gem.

Contemplating if it was worth hearing Aaron out in order to mend things between them floated in the air surrounding her, but with the many turns their relationship had taken in such a short time was a clear sign that they were better off apart.

Pulling her blanket up closer to her chin Nina glimpsed her engagement ring on her finger. She took it off and placed it on her bedside table. She felt lonely, isolated and empty and she decided that night staring at the flickering, fruity candle that burned on her nightstand, that she was going to do the job for Claire and disappear to Atlanta without telling a soul. A fresh start was what she required and she couldn't help but beat herself up for staying.

JORDAN.

The kitchen glowed as the house security light automatically came on signalling that Mark was walking up to the front door. Jordan had been awaiting his arrival all day and was curious to know how a couple of hours at the gym had turned into a fully fledged day out. The question was, a day out where? With whom? Trying not to let it work on her nerves and spoil what she had in store for him she mellowed and proceeded with her plans for their quality night in. Jordan was finally going to have his undivided attention, her plan was fail proof.

The front door swung open before Mark as if an automatic door. He hadn't even lifted his key to match the lock. "Oh," he took a step back astonished and surprised as if it were a magic trick.

"I saw you coming up the path," Jordan explained opening the door wider allowing him to enter. "Did you have a nice, long session at the gym?" She asked, placing emphasis on the word 'long' in hope that Mark would voluntarily confirm his whereabouts.

"Yeh but I'm really tired and I just want to go to bed," he said dropping his sports bag at the foot of the stairs and kicking off his Adidas trainers before heading up to the bedroom for a well earned sleep. He was exhausted mentally and physically.

"OK then," Jordan said with a malicious grin on her face, "I'll be up shortly."

Having already showered at his Mothers house Mark changed into his pyjamas and brushed his teeth deciding to speak to Jordan the following morning, he was extremely tired and lacked energy. Resting his heavy head on the cushy pillow Mark listened to Jordan scuttling about downstairs. He tried to stay awake for her to say goodnight, knowing he would be responsible for destroying her world the next day but he felt as if someone was sitting on his eyelids and it wasn't long before he fell into a deep sleep.

WHACK!!! "WAKE UP!!!!"

Marks eyes sprung wide open in a flash as a hand slapped him across the face leaving his cheeks burning. Unable to move and full of panic his eyes darted around the room as he tried to make sense of what was happening. He felt like he was in a nightmare dream.

"LOOK AT ME!" Jordan demanded him viciously.

Mark tried to calm his nerves and gather together his emotions, he was frightened. Realising his situation he finally held Jordan's gaze.

He was handcuffed to their bed and he was totally naked. Jordan was straddling him wearing a pair of lace panties and a bra that purposely exposed her nipples causing them to peek out. She wore a mask that covered her eyes with a netted piece that subtly covered her mouth. He made out her bright red lips as they twisted along with her crazy expression. Mark lay frozen and speechless. He prayed that it was all a dream and he would soon wake up but when she smacked his face once again the pain was too real to pass off.

"Do I look familiar?" Jordan stood up so she towered above him making him feel inferior. "Do I remind you of someone?"

Mark refused to speak, what the hell had come over her?

"WELL? DO I?" She commanded an answer. Jordan placed her 'Prada' heeled foot on to his stomach, her heel dug a little deep into his skin causing him to wince in pain. She slowly moved her foot lower journeying on towards his private parts.

"NO! NOOO!" He yelped bracing himself for whatever was to come next. "Please Jordan, stop playing now, let's talk about this."

"I'm trying to jog your memory baby, that's my game and you have no choice but to play," Jordan told him flicking Marks soldier with the toe of her Prada covered foot. "Don't I turn you on like she did?"

"OK, OK, OK!" Mark agreed.

Jordan climbed off the bed leaving Mark to wonder. She watched as he breathed a deep sigh of relief believing that it was all over. She trotted around the bed staring Mark hard in the face through her masked eyes. "Don't get to comfortable now," she warned him, "We have only just begun so brace yourself, it's going to be bumpy ride," she cackled crawling on top of him suffocating his face with her breasts, "suck them! Bite them! Do me the same way you did her." Jordan instructed grabbing his head and forcing him to do as she had told him.

Mark flipped his head from side to side trying to avoid Jordan's breasts in his mouth but no sooner had he started doing so he quickly regretted it as she whipped him with a belt on his thigh.

"YOWWWWW!!!" He screamed, "Stoppit! Please stop! What's wrong with you?"

"You still have no idea?" Jordan queried with a puzzled look on her face, "How about I go downstairs and get some ice cubes?"

"For what?" Mark whimpered anticipating Jordan's next move.

Jordan ignored him and giggled as she made her way downstairs to the kitchen. Within seconds she returned with a beaker full of ice cubes. "Oh, hold on a minute," she spoke to herself rustling around, "let me set up the camera so we can have a nice picture."

Mark squirmed trying to free himself from the handcuffs Jordan had secured him to the bed with, "Jordan are you mad? A camera for what?"

"I at least want a picture to show the world what a worthless piece of meat you are," she winked at him. She set the timer and positioned herself on top of Mark seductively as if she were riding him with a wicked smile on her face, rubbing ice cubes around her nipples making them erect. Once the shot had been taken she reviewed it and smiled with pure satisfaction.

Reaching over to the bedside table she grabbed what looked like a small book and flipped through some of the pages. Marks eyes widened in shock. Jordan read little by little of Nina's sordid journal acting out each part forcing Mark to play along, whipping him with the belt if he tried to disobey her. She watched as Mark closed his eyes trying to escape the truth.

"Please stop, please, please," Mark cried and begged Jordan. He couldn't take any more, he didn't want this.

Jordan read the last sentence and slammed the journal shut. She took off the mask and placed it on Marks face. She removed all the sexy underwear she had on and dressed Mark into them adjusting them as best as she could before smearing bright red lipstick on his lips. She took a step back and took a picture of him with the camera.

Mark lay there helpless, he couldn't do a thing. He was concerned that Jordan had lost her mind and if he uttered a sound she'd rip his heart out. He watched her as she put her pyjamas on as if nothing had happened and he was invisible although he was handcuffed to the bed wearing sexy underwear, a mask and red lipstick. He grunted in hope of receiving some form of attention but his attempt was lame as Jordan carried on regardless and disappeared from the bedroom.

"Jordan!" Mark called out, "Jordan, don't leave me like this!"

A few minutes later Jordan returned to the bedroom with Marks case and threw all he owned into it without even a sideways glance in his direction.

"Jordan I didn't know it was her."

"Does that make it right?" Jordan stopped and slowly turned around to face him, staring him down.

Mark could see the hurt and hate growing in her eyes.

"It's funny how you know who I'm referring to Mr Memory Loss!" She cried grabbing the bottle of Whiskey from the dresser top and swigging it back. She poured the rest all over Marks belongings in his case. "Hmmm, matches, matches..." she smiled tapping her lips trying to place them.

"Jordan noooooo!!!" Mark shouted, wiggling and tugging himself, feigning for freedom.

"It could have all been so simple but you'd rather make it hard with all your lies and deceit making out like you're the perfect gentleman. Did you think I wouldn't find out? I noticed how you look at her. And you had the nerve to punish me and treat me so cold for what I did? Really?" She said closing the alcohol soiled case and dragging it down the stairs, "What a nerve!"

Mark heard the front door open and felt the wrath of Jordan sneak up and kiss him. He wanted to be sure that she wouldn't set fire to his stuff but after what he had experienced that night he knew that any form of hope was pointless, he had pushed her over the edge.

Jordan made her way back to the bedroom and slowly walked over to where Mark lay handcuffed to the bed. She sat down on the edge of the bed and casually unlocked the cuffs. "Now get the hell out of my house and never come back!" She shouted in his face.

Mark backed up to the limit the frame of the bed would allow and scrambled off the bed ripping the outfit off that Jordan had dressed him in. He wiped his lips roughly with the back of his hand and ran down the stairs stark naked fearing for his life and what might be left of his belongings. He spotted his coat hanging on the banister and his Adidas trainers at the foot of the stairs and wasted no time putting them on for a small bit of coverage in order to leave the house with a slight piece of dignity. Mark opened the front door to his case in flames. He stood looming over it speechless. What was supposed to be a peaceful night in had turned into mayhem and madness and there was nothing he could do or say, nothing at all.

Not only was the security light shining brightly upon their house and the situation but the neighbours lights had come to life as they all had stepped out into the night on to their drives gathering to see what all the noise and commotion was about. Mark had never felt so embarrassed in the whole of his life. He ran inside and filled a big pot with cold water and threw it on to his burning case to put the flames out. Leaving the pot in the porch aiming to get away as fast as he could from the gawping neighbours, grateful for his coat and trainers, caring less about his bare chicken legs being on show, Mark picked up his case scurried off into the cold night air without looking back. He heard the upstairs bedroom window open and Jordan threw out what was left of the costume and mask shouting after him, "Give these back to her and tell her they don't fit, they're too big!"

CHAPTER 25

NINA.

"Hi Claire," Nina had eventually gotten around to giving Claire a call to arrange a date to discuss the 'favour.'

"Hey my darling, how have you been keeping?" Claire chirped back. Nina admired how sunny Claire always was regardless of all the doom and gloom surrounding her, she lived in her own sweet, rosy world.

"I'm fine, I just rang you for a diary date, I've decided to do that favour for you if the offer still stands?"

Claire didn't want to pressure Nina into doing it but she had a strong feeling from their night out and from hearing about the disruptive relationship she was riding with Aaron that she would give in and swim in the waters she belonged. After all, who could refuse the money and the glitz and glamour the job offered? Nina had an appetite for the tantalising lifestyle and Claire sensed that she was missing it. It wasn't that difficult of a task to tempt her, especially when she was down. Claire was a pro, she knew how to play the game.

"That's fine honey, or should I say Sunshine?" Claire laughed at her own joke as she flicked through her diary looking for a slot to fit Nina into. "How about Wednesday? We could have TGI Fridays," she suggested knowing full well that Nina loved her Jack Daniels Salmon.

"That'll be perfect," Nina agreed jotting it down in her diary to.

"Fab! I'll see you on Wednesday," Claire sang before she hung up.

Nina closed her diary and chewed the end of her pen thinking about the deed to come. She felt a mixture of feelings from excitement to nervousness. Her thoughts were interrupted by her phone bleeping, a text message from Mark.

'She knows, the crazy bitch knows!'

Nina hurriedly called Marks number but reached his voicemail. She tried again and again and each time over and over she reached his answer phone. "Damn!" She barked throwing her phone on to the bed. She got underneath her covers and hugged her pillow curious to know what had happened and how it had all been revealed. From Marks text message she assumed it wasn't very pretty.

AARON.

For the past few days Aarons life had consisted of work and home, occasionally checking up on his nephew Alec and trying to comprehend that Antoine was his Son and trying to figure out how he was going to accommodate him. He felt such a fool. Why didn't he see it coming? Why didn't he piece it together before, it was staring him in his face all along. He knew Tressa wasn't lying but he had to be sure, he needed concrete evidence, black ink on white paper. He was going to step up to the mark and do his best by Antoine.

He had agreed to meet Tressa and the boys on Wednesday evening to tackle the situation. As much as he didn't want to he couldn't help but feel that the sooner it was all out in the open and dealt with, the better.

Nina crossed his mind, he hadn't heard from her since the day she had left his flat in a frenzy. He craved for her attention, he wanted desperately to explain but she refused to hear him out. All he could do was hope that if he gave her the space and time she required she would give him the opportunity to explain.

Nina was certainly right, it was lonely living with lies. All he had done was lie upon lie in order to protect and please people and the pile had reached sky high and was falling down.

MARK.

Buzz! Buzz!
"Hello?"

"Nina, it's me, Mark."

Nina buzzed Mark into her apartment block. Once he had reached her front door she gripped him around his waist thankful that he was safe but then she noticed what he had on, the red staining on his lips, the bruises on his face and the way he trembled as he entered her flat. Something was seriously wrong.

"Mark?" She said touching his face gently. He jerked his head back frightened of her touch. "What happened?"

Mark dumped his barbequed case down in her hallway, "Where's your bathroom?" He asked scanning the unfamiliar territory.

Nina fought back her tears and pointed him towards the bathroom grabbing him a fresh towel and flannel from the cupboard and handing them to him before he went inside and locked the door. Hearing the shower run she made up the sofa with a pillow and a large fleecy blanket. She made a huge mug of hot chocolate and placed it on the coffee table next to the bed she had made up on the sofa for him.

Just as she finished up and was making her way back to her bedroom for the night the bathroom door clicked as Mark unlocked the door and stood in the doorway wearing her dressing gown. Nina knew full well that it was not a laughing matter, not right there and then after the trauma she could clearly see he had suffered but the sight of him standing there in her leopard print, tightly fitted dressing gown became too much to contain and she burst at the seams with laughter. Preparing herself to apologise she stopped, to her surprise Mark burst out laughing with her. They both fell into the bathroom, Nina sat down on the closed toilet lid to steady herself whilst Mark perched himself on the edge of the bath. The pair laughed until their sides were splitting and their stomachs cramped, a good five minutes it was until silence fell upon them. They both stared at each other, Nina spied the pain in Marks eyes, she stood up and embraced him. He snuggled into her breasts as she stroked his head resting her chin on top of his head, "What happened Mark? What did she do to you?"

That night consisted of Mark reluctantly relaying the events that had taken place with Jordan. He covered all the finest details serving it to Nina as it had been served to him, cold, hard revenge.

Stunned, astonished, shocked, flabbergasted were only the superficial emotions that attacked Nina's mind, body and soul after listening to what Mark had told her. He was right, Jordan had well and truly lost it.

As Nina lay in her bed that night listening to Mark snoring heavily from the living room, she knew for the first time what was awaiting her around the corner, Jordan and Aaron.

She couldn't help but feel that she was to blame for how Jordan had treated Mark. If only she hadn't kept a journal. The more she thought about it the more she itched to do Claire the favour so she could just disappear.

CHAPTER 27

NINA.

N ina watched as the minutes on her alarm clock changed from 6:29am to 6:30am before the piercing noise drowned the stillness of her bedroom welcoming her into another day.

She hadn't slept all night as she tried to play out the scenario as she thought it had happened how Jordan had mistreated Mark scarring him both physically and mentally.

She jumped out of her bed and darted into the living room only to find an empty sofa with a neatly folded blanket sitting on top followed by a note.

> *Nina,*
> ***Thank you for putting me up and lending me your shoulder. It's not right I stay here, I hope you understand.***
>
> ***Love Mark xxx***

Nina curled up around the folded blanket and flopped on it wiping a tear from her eye. She couldn't believe what Jordan had done and admittedly was dreading her next move.

AARON.

Aaron grabbed his belongings from his locker and made his way to the chip shop local to his work place as quick as he could. His morning had been hectic, he hadn't even had a mid-morning coffee break so hunger was hugging and squeezing him tightly.

Checking his phone in hope of something from Nina he shook his head. It didn't matter what he had to do Nina was constantly on his mind. His patience was wearing thin.

After work he was supposed to meet Tressa and the boys at TGI Fridays, not knowing what to expect he tried to put it to the back of his mind, he had to get through the afternoon first, he'd cross that bridge when he came to it, having a plan was useless especially when it came to Tressa.

Starving and grateful to eventually be getting his fill, Aaron reached the counter and ordered his usual. 'PING.' He had received a message on his phone from Jordan.

Aaron had difficulty making it out, it was a picture message. He zoomed in and realised that it was a picture of Mark tied to a bed wearing a mask and women's underwear. "What is this?" He tittered, forgetting he was in a chip shop during the lunch time rush.

His phone beeped once more, another message from Jordan,

'Mark and Nina slept together at the Masquerade Ball.'

Dread and humiliation suffocated Aaron at that precise moment, he stood staring at his phone re-reading the text message in hope of the words would re-arrange themselves, muddling together to read something different. Emptiness invaded his soul, everything that Nina and Mark had ever meant to him was diminished in a milli-second. Gone.

Thirsty to know the finer details for example how and why Mark was dressed in Nina's masquerade costume, Aaron contemplated ringing Jordan but selfishly changed his mind. He refused to comfort and console her when he was hurting too.

Trying to gather his emotions he reminded himself that in the back of his mind and deep down in his heart he had a feeling that the pair had come close or had totally become intimate at some point in time but he never would have guessed it was that night, the night his angel fluttered away from him.

He could still hear Nina's voice circulating in his head, "No more secrets..." he saw flashes of her face as the morning sunlight kissed her skin, smiling as she rolled into his warm embrace. If he had known he wouldn't have taken her back, Mark was supposed to be his friend. He touched his nose as he reflected back to when he protected Alec. 'Crazy,' he thought shaking his head, it seemed everyone was out for themselves.

"Mini fish and chips!"

He was so encapsulated in his whirlwind of emotions he didn't hear the shop worker calling to him.

"Excuse me," a smartly dressed lady tapped him gently, "I believe he's calling you, your order is ready."

Stepping back into reality Aaron thanked the lady, grabbed his order and left the chip shop.

NINA.

Sitting at her desk Nina devoured her favourite, tuna and mayo baguette. She had had a manic morning and was starving. On top of that she hadn't heard anything from Mark and was worried that he might have returned to Jordan's for round two. She refused to ring him in case he was in Jordan's presence as it would only make matters worse. The best thing for her to do was get on as normal, he knew where she was if he needed her.

'BLEEP.' Nina checked her phone to find a message from Claire reminding her about their dinner date at TGI Fridays that evening after work.

With all that had been occurring Nina had actually forgotten but good old organised and prompt Claire checked her back into reality.

After listening to Marks situation the night before Nina realised how important it was that she attended dinner with Claire that evening.

IRENE.

"Mark is that you?" It was 6am in the morning when Irene heard a key in her front door. It could only be Mark. She crept down the stairs switching on the lights as she moved along. "Lord Jesus!" She ran towards him and reached out to touch him.

Mark backed away and put his arm out to create a barrier so she couldn't get to close.

"What happened to you son?" She cried.

"It's alright mom, I'm ok, just go back to bed," he told her heading up the stairs to his room.

"But Mark -" she ran behind him.

"It's ok!" Mark shouted sternly. "I was attacked on the bus," he lied, "I just need to sleep mom, please," he begged before shutting his bedroom door in her face. He felt guilty and ashamed. He was supposed to be a man but at that moment in time he felt like a pathetic failure. Once again he had retreated to his bedroom at his Moms house.

AARON.

Aarons hunger pangs had vanished into thin air as he sat on a bench not far from the chip shop prodding and poking at his mini fish and chips. He didn't feel like returning to work for the remainder of the day but he knew that he had to, jobs were outstanding and needed to be completed.

Aaron felt like an idiot, he had set aside her past and welcomed her back into his life, both of them promising not to have any secrets. Should he be mad at her? Wasn't it similar to him fathering Antoine. Yes but she was with him at the time so no, not only did she cheat on him by escorting she also cheated on him with Mark.

The last time he had seen her was the night she fled from his flat without giving him the chance to explain the situation regarding Antoine and she had left it in his hands to make it right. After the text today he didn't see the point of making it right. He decided to leave her to come to him and also see if she would confess about herself and Mark in the process.

He composed a text message to Jordan:

'Hi Jordan, thanks for making me aware but please do not let on to Nina that I know. I will not ask if you are ok but don't let it stand in your way, you are better than that..

He felt sorry for Jordan, she had had it rough over the past few months and although that was the case she had still managed to be there for everyone. Nina's engagement party planning, Nina moving into her new flat and Mark being hurt. Even though she was partly to blame she had taken responsibility and taken him home and looked after him and this is how they repaid her?

CHAPTER 28

AARON.

"Table for how many Sir?" The waiter asked Aaron as he entered the restaurant.

"Erm…" he scanned the diner, "Oh I see them, I'm with that group over there," he pointed to Tressa and the boys seated in a corner booth.

Aaron made his way over to the table, "How are my favourite boys?" he addressed the table noticing how much Antoine resembled himself and the glum expression stretched across Alec's face.

Tressa rolled her eyes before telling Aaron that they had waited for him for as long as they could and had no choice but to order their food and drinks. "Antoine has been at school all day so of course he was hungry," she ranted on.

Aaron didn't want any fuss or an argument. "It's not a problem, I'll have a quick look at the menu and make my order don't worry," he said calmly.

Alec looked up from his food and mumbled something in Aarons direction.

"You will have to speak up if you want me to understand what you're saying," Aaron told him.

"I said, is it true that Antoine is your son?"

Antoine looked around the table, first at his mother, then his brother and last but not least at Aaron. Aaron held Antoine's innocent gaze cradling his pure soul in his hands and proudly replied, "Yes, that's correct."

"So whilst my Mom and Dad were still together you snuck through the back door and -"

"Alec!" Tressa put a stop to Alec's rude remarks, "Do not speak to Aaron like that!"

"Why Mom? Why shouldn't I?"

"Because he has been there for the pair of you a damn sight more than your Father ever was, that's why, now shut up and eat your food so that Aaron and I can discuss Antoine's care."

Aaron and Tressa shared ideas, made suggestions and even compromised in a civil manner on what they thought would be best when it came to Antoine. Aaron refused to do it all himself, he believed Antoine needed a balance in his life, Tressa wasn't getting out of it that easily, if she thought she could bail out she had another think coming.

Tressa excused herself to go to the Ladies. Alec watched her leave the table before he looked up at Aaron. "Listen Uncle, I'm sorry, I shouldn't have spoken to you like that. Mom's right, you have been there for us and for me. You've been there for me in ways that I could never repay you. Again, I'm sorry."

Aaron patted Alec's shoulder, "It's cool Alec, now understand that I wouldn't be a man if I didn't do right by little man over here," he said ruffling Antoine's curly hair.

NINA.

"Table for two please," Claire chirped at the waiter as he greeted her at the entrance of TGI Friday's.

"May I ask where the second person is?" The waiter enquired looking behind Claire.

"She's on her way," Claire confirmed, confused at what the matter was.

"It's just that we tend not to seat you until you are both present," he stated.

"Well excuse me," Claire frowned.

"Would you like to wait at the bar and have a drink until she arrives?"

"Only if you're buying," Claire chuckled leaving the waiter standing alone as she swished her hips making her way to the bar and adjusting herself comfortably on a bar stool.

Claire reached into her bag to retrieve her iPhone and sent Nina a text message to let her know she was at the bar before she was interrupted by a tall dark, handsome man wearing a classy suit, fitted in all the correct places. She scoped him from toe to head and then back again from head to toe inspecting his shoes.

"May I buy you a drink?" He asked her.

Claire smiled enormously, satisfied at the fine specimen of a man that stood directly before her.

"No because I got it, she's with me!" Nina chimed in, appearing form thin air hugging Claire and planting a kiss on her cheek.

The gentleman grinned, "Well in that case can I buy both of you ladies a drink?" He asked politely, hardly intimidated by Nina's presence.

"Sure," Nina responded quicker than a winning race horse, "I'll have a Pina Colada, no ice thanks being as you asked."

After fifteen minutes or so of fraternizing with Mr Fine and his friends, Claire and Nina were eventually shown to their table so they could order some food and get down to business.

"Long day?" Claire asked Nina.

"Way too long, and yours?"

"Not really," Claire said as she sipped on her cocktail that she had brought over from the bar, "but we have some business to put into order and some food to eat, I'm starving," Claire beamed, grateful that Nina was taking on her favour.

The ladies scoured the menu licking their lips at the thought of a delicious meal when they heard a little voice calling, "Nina! Nina!" Nina looked up from her menu to see a little, grey eyed, curly haired boy, running towards her. At first she had no idea what was going on but it didn't take long for her to recognise that the little boy was Antoine.

"Do you know this child?" Claire asked as she watched him run into Nina's arms and cling to her.

"I miss you Auntie Nina!" He screamed with joy, "When are we going bowling again?"

Nina squeezed him and kissed his forehead before turning to face the table he had fled from to see who he was with. There sat Aaron, Alec and a woman she didn't recognise. A new face. Nina locked eyes with Aaron. There she was holding his child's hand whilst he sat playing happy families. "Go back to your seat honey," Nina told Antoine.

"Come and sit by me pleeeease," he whined, tugging Nina's hand refusing to let go.

Nina felt Claire's eyes glued to her, "Sorry about this Claire, excuse me a minute." She approached the table where Aaron and company sat, her eyes still locked with Aaron's who hadn't yet breathed a word. "I believe little man here belongs to you," she said, freeing her hand from Antoine's, waving a hello at Alec and then walking away.

Tressa sat silently and diverted her attention to Antoine so she didn't have to witness how pitiful Aaron looked as he swooned over Nina. She hadn't met her before but she couldn't deny how pretty and expensive she looked and how well she handled Antoine.

"Nina wait!" Aaron called after her. "Please Nina wait," he yelled once more before pushing back his chair and scrambling after her, following her as she made her way to the ladies.

AARON.

Everytime he saw her standing before him in the flesh he couldn't deny her or hold on to the anger she caused him to feel, she stole his heart.

He caught up with Nina just before she was about to enter the ladies. "Nina please let me explain," he grabbed her hand and gently pinned her against the wall. Her smell captivated his nostrils and reminded him of home, of what once was. He tried to calm his breathing as he floated in the pools of her big, brown eyes. He wished that he could kiss her and they could travel back in time to when everything was perfect between them, when they loved the skin off of each other, when they were engaged to be married. He glimpsed her ring finger noticing that she wasn't wearing her engagement ring.

He knew what it looked like, him sitting with what one might assume to be a perfect family eating dinner together, but it wasn't that at all. He had to put his best efforts forward and not let Nina go without relaying the facts. He loosened his grip on her wrists and she folded her arms across her chest and pouted with an attitude.

"Nina this isn't what you think," he began, "I'm here today with the boys and their mother Tressa to sort out how I'm going to be a part of Antoine's life. I want to do right by him Nina."

Nina rolled her eyes and attempted to go into the ladies. Aaron followed her.

"Leave me alone Aaron, you carry on playing happy families, we are finished, there's too much rubbish sitting between us for it to work, it's ok, I don't care," Nina lied, hurt and jealous.

Aaron continued while he still had her in his grasp, "Nina, Antoine is six years old, Tressa was struggling with Alec, he wasn't the best behaved child due to things going on at home and my brother wasn't around to be a proper Father or a partner. He was constantly in and out of prison leaving Tressa and Alec with nothing. I was giving her money to help her out with bills, food and clothes for Alec. Then my brother got caught big time and was given a long prison sentence. I was just as upset as Tressa and after a few drinks to drown our sorrows and crying on each others shoulders, one thing led to another and that's how Antoine came about. Due to the timing we all thought without a doubt that Antoine belonged to my brother."

NINA.

Nina stood silently listening to every word that left Aarons mouth. She admired his kind nature immensely, he was always so neutral, he could make bitter lemons taste so sweet. She knew he was telling the truth, she couldn't be mad at him because it was before her time and she was respectful to the fact that he was wanting and willing to be an active parent in Antoine's life. She had seen him with the boys, even she had a soft spot for them, they had become a great part of her life too. She stared deep into his gorgeous eyes, she loved him but she loved him enough to let him go. She had to do this favour for Claire and leave the country, leave it all behind.

"Nina," Aaron broke the silence, "I love you, I want us to work and be honest with each other," he hinted, "Let's be a team and be happy, let's make a happy home and get married."

Nina wiped the tear that had dripped onto her top lip and remained quiet.

Aaron pulled the door open and left the ladies satisfied that he had said the necessary and also expressed clearly his feelings for her. She obviously didn't feel the same and he had a feeling as to why.

"Nina darling," Claire sang entering the ladies spying Nina wiping her eyes and blowing her nose.

"Right then," Nina said throwing her tissue in the bin, "Back to business."

She linked arms with Claire's and they made their way back to the table.

Aaron's table was empty.

CHAPTER 29

AARON.

Aaron sat on his sofa with his hands clasped together in a prayer like state with his fingers pressed to his lips and his eyes closed tightly. All he could envision were his days spent with Nina, how Antoine's eyes sparkled each and every time he saw her when she smothered him with her energy and love but then his vision dimmed to darkness as he saw the shadows of her with Mark. Immediately he opened his eyes and stood up and made his way into the kitchen, he was in desperate need of a drink.

He smiled as he poured himself a whisky, relieved that Antoine would be staying with him every other week. Antoine was young, he would adapt quite easily and that way the responsibility was split equally down the middle between himself and Tressa.

Standing in the doorway of the spare bedroom (the guest bedroom) he sipped his drink scanning the room, excited at the prospect of decorating it for 'Little man.'

"I'm going to do right by him and concentrate on the important things," he tried to boost himself, "it's time to forget Nina."

Aaron realised his glass was running low and made his way back to the kitchen for a refill.

"What the hey!" He laughed, tucking the bottle under his arm and heading for the sofa to lounge. Just as he was about to get comfortable his buzzer went off.

"Hello?"

"Hi Aaron it's me, Tressa."

NINA.

Nina drove home eager for the next day to arrive so she could go and buy the attire that was requested to play 'Sunshine' for the last time. That evening (after the drama) Claire had provided Nina with all the instructions and information she would require in order to conduct the favour for her.

There would be NO wining and dining, it was to be strictly sex. She would earn £2000 for two hours of her time. Names were not necessary, all the client desired was to touch, taste and smell her before she satisfied his desires.

This particular client was a very rich man who indulged deeply into bringing his sexual fantasies to life. The woman he chose had to fit a certain criteria, they had to be on point and once Claire had described Nina and enlightened him on her expertise he was more than happy for her to take Claire's place on this occasion.

"Is she pleasing to the eye?" He had asked, licking his lips as Claire described her physical attributes. "Mmmm, I can't wait," he grinned.

Nina's attire was to be a black, sexy thong, black, plain stiletto's, bright, red lipstick and a face mask (blind fold) He was to see her but she was not allowed to see him, he wanted to watch her react to each and every one of his tricks. She was to be prepared to play, participate and obey commands. "Oooh. A man who likes to be in control," Nina giggled.

"Are you ok with this?" Claire had asked Nina making sure that Nina was confident to carry out the job.

"I'm actually looking forward to it," she blushed, "It's been a while since I had a good time, I mean a really good time."

BEEP! BEEP!

The car behind her honked their horn, the traffic lights had turned to green but Nina was so caught up in her daydream and replaying the conversation at dinner with Claire that she hadn't realised.

Driving on she decided to take a detour to Aarons to finalise things. It was time to go their separate ways, yes she did love him but it was plain to see that they were drifting in different directions, Nina wasn't ready to play house, not just yet anyway.

AARON.

"What's up?" Aaron lazily asked Tressa over the intercom, holding his glass of whisky in his hand.

"I just wanted to check that you were ok after earlier on at TGI's, are you going to let me in?"

Aaron buzzed her in not really sure why, it was probably due to the fact that he couldn't be bothered with her loud mouth and attitude if he refused. He didn't want a big commotion on his doorstep, that wasn't his style.

Tressa huddled her way in though Aarons front door and found him sitting on the sofa drink in hand.

"Can I get one of those?" She asked throwing her coat over the arm of the sofa and slipping off her shoes.

"Not if you're driving," Aaron stated firmly, "and where is Antoine?"

"I'm allowed a tiny bit," Tressa said cheekily getting a glass from the kitchen and helping herself to some of Aarons whisky, "And why are you worrying about Antoine, he's fine, he's with my Mom."

Aaron gave her a sideways glance then focussed his attention back to the TV.

"So did you and Nina sort stuff out then?" She asked nosily shuffling closer to Aaron. Before he could reply Tressa's mouth ran away with her, "She is pretty isn't she? She looks like a lady with expensive taste, where did you meet her? I was surprised at how Antoine was with her, I've never seen him like that with anyone before except for with you and Alec. I'm just saying," Tressa babbled on, "Because it's rare that women like her have that maternal side, it's usually all about money, diamonds and -"

"ENOUGH!" Aaron shouted, holding his head, "Just leave it."

"Oooh touchy, touchy," Tressa teased rubbing his arm.

Aaron shrugged her off of him and carried on sipping his drink and watching the TV.

Ten minutes later Tressa was still sat beside him, "You can go now, I'm ok," he told her hoping she would feel uncomfortable and leave.

"Fine," she said placing her empty glass on the table and putting on her coat. "I hope you are not like this when you have Antoine in your care?"

"How dare you!" Aaron snapped thinking back to Tressa's drug addiction days and all the stress and upheaval she put the boys through, "Have you developed memory loss too?"

Tressa looked down at her feet and silently finished putting on her shoes, "I'm sorry..."

"No, I'm sorry." Aaron felt bad for throwing it back in her face especially after she was doing so well, "It's just me feeling sorry for myself that's all, it's just been a bit mad lately with everything going on."

Tressa gave him a hug and Aaron relaxed his entire body into her arms, it felt good. It had been a while since he had received any comfort of some sort. He pulled back to meet Tressa's lips enveloping his. He obliged and kissed her back. She removed her coat and kicked off her shoes their lips still interlocked. Aaron broke free and lifted his top up over his head revealing his toned body and broad shoulders before leaning forward to meet Tressa and reconnect their lips. With shaky hands, rushing to satisfy himself, Aaron undid the buttons on her blouse exposing her voluptuous breasts sexily seated in a lace bra inviting his tongue to play. He buried his head in her cleavage and pulled her bra aside so he could suck on her nipples. All the while Tressa wrestled with Aaron's belt buckle and before long they were both naked and caught up in the heat of the moment. "You feel so good," Aaron told Tressa as she sat on top of him riding him and biting his ear lobe gently. Aaron sat back and enjoyed the ride.

NINA.

Nina pulled up outside of Aarons flat, she intended on sitting down and having a civil conversation with him and splitting up with no hard feelings towards each other.

She scurried up to the main entrance and let herself in with her key reminding herself to hand it back to him. She climbed up a couple flights of stairs and stood outside of his front door. It was time to discuss everything, address all their issues, open up and be honest and then let each other be. She took a deep breath and put her key in the lock.

As she entered his flat she gulped as she spotted the trail of clothing that lead to the bedroom, She followed it, welcoming the hurt but intrigued as to who it could possibly be, preparing herself to see Aaron with Jordan. But to her surprise and demise, Nina stood in sheer shock, Tressa came into full view comfortably sitting on top of Aaron and Aaron was enjoying every moment of her, groping her breasts, his eyes rolling with painful pleasure.

The set of keys slipped from Nina's hands as they went limp and dropped heavily to the floor leaving her hands empty and hanging by her sides. The noise of the keys landing on the floor awoke Aaron from his blissful delight and Tressa turned to face Nina with a broad smirk on her face.

Aaron pushed Tressa off of him.

"I listened to your spiel and now look, already somebody else is in your bed and you lectured me?" Nina managed to say before simply turning her back on the naked pair and leaving.

"Shit!" Aaron barked causing Tressa to flinch.

CHAPTER 30

JORDAN.

"I'm gonna take that ring off my finger…!" Jordan sang loudly to her hearts content as she danced around her bedroom in nothing but her CK underwear set singing along to Toni Braxton and spraying perfume up into the air and running beneath it, letting the fragrant mist kiss her skin softly as Nina had taught her.

Her days of wallowing in self pity were over with, she refused to traumatise her poor blanket for the umpteenth episode with salty tears of self pity. She had tried to do her best by everyone and look where she had ended up. Admittedly she had done wrong but she felt she had paid her dues, it was time she fixed up.

Herself and Mark were no longer as were herself and Nina, Jordan had decided to wash them out of her hair and get on with her life making the most out of what she had and expanding on what she could. She planned to re-decorate her home and freshen it up, make it her brand new. Why should she sell up and move when she put in as much hard work as Mark did, just because he was now out of the picture it didn't mean she couldn't maintain. She had contacted a teaching agency in order to get some supply teaching work as her savings weren't going to last forever. It was time to get out there and enjoy life, see what she had been missing, starting tonight. It was pointless trying to fix the broken things that wanted to remain broken.

Noticing how thin she had become in her full length mirror, Jordan opted on a long black skirt with a slit up the left leg and a lace, black top with her strappy, Dune kitten heels. It was 7pm and she didn't have a date with anyone in particular but the mood she was in she wasn't going to let that stop her journeying on to wherever could pleasure her taste buds with sweet liquor, her insides were crying out for warmth.

Loading up her Marc Jacobs clutch with the essentials, Jordan grabbed her jacket and stepped out into the chilly evening breeze. It felt like the beginning of forever for her and she was going to enjoy every moment of it.

NINA.

Nina jumped down the stairs two at a time desperate for the exit to near her rapidly, suffocating, straining with urgency for fresh air to fill her lungs so she could breathe again. In such a hurry she miscalculated her steps and fell down the remaining few banging her legs and knees. "Owwwwww!" She clenched her teeth and squeezed her eyes shut tight trying to fight back tears and bear the pain shooting through her legs. Giving in to her sore knees Nina leaned back against the wall and cried silently. "This is my comeuppance," she told herself, "Only everything I deserve."

'Click,' hearing a door handle turn and locks unlatching, Nina quickly grabbed her stuff and regardless of the pain she felt she scurried out of the building as fast as she could, the last thing she wanted was Aaron or Tressa seeing her in that state.

Once inside of her car Nina drove a few roads down and parked up and dialled Marks number.

No answer.

Another stream of tears rolled down her cheeks, it seemed that whenever she needed comfort no-one was available.

JORDAN.

For a week day the vibes were quite lively as Jordan entered the bar. Mainly men littered the dance floor whilst women stood posted up the walls babysitting their drinks that sat on the ledges eyeing her as she made her way to the bar alone.

"A Tia Maria and Cranberry please," she told the bartender.

A few minutes later, drink in hand, she made her way to a corner booth and sat back to watch how individuals conducted themselves on a school night.

As she sat making up stories in her own mind about each individuals lifestyle her thoughts were interrupted, "Jordan?"

Jordan was irritated. The whole point of tonight was for her to branch out from familiarity. She intended to leave the old behind and when she looked up and saw Alec questioning her presence she shut off and got up to leave. "Excuse me," she said brushing past him, "Could you please leave me alone?"

Alec's face held a puzzled expression trying to figure out what he had done that was so offensive. "I was trying to be friendly," he said stepping aside in order for her to pass.

"Look where that got us last time," she said snidely, "I came here for a quiet drink not a chat with a young boy!" She snapped.

Her comment burnt Alec as he stood cradling a mouthful of hurtful responses in his mouth tempted to vomit them out all over her smug face but decided against it. Instead he admired her attire, her sexy leg peaking out of the thigh high slit in her skirt. The jet black colour against her complexion dominated his thoughts full of authority. The way her hips swung from side to side, hypnotising him as she walked away teasing him making him want her, making him want her to stay. He needed her attention.

"JORDAN!" He called out, but she continued her journey to the next bar purposely ignoring his call.

NINA.

Nina turned her key in her front door grateful to be home. She dumped her bag down on the floor and kicked off her shoes. She went into the kitchen and ran the tap before filling a glass with cold water and adding as many ice cubes as she possibly could before gulping it down to rid the drought in her mouth. She felt the cold rush through her body and waited a moment before flooding it once more. Breathing heavily she held on to the sink and gasped refreshed.

Nina had work the following day and unlike the saga of events that occurred when she worked for Mr Allen, she wanted discretion when it concerned her personal life in this job so she had to cover up the cracks.

Deciding on an early night, promising herself that she would get up half an hour earlier the next morning to sort herself out properly, she changed into her pyjamas and brushed her teeth. As she lay her head down on her pillow, the answer machine light flashing caught her attention. She pressed play.

> *"Nina it's me Claire. Just a quick ring to remind you and reassure you about Saturday.*
> *I hope you are ok, ring me if you need me, kiss, kiss!"*

Nina smiled, Claire always had a way of cheering her up, lifting her spirits and putting her right back on track.

JORDAN.

Unbeknownst to Jordan Alec sat admiring her from the bar opposite, he had taken a seat outside with his drink once she had left and he had spotted her next destination. He spied her as she drank drink after drink slowly getting tipsy and drunk as guys approached her and tried to take advantage of her sloppy state, groping and fondling her. She looked loose and easy and out of control and he couldn't allow himself to just sit back and watch, he had to get her home.

"You might hate me now Jordan but you'll thank me in the morning," he told himself as he darted across the plaza to the bar she was located.

Alec witnessed a guy dragging Jordan into a tight corner, pushing up against her, pinning her up the wall trying to kiss her. He could see that she didn't want to kiss him back but he persisted and man handled her even more so.

"She said NO!" Alec dragged the guy off Jordan and spun him around so they were face to face.

"Said who?" The guy spat. Shrugging Alec off and freeing himself, turning back to face Jordan ready to finish what he started.

"Says me!" Alec pulled him off Jordan for the last time and punched him twice, once in the jaw and once in his nose hearing cracks after both blows.

The guy staggered backward trying to regain his balance. Alec grabbed Jordan's hand and told her to run. Jordan did as she was told for once and held tight to Alec's hand as they left the plaza.

Jordan slowed down and began panting heavily, drunk and uncoordinated.

"I'm taking you home," Alec told her, "Jump on my back."

Jordan took off her heels and jumped on to Alec's back, folding her arms around his neck and resting her head against his.

"Thank you," she whispered in his ear.

They got into a Taxi and headed to Jordan's house in silence.

AARON.

Feeling uncomfortable as well as awkward, Tressa had decided to leave. It was obvious that Aaron harboured immense feelings for Nina and nothing could interfere with that.

Aaron stooped down and picked up the keys Nina had dropped on the floor. Holding them tightly in his hand he studied the keyring attached to it, it was a photo of them both from the night he took her Salsa dancing. He remembered that night like it was yesterday, he felt like the luckiest man alive to have her as his partner. Trying to dismiss the thought of two wrongs don't make a right, once again he didn't understand how they had reached this place.

CHAPTER 31

JORDAN.

Alec helped Jordan out of the taxi and guided her up the path helping her find her house keys under the security light.

"I got it!" She snapped pushing him away.

Once inside the house Alec headed straight to the kitchen to put the kettle on, Jordan was in need of a strong black coffee.

As Alec leaned against the counter top waiting for the kettle to boil, he reflected back to the time when he bought some flowers around to Jordan as a thank you for looking out for them the day himself and Antoine turned up on her doorstep. He remembered vividly what took place and how one thing lead to another.

'Click.' The kettle boiled snapping him out of his deep thoughts. Stunned he made Jordan's coffee and wondered around downstairs looking for her.

"Jordan!" He called. With no answer Alec made his way upstairs presuming she had conked out asleep on the bed.

Low and behold there she lay snoring on the bed in just her underwear with her dress and shoes on the floor in a pile by the bed. He gently placed the mug of coffee on the bedside table and tucked her into bed.

"Stay with me," she stirred clasping her hands around his neck as he leant towards her to get her into bed.

Alec roamed her sleepy eyes avoiding her glazed pain. She held his gaze awaiting a reply.

"I can't," he said removing her hands from around his neck and puling the blanket up to cover her semi-naked body.

"But I want you to. I…I…I need you to," she whispered.

Alec saw the yearning she contained inside for him but he knew it would only last a moment before it was followed by regret. He'd been there before with Jordan and a lot had changed since then.

"I just wanted to make sure you got home safely Jordan. I have to go now." He glimpsed a tear slide down her cheek. He adored her undeniably and the same hurt she felt from his rejection was the same hurt he felt having to reject her but he had no choice.

"OK. I'll hold you until you fall asleep," he said softly, climbing on to the bed and wrapping her up in his arms.

Jordan closed her eyes appreciative to him for his consideration of her fragile state.

'Ding dong!'

The sound of the doorbell caused Alec and Jordan to jump up out of their sleep.

AARON.

Having tossed and turned all night Aaron was good for nothing the next day. Nina catching him with Tressa haunted his mind viciously leaving little room for him to think about anything else including work. He couldn't care less about Tressa and was fully aware that she had deliberately played on his vulnerable state to get him into bed. He had concluded that she was jealous of Nina. He'd observed how she reacted to Nina's presence at TGI Friday's as well as the comments she had passed about how expensive she looked and how pretty she was. He noticed those superficial traits about Nina himself when he first met her but over time he fell for her. Her bubbly, lively personality, her excitement over the smallest of things, her cheeky face and generous heart and her independence. He had to talk to her.

After spending the morning ringing Nina's mobile and home phone off the hook he finally realised that she was probably at work. He decided to pay Jordan a visit to see if she had heard anything from Nina.

Surely it had to stop now. Nina had lied to him and worked as an escort whilst pursuing a relationship with him and also slept with Mark in the process and he, himself had discovered he was a father to Antoine and had a weak moment with Tressa.

MARK.

Knock, knock.

"Mark you cannot stop in there forever!" Irene shouted to Mark from outside his bedroom door as she set down a tray of food and drink. Just as she turned to walk away Mark's bedroom door swung open.

"Mum," he called out to her.

Irene turned around to face her son who looked like a fuzzy bear all grey and ashy. The stench of humidity flowed from his room due to lack of ventilation.

"Oh son, what's wrong?"

Marks legs felt like jelly and he collapsed on to the floor directly in front of his mother, embarrassed and ashamed that his feelings had gotten the better of him. Her only, big, strong son had crumbled into a thousand pieces right before her very eyes.

"Oh darling, oh no! Mama's going to run you a nice hot bath and I want you to tell me what it is that has forced you into this dark place," she soothed him, stroking his hairy face.

Ten minutes later as Mark lay in a Radox and Dettol bath, Irene scuttled around his room with a black bin bag in hand getting rid of the rubbish that he had accumulated. She changed his bed sheets and opened his curtains and his window to let in some life and fresh air.

Mark sank down into the bubbles listening to his mother humming along as she worked. Once she had finished she entered the bathroom with a fresh fluffy towel for Mark.

"I'll just leave it here," she said, placing it down on top of the wash basket.

Mark forced a smile, her efforts were more than commendable. He sincerely loved the bones off of his mother.

She walked over to him and placed her lips against his forehead. Mark pressed his head forward leaning hard and sturdy against her lips so she stayed a little longer. Irene surrendered to her son's silent cry for help and grabbed his cheeks to assure him she wasn't going anywhere.

"Come and sit down here by me," Irene patted the spot on the sofa next to her where she sat cracking and eating Pistachio nuts in front of the TV with her feet up.

Mark looked much better as if his soul was beginning to rise again and after his good shave and hot bath he smelled scrumptious. He obeyed his Mothers orders and sat down beside her and rested his head on her shoulder.

"Talk to me son."

Mark started from the beginning (some of which his mother was aware of) from when the ground was shaky beneath the feet of his marital home as they tried to conceive. The Bank Holiday when Alec and Antoine appeared on their doorstep. Mark discovering the pregnancy test sticking out of Jordan's handbag and what it read came after that. He confided in his mother about his secret hospital tests to see if it was his fault for the difficulty they were experiencing. "There was no way it was mine Ma, I'm all blanked out."

If he was going to tell it he was going to tell it all so he commenced inviting his mother to the night at the Masquerade Ball where the heavy, red, velvet curtains drew back to reveal the sexiest girl in the world. The girl in the mask with the net shielding her luscious red lips.

The unexpected phone call form a devastated Aaron appeared on the agenda. What he had suspected of Nina, the love of his life, his angel, was true.

"That's when it clicked Ma, according to Aaron she was working as an escort by the name of Sunshine…"

"The girl with the luscious red lips at the Ball?" Irene said tossing a nut into her mouth.

"Yes," Mark confirmed shuffling his head on his Mothers shoulder in shame. "I slept with her but I promise I used protection and I had no idea whatsoever who she was," he added bluntly. "After Aaron finding out that Nina was an escort imagine the pain he'd had felt if he knew I had slept with her. It would destroy him! I confronted Nina later on and she begged me to keep it our secret."

Mark paused trying to straighten out the order of events.

"You take a break, I'm going to get myself a ginger beer," she said smacking her salty lips together and heaving herself up off the sofa. Once she returned he picked up where he had left off.

"So myself and Aaron were in the same predicament as were the girls. I had finished with Jordan as you know and Aaron was no longer with

Nina. The girls had packed up everything on a whim and decided to go to Atlanta to stay with Nina's brother for a while. I was responsible for driving them both to the airport, that I could just about manage civilly, or so I thought until out of the blue Aaron appeared asking for Nina's hand in marriage."

"Hummph," Irene grunted, "Well well."

Mark ignored her and went on to tell her the rest of the situation how Nina accepted Aarons proposal and how they lived happy go lucky and he was left with the wrath of Jordan

"So son, are you now going to tell me how you REALLY ended up in that hospital bed?" Irene enquired as one would to a fool.

Mark reminded his mother of the time when Jordan had told everyone that she had miscarried when really she had had a termination. Then the day he was clobbered around the head by Alec replayed in his mind as if it was that very morning. He relayed every detail to his mother.

"What a great memory you have there son," Irene sarcastically remarked. "Carry on."

The memory loss game and the effort to make his lie a reality and maintain it reared it's ugly head along with using Jordan and playing on her emotions to get her back. It was too late to try and sugar coat the truth, not only did he tell the truth out of respect for his mother but to hear himself speak it loud and clear helped him come to terms with it all and see it for the complicated mess it was.

Irene was sitting upright at this point remembering the piercing hurt that ran through her veins having to see her son in the state he was in at the hospital but to top it all off the fact that he couldn't remember who she was stung her to the core. Biting her lips scared to release them in case the wrong words escaped her mouth she breathed in deeply and then exhaled, "And the final chapter?"

"Let's just say Jordan finished it Ma, good and proper, she tore me to shreds, she -"

"Alright son, that's enough, no more."

JORDAN.

Ding dong.

Alec opened Jordan's front door as cool as a cucumber, "Hey Uncle are you ok?"

"What do you mean are you ok? Alec what the hell are you doing here?"

"Who's at the door?" Jordan shouted approaching the front door wrapping herself up in her dressing gown.

"I don't believe this!" Aaron said catching an eyeful of Jordan's bare legs and Alec's lack of clothes apart from his boxer shorts.

Alec suddenly latched on to his Uncles line of thinking and tried to put him straight as fast as he could.

"No, no, no Uncle it's not what you think, tell him Jordan," Alec panicked. He had done right by Jordan the night before out of sincere care and he would be dammed if it was going to be twisted and him to end up portrayed as the brute and the menace. He was way past that and he needed his uncle to believe him. Alec glared at Jordan wishing her to tell the truth. He held her gaze his eyes replaying the day that he clobbered Mark, her beloved, around the head sending him into a deep sleep. He knew she hated him really and this was her chance to get even. Every muscle in his body tensed up in anticipation as he willed her not to tell a lie.

Jordan smirked sensing the lack of faith and trust he possessed for her. "He's right Aaron. I went out last night and some guy tried to attack me. Your nephew rescued me and made sure I got home safe and sound."

Aaron just listened awaiting an explanation for their semi naked attire.

"I asked him to stay and he refused. I pleaded, feeling a little scared and so he gave in and slept on the sofa that's why he got to the front door before me."

Aaron glanced back and forth between the both of them trying to work out if it was the truth. "OK," Aaron accepted as Alec walked back inside returning five minutes later fully clothed catching the end of Jordan and his uncle's conversation.

"What are you talking about?" Alec asked nosily.

"Nothing that concerns you," Aaron put him in his place.

"Well, can I have a lift home being as you're here?" Alec asked cheekily.

Aaron laughed for the first time that day and said goodbye to Jordan as they made their way to the car play fighting each other.

Feeling extremely proud of herself for letting go, Jordan closed her door and went into the kitchen to find something to nurse her hangover.

CHAPTER 32

JORDAN.

Jordan lay on her bed staring at the ceiling thinking. Thinking about all the drama that had taken place in her life over the past few months. She tried to figure out where it had all gone wrong, how she had become a divorcee living all alone. She chuckled in wonderment at how you could have it all one moment and in a blink of an eye it could all just disappear.

She turned on to her side to face the empty spot on her bedside table where the photo of herself and Mark once had a place. A tear slid down her cheek and dripped on to her pillow. She hated feeling overwhelmed with anger and frustration, sorrow and sadness and harboured hurt.

She didn't know why she was hurting so bad, she had always been alone. Her biological parents, whoever they were, had given her up for adoption and so she had never really had a stable, permanent upbringing, she'd spent her life flitting from place to place, a statistic floating around the system. That was her motivation in life and so she shined at School and whizzed through College and University proving her ability. To teach was her dream, knowing there were plenty of children who grew up like she did if not worse. Wanting a child to be born in a stable home was her intention and Mark was her perfect partner, but she blew him away into the arms of Nina, his childhood friend who his heart really belonged to.

Sitting up and swinging her legs over the edge of her bed, Jordan briskly wiped the tears that attempted to fall from her heavy filled eyes and sucked back her emotions.

"Stop it Jordan!" She scolded herself, "It's time to buck up and go get life, deal with it!"

Pulling back the curtains and letting the late autumn sun shine through she smiled, "I have a nice home, I can get another job, I'm healthy...I have foundations to build on."

Jordan switched on the radio in her bedroom to create a feel good atmosphere and danced herself ready to begin what she purposefully intended to be a fine day, starting with a trip to Ikea to buy a new bedroom set, the existing one held too many bad memories.

AARON.

"Come on Antoine!" Aaron hollered trying to grab Antoine off the bed in the show room at Ikea. "Stop messing before I throw you in the dustbin," he joked picking him up and holding him upside down laughing at his giggles.

"But I like that one the best," Antoine told Aaron once he was standing the correct way up on his two feet.

"I can see that," Aaron agreed grabbing a pencil and a slip of note paper off the stand to write down the codes in order to locate it later on, on their way through the warehouse.

"So can I have it then? Pleeeease!"

"Only if you're a good boy."

Antoine stopped jumping up and down and stood calmly by Aaron's side and held his hand, "I promise."

Aaron had decided it was time to step up to his role as a Father and begin by sorting out his bedroom at his flat. He had spent the last couple of days painting and decorating the spare room ready for Antoine to claim. He had to do something to distract himself from the madness that seemed to surround him.

He missed Nina in a way he couldn't describe. He craved and yearned for her presence regardless of everything that she had put him through and he couldn't understand why. Through it all he only saw her shine brightly like a star with the power to light up any dark sky, his dark sky.

"Jordan!"

Aarons deep thoughts were interrupted as he felt Antoine free his hand from his and flee into the direction of the pillows and duvets with excitement.

Jordan spun around at hearing her name being called to find Antoine running towards her with the most adorable smile on his face. She knelt down to embrace him as he ran into her arms and hugged him tightly.

Aaron arrived close behind as Jordan picked up Antoine and gave him a kiss. "Who's getting a big boy then?" She laughed as he kissed her cheek back.

"Meeeeeeee!" He squealed, laughing as she tickled him. "Where's Uncle Mark?" He beamed, twisting and turning in Jordan's arms trying to spy Mark.

"He's…"

"Are you harassing Jordan?" Aaron butted in saving Jordan from having to find an excuse for Marks absence.

"He's ok, he's harmless," she smiled handing Antoine over to Aaron, "In fact, he cheered me up."

Aaron noticed something different about Jordan but couldn't quite pin point it. "So how have you been keeping?"

"I'm fine Aaron," she smiled, "Honestly, I'm doing just fine."

"And…how's Mark?" Aaron queried hesitantly knowing it was a sensitive subject.

Jordan shook her head before replying, "Your guess is as good as mine but it's not a conversation I want to have in Ikea, in fact it's not a conversation I want to indulge in at all."

Aaron was a little taken aback at Jordan's calm but sharp response. "Jordan, are you sure that you are ok with it all?"

Again Jordan smiled that same smile, "I am Aaron, honestly, that's why I'm here in Ikea today to freshen up my home, out with the old in with the new. Life moves on Aaron and I'm not going to try and stop it, Mark and Nina are welcome to each other, I forgive them in order to get on with no heavy weight on my shoulders or in my heart holding me back and stunting my growth."

Aaron listened unsure if he was talking to the same Jordan he'd known all this time. "Good for you Jordan, I'm pleased to know. I think we've all had a rough time these past few months." He put Antoine down before continuing what he was saying, "I'm not sure if you are aware but you'll probably find out sooner or later," he looked down at Antoine and then back at Jordan, "Antoine is my son, I'm his biological Father."

"Wow!" Jordan smirked pinching Antoine's cheek, "That's not my affair to be concerned with but you'll both mean the same to me if that's ok?"

For some crazy reason Aaron felt a peacefulness attach to him whilst speaking with Jordan in the middle of Ikea and decided to latch on to it. He admired her attitude towards everything knowing she could spit fire. Yes she had nearly wrecked Alec's life just as much as she had saved it. She had taken her punishment and was handling it and at that moment he quietly thanked her for another lesson in life. "Yes, that's ok with me."

Jordan mouthed a 'thank you' and waved at Antoine before getting on with her Ikea shop.

"Byeeeee!" Antoine waved.

"Come on Son," Aaron said grabbing Antoine's hand.

"I like Jordan," Antoine sang as he skipped and hopped along.

"Do you?"

"Yes, she looked after me and gave me teddy and read me stories and…"

NINA.

'Three more laps and that's it for today,' Nina told herself as she swam beginning to feel tired. She had swam for the past couple of days to improve her stamina and to tone up in preparation for the grand favour to Claire. She aimed to be in tip top condition, with all that had been going on for the past few months she had hardly dedicated much time to her health and fitness. Food was any and anything she could grab that was quick and easy only to quieten the calling from her stomach.

As her body fought the water and glided across the surface so did her thoughts in her mind. Jordan had been ghost to her for a while now, which bugged her knowing what she had discovered and even revenged. Why hadn't Jordan confronted her via text, phone call, a visit…anything, especially after the abuse and torture she had crushed Mark with.

Reaching the edge of the pool Nina lay on her back and floated for a minute. Before panicking and saving herself from sinking, she suddenly experienced a petite, nightmare dream, Jordan scheming and conjuring up a punishment for her. She felt her heart bouncing off the walls of her chest and she pressed the palm of her hand against her breast to dim the thudding sound she heard echoing through her ears. Taking a long deep breath, Nina stepped out of the pool.

"Are you ok?" The Lifeguard asked her handing her a towel, recognising her face.

Taking the towel Nina nodded at him and smiled, "Yes thanks," and headed towards the locker and shower room. "Get a grip!" she sighed digging in her wash bag for her shampoo and shower gel. Checking her phone before she showered she noticed the time read 7:30pm and she had missed a call from Mark and two from Aaron. Claire had also sent her a text message wishing her good luck for the night ahead and once again gratitude for agreeing to do the favour for her.

MARK.

"Mum!" Mark called.

Irene appeared in Marks bedroom doorway, "Yes?"

"I'm going out tonight mum, I need a drink, I need time out, I need…" Mark began to justify his night out to his mother before she cut him off.

"You are a grown man Mark and yes, I agree after all that's happened I think a night out will do you some good," she lectured him, fixing his shirt collar and brushing off his broad shoulders proudly.

"Thanks Mom," Mark said, turning to face her and planting a kiss on her forehead. After venting to his mother the other day and putting himself back together as best as he could, Mark had pondered on a few things and had decided to exercise a few options. A few options he was hoping to relay to his friend Clive that night over a drink and see what he thought.

Having hit rock bottom and nestled at the feet of his own Mother reaching up to her with open arms, begging her to help him stand up on his own two feet like a small child was the most shame he had ever endured, it all seemed unreal, like a dream but it couldn't have been, the scars were proof and not just the visible ones.

Shaking the dreadful memories away shooing them, not wanting them interfering with his night out, he finished getting himself ready just in time to hear the honking of the Taxi horn outside his Mother's home.

He intended on drinking to his hearts content, so a 7pm start was perfect. Climbing into the Taxi and greeting Clive, Mark rang Nina to see how she was doing and what she had planned for that Saturday night.

She never answered.

AARON.

Antoine's heaving chest and gentle snores brought contentment to Aaron, he had enjoyed his Saturday with him in Ikea and seeing Jordan (for some weird reason) had left him with a sense of joy. He couldn't help but smile to himself in hope of things turning around and getting better.

He took out his mobile phone and unable to help himself, flicked through his photo gallery admiring the pictures he had of Nina and the boys. "Oh what the hell," he cursed himself going to his call list and dialling Nina's number.

Not planning on ringing her he had no clue what he was even going to say. Regardless of lack of intention and a prepared speech he didn't care, all he knew was that he wanted to hear her voice, her voice was his favourite sound and he needed to hear it to seal his day tightly.

Unfortunately Nina didn't answer.

CHAPTER 33

NINA.

I t was 10pm as a radiant and refreshed Nina stepped out of her Taxi at the specified location according to the received instructions. Her attire was as requested and on point and she was equipped and ready to indulge in the mysterious but intriguing night ahead.

Her stomach twisted with tight knots as she entered the hotel lobby as if she had never done this before. Weakness suddenly overcame her as she caught sight of a group of guys in the bar area raising tones of banter.

She scoured the group of suited men catching eyes with a couple of them trying to figure out which one of them, if any, were her mystery client for the night.

"Hey sexy!" A passing man whispered in her ear as he pinched her bottom.

Nina immediately slapped his hand away from her backside and frowned.

The reception desk seemed miles away from where she was standing and automatically her feet began to hurt. Michael Kors clutch in hand she confidently strutted towards the desk, after all she had promised Claire she'd carry out this favour and switching into work mode she was prepared to see it through in order to free herself from what felt like an awkward and uncomfortable, life situation.

"I have a reservation."

"And the name?" The receptionist politely asked.

"Erm...erm..." Nina hesitated, her nerves getting the better of her. "Sunshine Peter."

The woman behind the desk scanned the computer screen for a short period of time before clicking the mouse, "I found you."

A signature was required off Nina before she was handed a room key card along with the directions and a practised, plastic, "Have a nice stay!"

En route to the lifts Nina inhaled a deep breath disguising her feelings of a beginner. She had done this all before a hundred times so why did she feel so nervous this time around? In fact it felt more daunting than the first time around.

"America. America, America, America!" She laughed out loud to herself being as she was the only body present in the lift. She watched as the numbers increased on the small screen as the lift climbed higher and higher.

As the lift rode it's gradient Nina quickly whipped out her phone and checked the text message containing her instructions. This was the finale. Although nervous to the core a smile graced her face, she felt honoured that Claire had called upon her to do the favour. She had more than admired Claire from the moment she had clapped eyes on her, driving off in her Lexus all suited up, a woman of authority. A woman who succeeded at everything she set out to accomplish, she was no weakling.

Ninth floor. The lift came to a stop and Nina stepped out. Strutting sexily down the desolate corridor, Nina sprayed a couple squirts of perfume and touched up her lipstick before arriving at her destination.

MARK.

"How's moms?" Clive enquired to Mark as he brought their drinks over and took a seat at the corner table in the plush hotel bar.

"She's cool," he smiled, grateful for everything that she had done for him. She was both a mother and a father to him. His dad was abusive to his mother so she fled Jamaica when she was pregnant with Mark. She was sure as hell not going to let that man abuse her or her child, it was a life she was adamant against. A couple of years later she heard from relatives across the sea that he had died of a heart attack.

"She's always cool," Clive patted Marks shoulder, "No matter what she's always there for you and everyone else."

"Tell me about it," Mark agreed.

"Remember that time when…"

Mark drifted off from Clive's babbling about old times as he noticed the back of a familiar, female figure walking across the hotel lobby towards where the lifts were located. The way she swayed her hips sexily from side to side, her 'on point' attire, she exuded elegance and class, she stood tall and proud. He zoned in on her as her dainty, perfectly manicured finger pressed the call button on the lift. As she turned sideways her profile became exposed revealing herself to him to recognise.

"Nina," he swallowed hard before gulping.

"Nina?" Clive spat, "What has Nina got to do with it?"

Mark cut him off realising that he had been drowning deeply in a sea of Nina. "Oh yeah I forgot," he said trying to blend in with the one sided conversation that Clive had been indulging with himself.

Clive just gave him a puzzled look before guzzling his drink.

"So why did you choose this venue for tonight?" Mark asked Clive the events organiser.

"Oh to meet up with the others here makes a nice change from our local pubs doesn't it?"

Mark looked over in the direction of the lifts to find Nina had disappeared.

"Oh, you spotted that fine ass chick that was at the desk too?" Clive chuckled excitedly. "Something about her seems so familiar, she reminds me of that night we went…"

"Excuse me, nature calls," Mark said, getting up and backing his chair away from the table before heading to the men's toilets.

He splashed cold water on his face and shook his head. Surely Nina wasn't doing what he assumed, after everything, all the trouble and pain it had caused. The flashbacks attacked his delicate mind. The masquerade, his hands gripping her firm ass, his yearning to connect with her, her juicy lips and butter soft skin, she felt like a dream, she felt like home.

Grabbing a paper towel he patted his face dry, screwed it up and tossed it into the bin beneath the sink. For some reason he felt an ache in his heart at the thought of somebody else enjoying her. Jealousy stirred within his walls and he knew that he had to shake it off, Nina didn't want him and she didn't belong to him.

NINA.

Nina checked the time on her phone, she was five minutes early. Claire's voice echoed through her head, "Early is on time, on time is late." She fixed herself up and took a deep breath before knocking on the door of room 913.

She heard the door unlock but it did not open. Not knowing whether to enter or not at her own accord he decided to just stand and wait. Ten seconds later she heard a gruff voice command her to 'Enter!"

The twisting and pulling sensations inside of her stomach were a sign that danger lurked behind the door and encouraged her to turn and run away but the curiosity, greed and thirst won the battle as she gave in to temptation and gently turned the door handle entering the room.

Darkness greeted her except for a small glow coming from a lamp light on a small table a few steps away enabling her to find her way. Again she heard the same voice, "Follow the instructions on the piece of paper by the lamp."

Doing as she was told she walked over to the lamp to find a small sheet of instructions and an eye mask. Following the instructions Nina untied her Mack and hung it on the back of the chair that sat next to the small table. She placed her clutch bag on the seat of the chair, slipped off her simple DKNY LBD and laid that neatly on top of her Mack but kept on her heels.

She could feel her heart thumping at a ridiculous pace, pounding through her throat knowing that the moment she placed the mask over her eyes she would be helpless and devoted to the hands of someone else to do unto her as they pleased. She prayed silently for her guardian angel to protect her, trying to justify her reasons for being disobedient. With trembling hands she placed the mask firmly over her eyes refusing to taste a glimpse in case she disliked what she saw. A blanket of darkness enveloped her as she stood glowing by the lamplight.

MARK.

"Are you ok mate? You seem a bit jumpy," Clive asked Mark, sincerely concerned.

Clive was a renowned joker, always had been the class clown but at this moment in time he was seriously worried about his friends behaviour. Clive only knew a small fraction of what Mark had dealt with.

"I'm fine, honestly," Mark convinced him. "Thanks."

As the two drank up it wasn't long before the others began to arrive and the banter began distracting Marks thoughts from Nina and before long the group had decided to move on to another venue to continue their fun and games.

NINA.

The smooth, soft, sensual voice of Donnell Jones filled the atmosphere suddenly calming and relaxing Nina's nerves. She jumped as she felt the palms of manly hands caress her naked waist and roam around her semi-nude body. The hairs on the back of her neck stood to attention as she felt warm kisses (and facial hairs) travel from her right shoulder up to her neck before finally nestling on her earlobe. A familiar smell greeted her warming her into the arms of the owner.

Desperately aching to speak Nina remembered the rules and before she realised what was happening she was swept off her feet and carried off. She didn't know where to, she had no idea what her surroundings were, she just had to trust in Claire's word and play along.

He must have sensed the slight fear, "It's ok, I'm not going to hurt you," he whispered softly into her ear, his warm breath soothing her nerves.

Gently she was lowered onto a huge bed. "I'm going to pleasure you, don't be scared just enjoy," he whispered tying both of her wrists together above her head with what felt like a silk tie.

Nina gasped as a warm liquid touched the skin on her stomach followed by his tongue licking seductively around and around her navel sucking and slurping before travelling below her navel, removing her panties and exploring and savouring her further taking his warm liquid with him for assistance.

With her movement restricted due to her hands being tied all she could do was fidget with pure delight as the sensations drove her crazy. Just when she thought he had stopped and tried to catch her breath she felt his hands unclasp her bra and his hot, sticky mouth envelope her breasts driving her wild as he twisted one of her nipples relentlessly whilst biting and sucking on the other leaving her with a mouthful of moans and groans.

He began to pant and grunt as if he couldn't get enough of her and then she felt his saluting soldier pressing against her ready to attack. Again that familiar scent blessed her nostrils. Unsure of what was to come next Nina lay still trying to recover from what he had just pleasured her with. She heard a packet ripping and presumed he was capping his tool. (Claire had assured her it was strictly safe sex or no sex) Warm, gentle kisses rained upon her before his lips collided with hers tasting sweet like honey. (She put two and two together and realised it was honey he had poured all over her body)

"Do you like this?" He whispered to her in between kisses.

"Yes," Nina whispered back in order to satisfy her customer.

He changed his tune with a rough kiss before entering her unexpectedly with a deep thrust.

"Aaaaaah!" Nina screamed.

He swallowed her cry by covering her mouth with his and kissing her passionately as she whimpered, "Sssshhhh," he purred as he took pleasure from her and then returned it with gentle strokes.

Nina bit down on her bottom lip so as not to cry out, listening to his moans and groans as he stroked her sensitive areas as if he knew her body like the back of his hand. He positioned her in as many ways as possible occasionally pausing treasuring the moment. He untied her wrists but kept her mask on and placed her on top of him. He sat up to meet her, pulling her forward so she was close to him, so he could feel her skin against his skin, her legs wrapped around his waist. He kissed her ever so sweetly, she felt him stroke her hair and caress her facial features as if he missed her. He then re-entered her gripping her tightly.

Nina tried not to think, just comply with his actions and enjoy the ride but she couldn't dismiss the familiarity, feelings, smell and the sexual behaviour. Her thoughts were thrown as he clutched her backside and sucked on her breasts hard biting her nipples again, "Tell me you love me," he demanded in harsh whisper and repeated the same over and over again, "Tell me...tell me..."

Feeling that he was about to explode she said what he wanted to hear before he collapsed in a heap into her body breathing heavily. Nina became limp as he lay her down, she felt a trail of kisses descend off her body and she heard footsteps walk across the room. After a few minutes the music stopped and nothing but silence filled the air as she lay, sprawled out across the bed still blindfolded with nothing but her heels on.

A set of dim lights came on and Nina felt something touch her leg and heard the door close. She removed her mask to find a note beside her, 'Dress and leave.' She sat up and observed her surroundings to find nothing but an ordinary hotel suite, many she had visited of that calibre. There were no traces of any form of activity, no honey pot, no silk tie, no condom wrappers, no nothing but a messy bed with her sat in the middle of it naked. She looked across the room at the table with the lamp on and the chair with all her belongings on and noticed that everything was exactly how she had left it, the only difference was her underwear which had been neatly placed with her things and a white envelope on top.

Mustering up some strength, Nina climbed off the bed and headed to the bathroom to freshen up. She then made her way over to the chair and still standing naked in just her heels she opened the envelope to find a cheque.

She smiled to herself.

It was 1am as Nina stood in her shower lathering her body wash all over tingling from head to toe in disbelief at what she had just indulged in and how it had made her feel. Sunshine blew sugar coated kisses in her direction. She rinsed off the soap and reached for her towel. Drying off she sat on the edge of the bath and caught Sunshine's sweet candy. A feeling had invited itself into her system and she was more than happy for it to stay.

"Claire, it's me," Nina said. She had called Claire to give her the thumbs up.

"Hey honey, how was it?" Claire sang down the phone in her usual tone.

"Fine."

"Oh that's good. Thanks once again for...oh hold on a minute, I have a call coming through," she told Nina, "I'll get back to you tomorrow Darling, take care."

Nina hung up and lay her head against her pillow exhausted.

CLAIRE.

"Hello."

"Hi Claire it's me Tressa."

"Oh hi Sugar, did you get it all?"

"Sure did."

"And is Frank happy now? Not to mention satisfied?"

"He sure is. He told me that he won't be able to meet up with you to give you your reward and if you don't mind me passing it on to you at your convenience?"

"Sure, no problem," Claire agreed before hanging up the phone.

CHAPTER 34

JORDAN.

Unlocking her front door Jordan hurried into the kitchen and grabbed a bottle of water from the fridge, she had just been on a morning run to cleanse her mind and exercise her body. Listening to the weird yet wonderful sounds of Lana Del Ray through her earphones during her run Jordan had come to realise that it was time to confront and converse with Nina. They were supposed to be best friends and admittedly (and who could blame her) she felt differently towards her from how she used to, but she wanted to give her the opportunity to justify her behaviour and air anything else that might be bothering her, make a fresh start.

Choosing to be forthright with her decision she dialled Nina's number but as usual reached her voicemail.

NINA.

Nina felt her phone vibrating beneath her pillow but she was too tired to move, not really bothered about who it was who was calling her that Sunday morning, If it was important they'd leave a message, she thought as she closed her eyes and drifted off back into slumber land dreaming up her next adventures.

MARK.

Mark hadn't slept all night, he had discretely slipped away from the group finding it difficult to enjoy himself. Spotting Nina had caused an abundance of scenarios as to what she could have been up to, to invade and conquer his mind

Laying on top of his duvet covers still in his jeans and shirt, arms resting behind his head, he stared at the ceiling and thought hard. He thought about how much life had changed for all of them.

AARON.

Buzz! Buzz!

"OK, OK!" Aaron shouted as he placed Antoine's breakfast on the table in front of him. "I'm just going to answer the door, eat up your breakfast son."

"Hello?" Aaron answered through the intercom.

"Hi, it's me, Tressa."

Aaron buzzed her in checking his watch, she was an hour early.

As Tressa entered Aaron was making his way back in to the kitchen to join Antoine at the breakfast table when he noticed her attire. She wore a pair of skin tight, plastic pants and a top that resembled what he would call an undergarment, her heels were sky high and her hair was slicked back in a long ponytail.

"Good morning," she winked at him entering the kitchen.

Aaron turned his head in disgust at her disregard for Antoine's presence not to mention his anger towards her for the night that Nina had caught them in bed together.

"Oooh I'm just in time for breakfast," she smiled taking a seat next to Antoine and ruffling his hair. "Did you have fun with Daddy this weekend?"

Antoine showed her a mouthful of scrambled egg on top of which he was forcing pieces of bagel in and trying to speak, "I did," he giggled as Aaron poked him for talking with his mouthful.

"Antoine take your time there's no rush," Aaron said ashamed at his poor table manners.

Tressa got up and made herself a cup of tea because Aaron had no intention of showing her any hospitality. "Well I suppose I'll sort my own breakfast out then."

Not wanting to make a scene in front of Antoine, irritated by her and what she was wearing he replied, "I suppose you better considering we weren't expecting you for breakfast anyway." He ate up quickly and then got up to pack Antoine's belongings together. "Make sure he eats up," he told her before leaving the kitchen.

Tressa just rolled her eyes, peeved that she had deliberately kept her outfit on from that night to get his attention only to be ignored and treated like a 'nobody.' A devilish grin spread across her face as she thought about the simple video recording job she had come across for a friend of a friend. Discovering it was Nina and managing to disguise the shock and complete the job, she had not only enjoyed it and made a nice little profit but she now had some dirt to throw. Now that Aaron was adhering to his Fatherly duties she was becoming a stable part in his life and she was fully aware that he had great feelings for Nina. That was going to have to change, she was going to make Nina disappear, become a thing of the past, it was her turn now, she wanted Aaron to herself, a nice little happy family.

Aaron had finished packing Antoine's stuff and once again stood scrolling through his phone admiring the pictures of Nina devastated that she had caught him in bed with Tressa.

"Have you heard from her?" Tressa's voice pierced his thoughts like a sharp arrow.

He put his phone away and turned around to face Tressa peering over his shoulder, "That's none of your business, Tressa now where's Antoine?"

"He's in the living room watching children's TV," she said giving him a dirty look and blocking his way.

"Would you excuse me please," he gently pushed passed her trying to avoid touching her. "Antoine, time to get your shoes on your Mom is taking you home now."

Antoine did as he was told and Aaron scooped him up and swung him up to the ceiling pretending to make him fly like Superman down the hall to where his shoes sat on the doormat. Antoine laughed and caught his breath, beaming with joy.

"Did you see Nina this weekend?" Tressa sneakily asked Antoine.

Aaron glared at her clenching his jaw wondering where she got off using her own child as a tool for something that didn't concern her.

"No," innocent Antoine replied, "But we saw Jordan in Ikea and she made us happy."

"You better get home before you catch a cold," Aaron said sarcastically hurrying her off and having a dig at her lack of clothing

"I need sleep not so much warmth as I came here straight from my night out. Antoine is going to Alec's now and I'm going to get some rest," she informed Aaron as she adjusted her breasts and pulled up her plastic pants, wiggling her ass in front of Antoine.

"What a disgrace," Aaron muttered opening the door for her to exit. He bent down and kissed his son.

"Disgrace hey?" Tressa whispered in his ear as she passed him at the door, "I'll show you disgrace."

NINA.

Nina tossed and turned furiously in her sleep as mysterious lips kissed her seductively, suckling on her intimate areas causing her to squirm in pure delight. Familiar hands caressed and groped her and a warm breath whispered sweet nothings in her ear causing her skin to tingle. The tingling escalated through her entire body vibrating...That's when she awoke realising that she was dreaming and her phone was vibrating next to her.

"Hello."

It was Jordan, "I've been trying to ring you all morning," Jordan said impatiently. Not even a 'Good Morning' or 'Hello.'

Nina remained quiet, a little set aback that firstly, Jordan was actually calling her and secondly that she was conversing with her as if nothing had happened over the past few weeks.

"Can I ring you back in ten or fifteen minutes," Nina asked, "I have just literally opened my eyes." Something told Nina that she would need to be alert and attentive for whatever it was that Jordan was calling her for.

"No need for that," Jordan said, "How about we meet up today for a chat and some Sunday lunch, we both know we have a lot to discuss. The Kings Head at 3pm?"

"Ok," Nina managed to muster, under the impression that she didn't have any choice over the matter. Jordan didn't sound as Nina had expected, her behaviour was peculiar and something felt different. The only way to find out what it was, was to attend the meal at 3pm.

Nina lay in the centre of her bed comfortably confined by her many pillows and stared up at the ceiling trying to comprehend what had just happened. One minute she was enjoying dream state sex with Mr Mysterious and within a split second she's on her phone listening to Jordan dictate to her about her days arrangements.

Reverting back to last night and the favour she had carried out for Claire, a chuffed Nina smiled pleased with herself and full of excitement then eventually stretched and climbed out of her bed. As she did so her phone beeped, it was a text message from Claire;

> 'Sorry I had to end the call last night. Thanks once again for doing the favour.
> I don't know how you'd feel about doing it again? My client has politely ditched me
> In request for your services but only if you agree.'

Nina jumped up and down like a jolly child full to the brim with glee. Claire had saved her from asking to get back in the game and if she only dealt with this one client once a week it wouldn't interfere with her work, he would become even more familiar and comfortable to service and she'd receive her fat pay cheque each time, not to mention the sexual satisfaction of her own. It was the perfect opportunity and although she would be stealing Claire's client she knew Claire had plenty more.

She replied to Claire's message, the answer simply being; 'yes!'

JORDAN.

After finally getting through to Nina and purposefully not allowing her an inch of breath to speak but to just listen, a Sunday lunch date had been arranged.

Standing in the shower freshening up after her morning run, Jordan thought about all the things that she wanted to say to Nina, all the things she wanted to get off her chest but having showered and dried off she wondered if any of it was necessary.

Nina knew what she had done to upset her and she guessed that Mark had gone running to her the night she threw him out. Buttoning up her jeans and tucking in her t-shirt, Jordan flung on her striped GAP blazer and smiled. Reflecting back on her previous behaviour she no longer felt that anger and frustration, that bitterness. She now had clarity and she wanted to show Nina that. Grabbing her clutch and keys she left her house.

NINA.

Heading towards The Kings Head, Nina stared at the line of traffic ahead of her. Although it was late autumn the sun was out and the chill was tolerable. It seemed like everybody had the same idea, a spot of pub grub for Sunday lunch.

As she pulled into the car park Jordan's car came into view. Fists threw punches inside of Nina's stomach causing it to cramp and twist in pain. Searching through her glove compartment she found a pack of mints and hastily shoved one in her mouth to try and disperse the terrible feeling that viciously bounced around her stomach.

Nina knew that the feelings she felt were due to her guilt. Jordan's secrets had been exposed and she had dealt with the consequences of them. Whether she had dealt with them appropriately was another question (the saga with Mark) and now karma was journeying in her direction and she knew she couldn't keep running, so today was the first stage of facing it.

JORDAN.

Jordan watched as Nina strode over to the table where she was seated.

"Hi," Nina said and bent down to kiss Jordan's cheek before taking a seat opposite.

"Hello," Jordan smirked full of confidence.

"You're looking well," Nina complimented Jordan.

"Thank you," Jordan smiled and left it at that.

Nina fidgeted uncomfortably in her seat anticipating the first bout of confrontation guessing there would be hoards of it.

"I've ordered us a virgin cocktail pitcher," Jordan informed Nina.

"Nice," Nina said devoting her attention to the menu, scouring it with a fine tooth comb, still waiting. She hadn't eaten a thing all day and she decided that if she constantly filled her mouth with food her speech would be limited and there would be less room for regretful words.

The waitress came over with their glasses and their virgin cocktail pitcher. After what felt like forever she left their table.

"I know you slept with my husband," Jordan just blurted out.

Nina looked her square in the eye, unafraid, waiting for her to continue but she didn't. The silence begged to be filled.

"I did," she answered honestly.

"I also know that you have been escorting," she added.

"I know you do." Again Nina waited for more but it never came.

Jordan sipped her drink and glared intensely at Nina waiting for a reaction of some sort but just the same it never came. "Well?" She prodded.

Nina took a sip of her drink and firmly placed it down on the table, clasping her hands together she looked at Jordan. "You found my box Jordan, you read my diary so you don't need me to tell you what you already know. You even used the contents of my box against me."

Jordan sat in silence with pursed lips.

"I don't believe the issue was my escorting or even sleeping with Mark because as we both know your halo is hardly sparkling clean is it?" Nina paused again leaving a football pitch worth of space for Jordan to say something but surprisingly she just sat and let Nina speak with no attempt to gain control of the situation.

"You were angry that you never knew, you love to be 'in the know' and in everybody's business but when you have things going on you keep it to yourself. Why did you scatter bits and pieces of my box around Jordan? Why did you treat Mark in such a way? Why did you do that?"

At last Jordan spoke, "I wanted to spoil your relationship with Aaron just like you spoilt mine with Mark. Why should you come through the other side smiling after damaging other people and messing with their feelings? Why should you get engaged and live all cosy?"

It took all Nina had not to butt in and tackle Jordan's reasons but as soon as a gap presented itself she leapt right in, "But your behaviour was horrendous, that of a crazy woman!" Nina chuckled although it wasn't in the slightest bit funny.

"I'm past that now," Jordan calmly stated.

The waitress re-appeared once again at their table with a cargo of food flagging healthy appetites, she even had difficulty arranging it on the table.

Nina was about to tuck into her food when Jordan passed a remark, "I've paid my dues, funny you haven't," and she began shovelling food down her throat.

"Excuse me?" Nina's eyes bulged out of her head and she instantly lost her appetite.

"You heard me," Jordan mumbled with a mouthful of food blocking her vocal cords functioning.

"Oh I see," Nina rolled her eyes at Jordan's childish behaviour, "I haven't paid my dues?"

She was about to reel off her dues, no longer engaged, living alone in her own place once again, having to change jobs, discovering Antoine is Aaron's son, catching Aaron and Tressa in bed together, comforting Mark and his mother because of Jordan's despicable behaviour and putting up with her bullying, but she knew it wasn't worth wasting her breath and she didn't want Jordan to be a part of her life anymore especially how she conducted herself, she could easily do without her presence. She refused to give her the satisfaction of knowing what was occurring in her life.

"I have taken responsibility for mine everyday Jordan. The difference between you and me is that you always have to have someone to blame because that's easier than accepting your own actions." With that said Nina pulled out a wad of cash (purposely to rub salt in Jordan's wounds and keep her wondering) and slammed it down on the table, "Here's to our last supper!" Unable to stay seated in Jordan's company any longer Nina got up and left the pub.

Nina opened the windows in her car to let a gust of fresh air through, she was furious but relieved at the same time. So much for minimal speaking, she'd been bursting at the seams for a while now so better out than in.

Still sitting at the table alone surrounded by piles of food Jordan tucked in as if nothing had happened that afternoon.

CHAPTER 35

AARON.

Aaron stood in the shower for what seemed like an eternity as he tried to eliminate Tressa from his thoughts. He didn't understand her and cursed the day he had comforted her through her domestic problems because now he had a permanent attachment to her - Antoine.

Yes he was proud to be Antoine's father but it seemed that Tressa was taking full advantage of the tie they had and it was gnawing away at him slowly. It was obvious that she had a chip on her shoulder because all she did was rant on about Nina which didn't help because Nina was his weakness and Tressa knew it. If Tressa thought she could win him around and play happy families she had another thing coming, if he couldn't have Nina he didn't want anyone. Stepping out of the shower he prepared himself to pay Nina a visit.

NINA.

Nina drove home after her meal with Jordan dumbfounded, trying to figure out what the purpose was. Proud of herself for not blurting out the tribulations she was contending with and for plucking up the courage to eventually face her, Nina decided there and then to leave it all behind and get on merrily with her life. She had a lot to look forward to, her mysterious client for one, planning to move and she still had Claire and Mark with the added comfort of his mother, Irene.

As she pulled up to her apartment she spotted Aaron's Audi parked up and as she drove a little closer she saw him ringing her buzzer at the main entrance. Automatically she put her car in reverse and drove off to nowhere, anywhere was better than seeing Aaron. Nina pulled over down a random side road and sobbed, seeing Aaron ripped her heart out. She knew why and had to admit it to herself. She didn't know what she had until it was gone, she thought she could have it all, she got wrapped up and lost in the exciting escorting world and realised too late. It did hurt her when she caught him in bed with Tressa but she deserved that after her history of cheating and it did hurt her that Antoine was his child (although she adored him) hoping that one day she would bear his first born, but it was what it was and now she knew how he felt the night of the Masquerade Ball.

Aaron standing outside of her apartment reminded her of the Bank Holiday when he surprised her with a Chinese takeaway, their first kiss and his charming lyrics. She shook her head and wiped her eyes, she had plans and she had to stick to them. Unsure of where to go she headed to Marks moms house.

MARK.

Mark opened his Mothers front door shocked to see Nina standing there, he had done nothing but think about her all night and all day.

"Hey," he greeted her.

"Hey to you to," she smiled.

He admired her attire and couldn't help but smile back. From when they were little kids growing up she always brightened up his mood with just her smile. Over time he had learnt that Nina's smile was her make-up to cover up her true feelings, even when she was up she was feeling down but no one would ever guess.

"To what do I owe this visit?" He asked, curious as to why she had turned up on his Mothers doorstep out of the blue with no warning.

Nina looked away across the road to hide her genuine emotions, she sucked it up and smiled once more, "Well if you let me in and make me a 'cuppa' I'll explain," she joked.

Nina hadn't stepped inside enough for Mark to close the front door before Irene pounced on her, "Oooohh my Baby!" She squealed hugging her tightly to her bosom, "I thought I heard your voice. How are yah keeping? Looking beautiful as always," she said breathlessly from all the excitement.

"I'm fine thanks," Nina said kissing Irene's cheeks respectfully, "I just need to talk to Mark if that's ok?"

"Sure Sweety, I'll pop the kettle on and make some tea, please say you'll stay for some of Aunty Irene's dinner?" She asked hopefully, glad to have a guest and her favourite one at that.

Irene had always had a soft spot for Nina from when Nina was a little girl. Nina's Mother had died in a car crash when she was just five years of age and she never knew her Father so her and her older brother were to be cared for by their Aunt. Nina's Aunt worked all hours god sent to keep a roof over their heads and make sure that Nina and her brother had everything they needed and wanted. She was good to them but cuddles and quality time was where Irene fitted in.

Nina met Mark in Primary school and they became the best of friends which meant Nina spent a majority of her time around Marks house. Nina's brother was much older and did his own thing with his own friends and although he was very protective of his little sister he felt comfort knowing that she was happy and safe with Irene and Mark when their Aunt was at work. Irene welcomed her into her home because she was full of manners, very polite and gentle regardless of losing her Mother at such a young age. She was never rude or disrespectful and a smile always graced her pretty face. She was the daughter she never had. Nina would always help Irene in the kitchen and learn how to cook Jamaican food and bake cakes. Nina would help in the garden that Irene was so very fond of and sometimes if her Brother and Aunt let her she would go to church with Irene and Mark on a Sunday.

AARON.

After ringing Nina's buzzer three times and getting no response Aaron decided to give up, but still couldn't help but wonder where she was and what she was doing. He hadn't noticed Nina pull in and pull out of the car park in order to avoid him. Feeling low and disheartened he picked himself up and whilst still in the mood of making amends, Mark was next on his list but a Chinese meal was in order first to feed the growling hunger in his stomach.

NINA.

Nina sat crossed legged in the middle of Marks bed, Mark sat leaning against the headboard facing her. Nina quit pretending and expressed her true thoughts and feelings.

"Jordan?" Mark frowned, curiously, "What has she done now?" He questioned with concern.

Nina saw a slight panic loom over him and eased him, "Nothing drastic or crazy Mark, she invited me to a pub lunch just and she confessed all. She said she knew about us and what happened at the Ball from finding my secret box when she helped Aaron move my things into my new flat, "Nina took a deep breath before continuing, "She admitted to haunting and stalking me using my own possessions against me, she wanted me to suffer, she wanted me to hurt, she wanted me to pay for what I did and she began by destroying my relationship with Aaron, how dare I be engaged and happy."

Mark sat silently biting his cheeks as he listened unable to speak. At the mention of Jordan's name he felt queasy especially after what she had put him through.

Nina sensed his sensitivity and remembered the fright displayed in his face that night Jordan had her wicked way, "I'm sorry Mark I didn't think, I shouldn't have brought this here, silly me, please forgive me."

Mark grabbed her hands and held them tightly reassuring her it was ok. "Did you eat then?" He asked changing the subject.

Nina cracked up laughing, "No! I left her at the table in front of a mountain of food for her to plough her way through. I just don't understand how someone could be so mean."

"Well, Mom will fill your belly with her good home cooking that'll soon get rid of that nasty taste," Mark said sniffing the aroma in the air anticipating his Sunday dinner.

After a catch up and a bit of reminiscing, Nina felt much better and grateful for Mark and Irene in her life. In Irene's home she felt like a little girl again without a care in the world, safe and secure and with Mark as her friend she felt she could always be herself, honest and true. As for them sharing intimacy, in Nina's eyes it wasn't her and she didn't feel for him in such a way, it was him lusting after 'Sunshine.'

"I tried to ring you Saturday night to see if you wanted to go out," Mark suddenly threw her way, "But you never answered your phone."

Nina thought back to her mind-blowing Saturday night with her mystery client. A slight giggle escaped her before she replied, "I erm...I decided to stay home and chill out, you know, watch a movie in bed," she blatantly lied.

Mark knew that it was her he had seen that Saturday night in the hotel but he knew not to push it, he heard the sweet, little giggle that had left her lips and he had watched her glow when she answered him. He felt there was much more to this than Nina was letting on, she was up to something and maybe she had her reasons for carrying out whatever it was she was doing but he knew it was going to end in tears, he could see behind her smile. His Mama always said, 'the same thing that makes you laugh makes you cry.' He felt it his duty to protect and protect her he would.

It wasn't long before the two of them heard Irene hollering to them that dinner was ready, she didn't have to call them twice as they raced down the stairs like a pair of ravenous school kids hungry after a long day. They said grace faster than the speed of light before attacking their food with no mercy creating an A star Sunday entertainment for Irene.

Nina acquired her dose of love and hugs from Irene and thanked her again for her hospitality and generous heart before opening the front door refreshed and ready to conquer the week ahead. "Oh," she stopped dead in her tracks at the sight of Aaron standing in front of her poised ready to ring the doorbell.

Aaron didn't move, He just arched his eyebrows as if waiting for Nina to explain what she was doing at Marks house.

Nina had a flashback to the night she had caught him in bed with Tressa and it disturbed her. Gripping on to her feel good mood she politely said, "Excuse me," and made her way to her car without looking back.

"What's going on?" Irene questioned, "Who's upset my baby girl?"

Mark ignored his mother, "Are you ok mate?" He asked Aaron feeling his embarrassment but secretly amused by the fact that Nina, his Nina had paid him no mind.

Aaron sighed with shame, "I came to speak to you actually, I had no idea she would be here."

Mark opened the door a bit wider, "You better come in then," he invited Aaron in and Irene scuttled off into the kitchen to wash up the dishes.

Mark went into the kitchen and grabbed two cans of beer from the fridge and handed Aaron one as they made their way into the living room. "So what's up?"

Aaron felt a familiar security and remembered how close he used to be to Mark before the saga with his nephew and Jordan. "I can't keep living like this Mark."

Mark knew exactly what Aaron meant but still he needed to hear his reasons why.

"I miss you, I miss Nina so much and when she pretends I don't exist it kills me inside. I even miss Jordan after seeing her in Ikea the other day."

Mark shuddered at the mention of Jordan's name but he understood. Those times had gone and things had changed.

Aaron decided to tell Mark everything, he had nothing left to lose and then there was the hope that Mark would open up too. Aaron dived in and informed Mark about Antoine being his son and how Nina caught him and Tressa in the act. He told him about the escorting objects lying around and how it encouraged his suspicion of her old ways still in play causing them to split. He told Mark everything until his shoulders felt light and his chest no longer heavy. He sat and waited for Mark to confess his feelings for Nina, to tell him about the night at the Ball that Jordan had revealed to him. Wasn't it funny how he felt comfortable confiding in a man who had similar if not the same or even more feelings for the same woman.

Marks head felt fit to burst after hearing Aarons stories, he was clueless to it all, Nina hadn't uttered a word to him about an ounce of it, then on top of feeling bad for Aaron he felt worse for Nina. It seemed like everyone had piled their rubbish on to her with no regard for her feelings or what she was able to cope with. He thought back to last night at the hotel when he saw her and then he remembered the Ball and Martin, yes that was his name, Martin the host, setting a price for him to have 'Sunshine' for a time. He knew Nina and she didn't do something for nothing, Nina was out to make money to get away from everything, her fake smiles disguised her burdens and sadness. He could tell that Aaron loved her and deep down he knew Aaron was good for her but Nina didn't need further complications in her life and Aaron had accumulated baggage.

"Hey Mark!" Aaron shouted, clicking his fingers in front of Marks nose to wake him from his daydream.

"Sorry I was erm…"

"Are you ok?"

Mark gathered his thoughts and played his part, "I'm ok, it's just after hearing everything that you have been going through it seems like we all have our problems and we should be getting together and helping each other."

"Very true," Aaron agreed, "That's why I came here today to make it right, it would have been nice if Nina had acknowledged me and given me a chance as well."

Aaron and Mark spent the evening chilling and catching up and then Aaron was sent home with a container filled with Irene's delicious cooking and a welcome back ticket whenever he felt like it but nothing could fill that empty space in his heart that Nina had left and he didn't know what to do about it.

CHAPTER 36

JORDAN.

Monday morning and Jordan had to literally rise and shine in order to impress a panel, it was time she went back to work. Mark was no longer a part of her life and he had made that perfectly clear and due to the revenge dish she had chosen to serve him she knew there was no way in hell he was ever going to come back.

She no longer had the blessing of a best friend, that bridge had been burnt. She now stood alone and had to brave it and face the storm, she had to start all over again, divorce, new job, new friends and maybe sell up the house and downgrade to a smaller property.

'It's just me, myself and I', were her last thoughts before she prepared herself for her interview.

AARON.

Aaron woke up with a different frame of mind in comparison to his previous days. Today he felt refreshed and he had a spring in his step, he put it down to the conversation he had with Mark the night before.

As he sat in Irene's living room yesterday with Mark, Aaron admired the numerous framed pictures that decorated the cabinet surfaces of Mark and his family and he had learnt that Nina was a major part of his life, practically family. In the time that he was with Nina she never really went into detail about her past. He was aware that her mother had died in a car crash but that's where she would become mute and speak no further on the matter.

After receiving a family history briefing from Mark and his mother he learnt that they cherished her in an adoptive way, she was their family and they were hers, she was Mark's best friend and his sister and suddenly Aaron felt a little bit silly for thinking otherwise. Mark no longer felt like a threat he was a friend once again. Mark had been tricked into sleeping with 'Sunshine.'

A piece of hot toast popped up out of the toaster, Aaron grabbed it, slathered it with butter, grabbed his belongings and left his flat for work with a smile on his face.

NINA.

Nina woke up to the funky sounds of Maxwell, she jigged herself up on to her feet and danced around her room to the music giggling to herself. Her bum accidentally bounced the bedside table knocking her engagement ring to the floor. She picked it up and placed it into her jewellery box trying to fight the urge of granting it attention but she failed miserably and found herself in the bathroom splashing cold water on her face to dilute her tears. 'It's a new day,' she told herself.

Just as she was leaving her flat for work she heard her phone make a beeping noise. It was a message off Claire providing her with the contact number of her mystery client followed by a rule.

> 'Not for you to use but for you to recognise it is him when he contacts you.'

Nina smiled but at the same time she found it quite odd that Claire was so co-operative about the whole situation. Nina assumed that with Claire's demeanour and reputation, she probably got a massive pay off for recommending 'Sunshine.'

Driving to work Nina began wondering to herself, questioning what her mystery client found so amazing about her, all she did was follow his command whilst he did all the work, satisfying her bodies cries and taking pleasure from it. She laughed to herself, she wasn't complaining certainly not for the amount of money she received her such a pleasurable deed.

MARK.

After spending the best part of Sunday with Nina and even Aaron, Mark woke up feeling much better than he had in a long time. Aaron's visit had settled him and he had begun to feel a bit more like his old self once again, he felt as if he was waving goodbye to his lonely days.

One thing Mark knew for sure was that there would never be any form of voluntary communication or acknowledgement between himself and Jordan, not after everything she had put him through and if he was to be honest he did fear her and carried concerns for her mental health, but she was no longer part of his life.

He had not yet informed Nina or Aaron, having made the decision yesterday with his Mom, but he was going to Jamaica to stay for a couple of months to get some head space and figure out what he wanted to do with his life. He didn't want them coaxing him to stay or influencing his already made plans. A lot had happened in such a short space of time and he was finding it hard to cope and if it wasn't for his Mother he probably wouldn't have got back on his feet.

Jordan popped into his mind as he remembered the somewhat positive reference Aaron had made about her last night but he shrugged it off, if Aaron wanted to maintain a friendship with her then that was his choice, after the whole Alec incident he personally wouldn't but that was Aaron all over, a forgiving soul. Mark sighed thinking about Aaron, when you loved so deeply like Aaron did, trouble would always end up being his best friend.

Leaving his thoughts in bed he jumped into the shower, today he had to take his Mom to the supermarket and then to the Doctors.

CHAPTER 37

NINA.

The week had flown by, Nina had been busy with work due to a visit from head office in order to inspect certain files most of which she was responsible for, therefore for a majority of the week she had taken work home with her and nourished herself with ready meals.

Thankful it was Friday and the pressure from work had eased up immensely, Nina clocked out of work containing high spirits. She had received her anticipated text message from 'Mr Mysterious' with her attire requirements for her special, Saturday night rendezvous. Her stomach fluttered when she read the text.

"What are you smiling about?" Her nosey co-worker asked getting up to take a seat next to her in hope of getting a peek of the text.

"Mind your own business," Nina laughed clearing the screen and putting her phone away into her handbag.

"Well boo you!"

Nina hugged her giggling and wished the rest of the office a lovely weekend because she knew full well hers was going to be magnificent.

AARON.

"Where's Alec?" Antoine asked Aaron as they made their way to the car. Aaron had finished work and gone straight to pick Antoine up from after school club. It was Tressa's weekend to have her son but she had asked him to cover her and then she'd have him for two consecutive weekends to put them back on track. Aaron had made plans to go out with Mark on Saturday night and thankfully Alec had come to the rescue and offered to baby sit his little brother.

"Alec will see you later when we get home," Aaron told him, "Let's go to the supermarket and get some goodies for your busy weekend. Now the last one to the car smells!" They both picked up their pace and ran as fast as they could to the car.

NINA.

Nina casually wondered the aisles of the supermarket placing random items into her trolley. If there was one thing she hated it was food shopping but with cupboards resembling those of 'Miss Hubbard's' she didn't have much choice and another week of ready meals was a definite no. It was at that thought that she realised most of the dates her and Jordan had had revolved around food, either attending restaurants or girly nights in with a take-away and ironically their 'last supper' signified a bitter end to all of that fun.

Nina suddenly felt a hand touch her waist and she shivered. She turned around to see Frank. Her heart stopped for a brief moment and her legs turned to jelly. He totally ignored the horrified expression plastered across her face and planted a gentle kiss on her left cheek. She closed her eyes as he leant towards her to do so allowing her to get a whiff of his cologne. Hastily she backed away and he grabbed her hand. Briskly she shook him off of her and pushed her trolley down the aisle ignoring him but he remained hot on her heels.

"Sunshine, I'm not going to harm you in any way, let us forget about the past and start again."

"My name is no longer Sunshine," she told him through gritted teeth reinforcing her hatred towards him.

"I'm trying here, please," he begged her.

"Well I'm not interested," she declared.

"OK, well I'll see you soon," he grinned before walking away.

"Not if I have anything to do with it," she spat after him.

Frank heard her and slowly turned around, he walked right up to her and whispered in her ear, his lips caressing her ear lobe feeding her a final whiff of his cologne, "That's what you think," before striding off in the opposite direction.

Nina held on tightly to her trolley in order to regain her balance. His touch, his kiss, the way he whispered in her ear not forgetting his cologne, it was all so familiar.

"No," she told herself, "He's familiar because I had grown accustomed to him, he was my most frequent client," she told herself trying to warrant her own excuse for his familiarity.

Unsure of which direction he had travelled and feeling nervous of his presence she scooted rapidly around the supermarket in hope of getting the hell out of there and freeing herself from the haunting of the ghost from her escorting past ASAP.

AARON.

"Nina! Nina!" Antoine shouted running towards her.

Before Nina knew what was occurring Antoine had jumped into her arms and was climbing up her body hugging her tightly.

"Antoine, stop that you know better," Aaron ordered him.

"It's ok," Nina assured him, smiling and hugging Antoine grateful for the sweet distraction, "I miss you too beautiful."

Antoine clung on to her like a lost puppy whilst Aaron took control of Nina's trolley as her arms were obviously full. Aaron knew that Nina was only being civil due to Antoine's presence but he was satisfied with that.

"I miss you sooooo much," Antoine sang at Nina placing emphasis on the word 'so.'

Nina giggled warming Aaron's heart, he hadn't seen her smile so much in a long time.

"I miss you too little man," she tickled him planting kisses all over his face making him laugh even more. "So what are you doing in here?" She asked him.

"I'm staying at Daddy's house this weekend and Alec is too, he's coming around later so we are buying some goodies."

Hearing Antoine refer to Aaron as 'Dad' tore her heart in half but she could never be mad at Antoine he was faultless. She disguised her feelings with a broad smile and pretended to be as excited as Antoine about his goodies, "Ooooh, sounds like you're going to have loads of fun."

As they reached the end of the aisle Aaron attempted to make conversation, "So how are you keeping?"

"I'm fine thank you," Nina replied shortly.

"How's work?"

"That's fine also."

"I bet you're glad it's Friday," he said in hope of a greater response.

"Yes," she said complacently.

Aaron got the hint, "Come on Antoine, say 'bye so Nina can finish off her shopping," he rolled her trolley over to her and Nina bent down to place Antoine onto his feet. He grabbed Nina's face slobbering kisses all over her, "I got you back," he chuckled, pleased with himself.

"Come on now," Aaron said becoming impatient not to mention jealous that Antoine was getting all of Nina's attention.

"When are you coming around?" Antoine questioned her staring her square in the eyes full of hope.

"Erm…maybe soon," she said stumped.

Nina waved after them both and pushed her trolley to the checkout without looking back. She heard Antoine's little voice trail off…"Nina always smells nice daddy."

As she packed up her shopping she couldn't help but feel joyful, Antoine was such a cutie and his little face bought back an assortment of memories.

Aaron and Antoine joined the checkout, Antoine struggling with the weight of the basket but refusing to let Aaron relieve him trying to prove his superman strength. Aaron laughed quietly to himself.

"Look at all of those flowers," Antoine said amazed as he noticed the man in front of them placing a bucket of red roses on the conveyor belt.

The gentleman turned around to see who the little voice belonged to and winked at Antoine.

Aaron noticed the amount of flowers himself as well as a couple boxes of strawberries, some Tia Maria and a box of chocolates. "It looks like someone is going to have a nice evening, a very nice evening indeed."

"It's actually in preparation for tomorrow night," the man in the expensive, starched suit confirmed with a proud smile.

"Well I hope she appreciates it."

"Oh no, this is for me to show my appreciation to her," the man smiled.

Antoine wasn't listening and had started placing the items from the basket on the conveyor belt.

"She must be very special," Aaron continued nosily.

The cashier nodded in agreement as he carefully packed the roses.

"She's a ray of sunshine," the man said placing his card in his wallet and grabbing the bags of gifts, "Have a marvellous weekend all," he said before walking off.

"You too, Frank," the cashier waved before he served Aaron and Antoine. "He's a regular customer, a real gentleman," he stated.

Once inside the car and Antoine was buckled up and the shopping was packed away in the boot, Aaron started the car. He stopped and pulled the key back out of the ignition staring into space lost in his thoughts. Unaware to himself he began speaking out loud. "Sunshine." he breathed, realising what the man with the roses had said at the checkout. "Frank." He recognised that name for some particular reason. Suddenly he had flashbacks to when Nina was escorting and woke him up panicking and fighting in her sleep calling out the name 'Frank.' "No," he said. But they had just seen her in the same supermarket, she was at work, she didn't escort anymore he tried to convince himself.

"Who are you talking to?" Antoine butted in, knocking him off his train of thought.

"No one, no one Son," he frowned starting the car. Luke James filled the speakers of the car singing a song that represented his feelings for Nina and their situation.

> 'When you get lost in just loving someone baby,
> You'll always find,
> Trouble, trouble,
> It happens every time...'

CHAPTER 38

AARON.

Aaron carried the shopping bags through the residential car park to his flat. Antoine dawdled behind with the milk in one hand and the pack of toilet rolls in the other.

"Come on slow coach!" Aaron laughed at him.

"You're going too fast," Antoine whined stopping to swap the milk and toilet rolls over in each hand.

Once inside Aaron took the pizza out of one of the bags and put it in the oven knowing that Antoine was hungry. "Go and put your school stuff and your overnight bag in your room while I put the shopping away," he told him, "And don't forget to wash your hands."

Ten minutes later an excited, energetic Antoine bounced into the living room and jumped all over Aaron for hugs and to show him the toys that he had packed for the slumber weekend. He was overwhelmed that he would be spending the entire weekend not only with his Dad but with his big Brother too. He hardly saw Alec much since he got his own place and his mother had been granted custody of him again.

Just as Aaron was about to sift through the pile of DVD's that Antoine had handed him his phone rang, "Hey Alec, are you ok?" Antoine's ears perked up at the mention of his brother's name, "Ok, I'll let him know then," Aaron said before hanging up.

"Let me know what?" A forward Antoine cheekily asked.

Aaron couldn't help but chuckle, "How do you know it concerns you?"

"Because he's my Brother," was his reasoning.

"He said he's working until later so you'll probably be sleeping when he arrives and he'll see you in the morning when you wake up."

Antoine's face dropped and he pushed out his bottom lip, "You'll see him in the morning," Aaron repeated himself trying to cheer him up.

"I'm going to stay awake and wait for him," Antoine stated.

"If you say so," Aaron nodded knowing full well he'd be snoring before 9pm.

JORDAN.

It was Friday and Jordan was feeling happier than she had felt in a long time. She had received a call from the interview she had attended and they had snapped her up and given her the position she had applied for. She thought she would see how teaching evening classes for Adult Education would go, after all, her days she could easily fill with chores and work preparation, it was the nights that were dim and lonely so it seemed like the perfect option. Luckily the ordeal with Alec hadn't breathed enough air to live and give her a stained teaching record and for that she was grateful.

Tonight she was going to relax, have a deep bubble, put on a homemade face mask, paint her nails and then lounge on her sofa with a bottle of wine. She couldn't help but yearn for the Mark she used to know to be there with her for her to snuggle up to. Things were slowly getting better for her, slowly but surely.

NINA.

Nina dropped her shopping bags on the kitchen floor and huffed, she'd rather struggle with a load of bags instead of making two trips to the car. First thing was to put the kettle on she was desperate for a cup of tea it had been an extra long day and that jolly feeling that had filled her up when she had left work had faded into the background.

Something didn't feel right, she felt as if a dark cloud was looming above her head. Smelling herself where Frank had touched her caused her to feel nauseous. "He's my mystery client, I know it," she said as she poured hot water into her mug over the tea bag, her hands shaking at the thought of it being true.

She began listing the reasons as to why she had reached that conclusion, "He said he would see me soon," she said adding a spoonful of sugar to her tea, "His touch and his kiss felt very familiar," she continued adding a drop of milk, "And his cologne, it's him, I know it's him. He always did go all out, Mr extravagant and Claire knows him more than she's letting on, he was one of my first ever clients that I met at Martins party that she took me to." Another frightening thought crossed her mind, "Isn't it ironic that it was her I caught pleasing Mr Allen and Frank turns out to be his cousin and a close one at that."

At that point Nina realised that Claire wasn't as sincere as she had made out to be and she became paranoid at who to trust.

Leaving her shopping bags on the kitchen floor Nina took her tea into the living room. Instead of turning on the TV she sat by the lamp light in silence, sipping her tea and collecting her thoughts. Antoine's little face popped into her mind from the supermarket trip, his loving hugs and kisses, she heard his voice echo referring to Aaron as 'Daddy' and she cried silently inside. Jordan was right, she didn't deserve him after everything she had put him through when all he did was try to love her. The Antoine situation was before her so she couldn't be angry with him for that she had no excuse to hate him, it was all on her. She was lucky to still have Mark as part of her life, again another person she had cheated.

Fed up of thinking and beating herself up she began unpacking her shopping and putting her plan together for Saturday night when she was going to confront Frank and after that was finished and closed she would call Aaron and arrange a Sunday lunch and see if they could save what was left of them.

MARK.

Exhausted from helping his Mom with the gardening and moving the kitchen appliances for her to clean behind Mark sat in front of the TV with his dinner resting on his lap, indulging in his Mothers cooking, the best Chef ever. That night was all about spending it with his mom as Saturday he was out with Aaron, he had decided to tell him about his plans to go to Jamaica for a while.

CHAPTER 39

NINA.

Opting for a professional pamper as opposed to her usual home pamper, Nina left her Beautician's premises late Saturday afternoon feeling wonderful and refreshed and in tip top condition to carry out her plan. She was more nervous about this night than any other night she'd carried out her service but she needed to do this.

A visit to the supermarket on her way home was a must, she was in desperate need of a huge bar of chocolate to calm her nerves not to mention a couple of other things she forgot the day before because she was trying to hurry away from Frank.

Claire hadn't done her usual 'Good Luck' call or even text so Nina decided to call her. As she walked around the supermarket with her phone to her ear hunting for her items and waiting for Claire to pick up, she heard a phone ringing close by. Turning around to locate it, to her surprise there stood Mr Allen further down the aisle staring at his ringing phone. Nina scurried up to him to surprise him having not seen him a long time but she stopped dead in her tracks as Claire appeared from around the corner and stood by his side placing an item in his trolley. Their trolley.

"Your phone Honey," he said handing it over to her, "it's Nina."

Nina immediately ended the call, her mouth wide open in shock. Did Claire just appear and Mr Allen refer to her as 'Honey' as she put groceries in the trolley that he was pushing and took her phone out of his hands? Nina disappeared down the adjacent aisle and listened to their conversation.

"Oh she's hung up, I missed it, I'll ring her later, remind me to ring her when we get home," Claire babbled.

Nina tried to stifle her emotions at what she was hearing, 'We get home.' Did they live together?

"Ok, have we finished now, can we go home?" A tired and fed up Mr Allen huffed.

Nina peeked around the corner and watched as they behaved like a typical couple, she felt foolish, she felt like she'd been walking around in cuckoo land for the past how many months.

"Alright misery guts let's go and don't forget to remind me to call Nina back when we get home."

"How long does Frank think he'll get away with this?" Mr Allen raised his eyebrow as if Claire knew the answer. "Nina's not stupid, she'll figure it out soon and it won't be pretty, she can't stand the man," Mr Allen said in Nina's defence. "I don't understand why Frank doesn't just leave her alone and let her get on with her life-he's put her through enough already."

Claire rolled her eyes as she listened to him favour Nina but she couldn't care less it was business to her and Frank had paid her off for this favour. "Well she can't be that clever if she hasn't figured it out yet and I'm sorry honey but business is business."

As Nina listened she began to feel breathless and claustrophobic, she suddenly felt weak and dizzy like she was spinning around on the spot. Her whole world had suddenly collapsed around her and turned into a pile of trash at her feet. She wished she hadn't chosen to play the fly on the wall. Was she dreaming? Nothing mattered except getting the hell out of the supermarket and fast!

Nina drove straight home and struggled to enter her key into the keyhole for the sake of her trembling hands regretting the fact that she hadn't purchased the bar of chocolate. She eventually entered her home and leaned her back against the back of her front door and gave permission for her tears to journey down her cheeks.

"Claire's right, I am stupid," she scolded herself, "Of course it all makes sense now."

Laughing out loud at how naive she had been considering all the clues (or should she label it the truth) were laid out right before her very eyes for her to see but she had been walking around with her eyes wide shut.

Claire and Mr Allen were an item, a married couple, Husband and Wife and they kept their relationship 'alive' by either keeping it open and Mr Allen accepting Claire's line of work. This then explained why Mr Allen didn't convey an ounce of shock and was quite sympathetic towards her when her secret was exposed in the work place due to Frank and he's malicious, obsessive ways. Then there was Frank, Claire knew him all along, she probably knew that he was the one who wanted to scoop Nina up and have her to himself. He was Mr Allen's cousin and a very close cousin at that. She reflected back to the staff party at his restaurant. Nina had to admit to herself that she had been taken for a ride...Claire had been playing her.

Nina began selecting the correct attire for her 'mystery client' as she sang along to Eric Benet seeping through the speakers,

> 'Why you messing with my feelings,
> Why do you follow me...'

AARON.

"Right you two I have to get ready now, I'm meeting Mark in an hour," Aaron told the boys. "Antoine have you decided which DVD you are going to watch yet?"

"I can't find them," Antoine moaned throwing cushions across the room and trying to crawl underneath the sofa.

"Where did you leave them last night?" Alec butted in getting irritated as a cushion bounced off his head.

"I didn't get to watch one last night," Antoine admitted and carried on looking.

"Why?" Alec teased him knowing full well he fell asleep.

Antoine ignored him and crawled further beneath the sofa before shouting, "Because I fell asleep!"

Aaron stood in the doorway watching and listening and told Antoine where he had left them the night before, before the situation got out of hand.

As he showered Aaron's mind drifted to it's usual place, Nina, but the sound of his mobile phone ringing, Alec's mobile ringing and the house phone ringing disturbed his thoughts. "Alec!" He hollered, "Who is that?" He turned off the shower all flustered at the noise and wrapped his towel around his waist leaving the bathroom. He checked the living room to find Antoine slumped over a cushion on the sofa sucking his thumb whilst watching his Horrid Henry DVD.

Alec followed Aaron into his bedroom, "It's mom," he said, "She said she's left something of hers in Antoine's overnight bag by accident and she needs it for her job tonight. She's on her way now but not to tell Antoine, she'll sneak in and sneak out."

Aaron was tired of Tressa and her excuses in order to be his presence, When would she realise that he wasn't interested in her. He had heard everything that Alec had reiterated and quickened his pace in getting ready in hope of missing her.

"So where are you and Mark off to tonight?" Alec asked his Uncle.

"I'm not sure, he's organising it all," Aaron answered putting on his socks. "Alec these don't match I must have folded them together in the dark," he laughed, "Look in my drawer and see if you can find the other one to match this please," he handed Alec one of the socks.

While Alec rummaged through his uncles sock drawer, Aaron finished buttoning up his shirt when all of a sudden Antoine came bounding into the bedroom, "Nina's on my DVD!" He screamed jumping up and down, grabbing both Aaron's and Alec's hands and dragging them into the living room to look at the TV. "Look! Look!" He said pointing at the TV screen.

Aaron and Alec glared in awe at the TV screen, it took a brief moment for it to register what they were actually watching.

"Antoine go and look in your room and find another DVD please," Alec said trying to distract him from the adult goings on displayed on the TV. Antoine saw the look in his brothers eyes and watched as his Dad just stood still as a statue without uttering a word and knew that something was wrong so he just did as he was told.

Alec saw his sad little face and tried to reassure him that he hadn't done anything wrong, "It's ok little man, if you look in my bag you might find the entire Spiderman collection."

A massive smile spread across Antoine's face as he ran at full speed into his room.

"Set it up in there and I'll come and watch it with you shortly," Alec told him.

Aaron hadn't moved a muscle, what he was watching was playing out in extra slow motion right before his eyes.

Nina had entered a room, a hotel room it looked like. She was stripping down to barely nothing, string. She then placed an eye mask over her eyes.

Alec picked up the remote control to turn it off but Aaron grabbed his hand sternly, "NO!"

Alec could see the hurt and pain in his uncle's eyes, he felt the tight grip on his wrist and knew to do as he was told but he couldn't allow his uncle to torment himself by watching anymore. "But Uncle…" he began.

"Just go and entertain Antoine, I need to watch this."

Reluctantly Alec left the room walking backwards in hope of Aaron changing his mind.

"And shut the door!" Aaron sustained his attention to the TV screen scanning every fine detail rewinding it back and forth, back and forth. Tears dripped from his eyes and his heart pumped hard and fast, his emotions became a congealed mess, he felt humiliated, perplexed, tricked but most of all empty.

BUZZ! BUZZZZZ!

Aaron didn't even hear the buzzer go off, he didn't hear Alec shut Antoine's bedroom door and go and answer it letting Tressa in, he was even oblivious to Tressa standing next to him watching the TV screen to.

Alec had seen enough, enough of the DVD and enough of his Uncle punishing himself. He didn't need the remote. He walked over to the DVD player and directly turned it off removing the disc from the plate. Tressa snatched the disc from her Son's hand and turned to walk away but not before Aaron grabbed her by her arm and shoved her across the room.

"Ouch!" Tressa shrieked as she landed on the sofa.

"Uncle NO!" Alec shouted restraining him from attacking her, "What are you doing?" I don't understand any of this," he said, all confused, maintaining his restraint and staring at his Mom awaiting an explanation.

Tressa stood up and walked right up to Aarons face, "And I'm a disgrace?" She cackled in his face.

"GET OUT!" Aaron roared at her as he freed himself from Alec's grip and chased after her.

"Mom, what's going on? Alec asked yet again uncomfortable at seeing his usually calm and collective Uncle behaving like a monster.

"Just stay out of this Son," Tressa warned him at the front door ready to leave.

Aaron spun her around to face him, "Why?" he asked her staring her straight in the eyes.

Tressa stared back at him with his 'puppy dog' eyes, his caring, soft and gentle eyes. The same eyes that had welcomed her into his loving heart, a heart that had offered her security and safety. The same heart that had dusted her off and made a new sanctuary for Nina. She didn't want Nina to take her place, she didn't want to be forgotten. "I wanted you to see her for what she truly is. I didn't want you wasting any more of your precious time moping around after her, she's not worth it, she's making a fool out of you Aaron, can't you see that?"

After what he had just witnessed he knew Tressa was right but he also knew Tressa and she only did things to benefit her own selfish needs. "You did it on purpose didn't you?"

"Did what?" She asked playing ignorant.

"Where did you get that DVD?" Aaron asked wanting to get to the bottom of it.

"It doesn't matter," she replied nervously. Frank was expecting that DVD in his hands tonight and he was also expecting her shortly to set up for the recording of part two.

"You wanted me to see that DVD. You packed it into Antoine's bag deliberately in hope that afterwards I would collapse like a wounded deer into your comforting arms. Did it not ever occur to you that Antoine might have watched it? Has your parental guidance totally disappeared? Oh yeh, you never had any to begin with!"

SLAP!!! Tressa hit Aaron across the face, "I don't have to listen to this," she said opening the front door and leaving.

Alec looked at his Uncle, "I'm sorry Uncle."

"You have nothing to be sorry about," and with that (to Alec's disbelief) he put on his socks, shoes, jacket, sprayed on some cologne before grabbing his wallet and keys, bidding them goodnight and left for his night out with Mark as if nothing had ever happened.

CHAPTER 40

FRANK.

Frank plucked handfuls of rose petals from the bouquets he had purchased the day before when he had bumped into Nina. He scattered them over the king-sized bed and made a trail leading from the door to the bed in preparation for Nina's arrival.

A smile graced his face as he did so thinking about the times he had shared with her and after thinking he would never get the chance to re-unite, here she was once again a part of his life. He had her firmly in his clutch (so he thought) she was like putty in his hands. He knew that he wasn't the man she wanted to give her all to, she probably even hated him but that mental battle, that game they quietly and personally played was what he thrived off. He loved her to the core. Her angry face, the venom she spat at him, it was all part of what made her beautiful in his eyes.

He set the chair by the table with the lamp on it and placed the eye mask next to the lamp with a set of simple instructions on a small piece of paper for her to follow. His nature began to rise as he became excited at the prospect of it all, he could already imagine her standing before him rolling her back to rest against his chest as he savoured her.

Checking his watch he frowned. Tressa should have been there by now, not only to set up the cameras but to present him with the disc of last week's recordings to add to his shrine of Nina. Time was ticking away and he was getting impatient, like every encounter with Nina he wanted it to be perfect.

Just as he was about to dial Tressa's number there was a loud knock on the door. Frank looked through the peephole and saw that it was Tressa, "Speak of the devil," he sighed.

Tressa bustled her way into the room red faced and frustrated, "I'm sorry Frank," she apologised handing him the disc from last week's performance, the same disc she had rescued from Alec's grasp.

"What took you so long Tressa? You nearly messed up my plans," Frank barked snatching the disc from her, "Just hurry up setting up and make sure you include all angles in the bathroom to then disappear from my sight."

Tressa opened her mouth to say something but decided against it, she just wanted peace and quiet so with a forced smile she got on with what had been asked of her after all she was getting paid for it. She had a feeling that tonight would be Frank's last rendezvous with Nina, especially after today's events with Aaron. She could only assume from the devotion and attachment that Aaron embraced for her that he would be on the hunt for Nina to track her down for an explanation but she didn't have the heart to tell him, instead she left him in his happy bubble. He saw her to the door and handed her an envelope with some money in for carrying out her job.

He stood back and admired the setup, proud and excited. All that remained was to select some sexy music in order to set the scene and light the candles. Tonight was all about loving her and satisfying her in the warm, serene, calming atmosphere of the bathroom. Essential oiled bubbled bath, her slippery, soft, smooth skin…he yearned for her and if he couldn't have her any other way at least he could have her this way.

NINA.

Nina sat on the edge of her bed oiling her skin with her camomile baby oil, she sprayed her lingerie and her black dress with her Prada perfume then she sprayed some up into the air and stood underneath the mist letting it rain down on her skin.

She was confident that she could handle Frank so she didn't alert her personal security for that night.

As she applied her make-up she fought back the tears that were begging to fall so she didn't mess up her face or show any signs of weakness, not until it was over. She considered not attending but she couldn't deny the need to confront him once and for all and for her to leave her alone for good. She slicked her hair back into a perfect ponytail and finished off with her lipstick. She kissed the mirror and winked at herself, she grabbed her clutch with the essentials inside making sure her pepper spray was sitting on the top ready at hand. "No taxi tonight," she said, "When it's time to go, it's time to go."

JORDAN.

Jordan lay on her sofa wrapped up in her faithful blanket shedding her usual tears. One minute she was up, full of self motivation and the next minute she was down in the dumps missing her lost friends and soon to be ex-husband.

She sat contemplating whether to dress up and go out for a night on the town, maybe just a drink at a quiet bar, maybe a hotel bar.

Having blown her chances with Nina she thought that maybe it was time that she spoke to Mark in an approachable manner, all she wanted was for them to be civil to one another.

MARK.

"Aaron's outside in a taxi waiting for you," Mark's Mother reminded him yet again, "Don't keep him waiting."

Mark grabbed his keys and wallet and headed downstairs to where his mother stood at the bottom her arms akimbo. He kissed her on her cheek, "Shouldn't you be in bed?" He laughed opening the front door.

"You just have a good night and don't be cheeky."

Mark got into the taxi and greeted Aaron. "What's up man?" He asked noticing the distraught expression written all over his face.

"Where to?" The taxi driver interrupted them impatiently.

"Oh sorry," Mark said giving him the location but still staring at Aaron, waiting for a response.

"I'll tell you when I get a drink or two inside of me," Aaron muttered staring out of the window.

Mark tried to figure out what could possibly be wrong, there were no more secrets to tell as far he was aware. Everyone had cleared out their closet and reaped the consequences.

Fifteen minutes later after what seemed like a long silent drive, they pulled up at the hotel Mark had picked to make good use of the bar and for Mark to hopefully spot Nina and get to the bottom of what she was up to.

"This is a bit lush," Aaron complimented the hotel premises as they headed straight to the bar.

"You grab those seats over there," Mark purposely pointed out. They were the exact same seats he had sat in the weekend before and had the perfect view of the surroundings, including Nina. "I'll bring over the drinks and yes I'll make yours a double," he assured him.

Aaron walked over to the empty seats avoiding other people coming and going and as he went to sit down he smelt a familiar smell kiss his nostrils as a lady hurriedly manoeuvred past him. As he turned around all he managed to get was a glimpse of a sexy woman in a fitted black coat and a pair of red soled heels. As quick as he went to smile he stopped and turned back to face his table.

Mark tried sipping his drink and sitting at same time but he failed as his drink slid down the wrong pipe causing him to choke as he spotted Nina waiting for the lift. He needed to know what she was up to.

Aaron stood up and began patting Marks back, "Are you ok?"

Mark couldn't speak, he squeezed his eyes tight gasping for breath and when he opened them Nina had disappeared.

CHAPTER 41

NINA.

Nina had grown accustomed to the routine after just one visit and carried out what was expected of her. Nothing mattered as she sauntered across the hotel lobby to the main reception and gave the necessary details so she could be granted her room number and key card. She felt a sea of eyes washing over her but she didn't care, she knew what she had come to do. Taking her key card she made a quick trip to the hotel bar and bought a whisky shot which she downed in one. Lost in her thoughts, floating around in her own world, she walked over to the lifts and pressed the call button. She heard a small commotion happening behind her but she didn't have time to be nosey because the lift had arrived. It sounded like someone was choking on their drink but she didn't care she had other things to deal with.

As the lift ascended Nina took her pocket mirror out of her clutch and re-applied some more of her lipstick, she put her game face on, stepped out of the lift and marched down the corridor to her destination.

Nina was supposed to knock on the door twice and when told to enter she was to use her key card to unlock the door and then as before make her way to the lamp light on the table.

AARON.

Mark had calmed down and returned back to his normal state. Aaron had followed Marks eyes to the lift area and again saw the back of the woman in the fitted black coat and the sexy heels.

"What is it Mark?" Aaron couldn't help but ask due to Marks suspicious behaviour. "What's going on Mark? Who is she?"

Aaron remembered the smell and how it reminded him of Nina. He began having flashbacks to the DVD he had watched earlier on, over and over until Alec had switched it off and put him out of his misery. "That was…"

MARK.

"…Nina, yes Aaron that's Nina and we have to find out what she's doing here," Mark panicked standing up and pushing his chair back rearing to go. "I need you to come with me."

Aaron's face dropped and he gulped down what was left of his drink. He stood up so he was level with Mark, "I already know what she's doing here Mark and so do you. I don't want to know any more about her and what she chooses to do," he firmly stated grabbing his jacket preparing to leave, "I suggest you do the same and walk away, you're only hurting yourself."

Mark grabbed his arm, "Please Aaron, I have a bad feeling about this, I think this time she may be in danger."

Aaron saw the desperation in Mark's eyes and he knew that if he walked away and something did happen to Nina he wouldn't be able to forgive himself.

They made their way towards the lifts. "How do we know what floor or what room?" Aaron questioned Mark.

"I saw that the lift was empty when Nina stepped into it and it didn't stop until it reached the eleventh floor."

Aaron was impressed at Marks vigilance. "Ok but how do we know which room?"

Mark was stumped, "We'll just have to listen at each door I suppose," was all he could suggest.

They stepped into the lift, "I can smell her," Aaron said inhaling Nina's lingering scent. His heart began to race because deep down he knew he wouldn't be able to cope with what he was about to see before him.

NINA.

Nina slowly and steadily entered the hotel room and pushed the door to pretending to lock it. Again she stood lost in darkness travelling to the dim lamp light. A sheet of paper lay on the table with written instructions. She began removing her clothes reading the list at the same time noticing that the instructions were different to her last visit. She was to remove every garment and remain in her string thong and place the eye mask over her eyes.

Her hands began to shake as she followed the demands. She placed all of her clothes underneath her coat so at least she could grab it to cover herself up on her escape.

This was it, she placed the mask over her eyes and stood swaying to the sweet sounds of Tyrese knowing this would be her theme tune for this chapter of her life for years to come.

"You're are so beautiful," she heard a voice whisper to her through the air, "So so beautiful," he whispered into her ear appearing out of nowhere, kissing on her neck and holding both of her hands together leading her blindly into the bathroom ready to feast upon her tantalising treats.

Nina stopped him from leading her to wherever he was taking her, she wanted to stay close to the lamp, "Kiss me," she whispered into the air, "I want to feel your lips on my skin, I've missed you," she teased and lied at the same time.

He spun her around to face him, her eyes still covered with the eye mask and blew gently on her lips before tracing the peripheral of her mouth with his tongue. Nina faked a seductive moan and then he kissed her and she allowed him to explore her mouth and play house with her tongue.

He became caught up in the moment especially when Nina freed her hands from his grip and wrapped her arms around his neck. He closed his eyes lapping up her caress as she stroked the back of his neck and took control kissing him hard gliding her hands down the top of his spine. She touched and rubbed his chest and felt him surrender to her, happy that she had gained control so easily. Then with one swift movement she slid the eye mask back over her forehead and let it drop down her ponytail, and land on the floor revealing her mystery client.

Enveloped in what he thought was her love he hadn't realised what Nina had done until she released herself from his arms, "I knew it was you, how could you?"

FRANK.

Frank couldn't believe that he had let himself lose control, he was supposed to have handcuffed her with his comfortable, soft cuffs but she had distracted him and now he knew why. He watched her sexy figure walk over to the lamp and reach for her coat and he tried to think quick, he couldn't let her leave because he didn't want her to leave, he didn't want it to end, especially not like this.

Without thinking he picked her up and threw her onto the bed, he crawled on top of her clasping her hands and pressing her arms flat above her head pressing his weight down on her so she couldn't move.

"FRANK NOOOOOO!" Nina screamed repeatedly fighting to free herself.

"Shut up and just cooperate, stop acting like a baby, you know I don't want to hurt you, all I want is to love you and I know you enjoy it otherwise you wouldn't be here. You can't deny me Nina, if you knew it was me why did you come back?"

"Get off," Nina said struggling to breath from the pressure of Franks bodyweight.

Frank ignored her cries and covered her mouth with his in order to muffle her screams.

AARON.

BAM!

Frank looked up in horror as the hotel room door flew open and two male figures stood in the doorway. He automatically got up off Nina standing in just his boxer shorts and began frantically searching for something, anything to defend himself.

Mark and Aaron entered the room, Mark closed the door and flipped the light switch and before their eyes Nina lay on the bed in just her thong shaking and trembling with fear and embarrassment .

Aaron refused to look at Nina and instead focused his attention on the muscular built character that stood in the corner of the room alert and ready for a fight. He recognised him from the supermarket, the man who had amazed Antoine with all the roses. He scanned the room and saw Nina's clothes strewn across the chair and her red bottom heels sitting neatly underneath it. He observed the petals scattered everywhere and squinted as he spied a few cameras dotted around. He strode around the room switching them off angrily, still refusing to look at Nina who was now receiving attention off Mark. Mark helped her into her coat and began collecting her other clothing items and placed her heels at her feet.

"Are you able to walk?" He asked her worried but grateful he had followed his instinct.

Frank still lurked in the corner in a braced stance ready for attack but it never came. After switching off the last camera and staring at Nina sitting on the edge of the bed with Mark about to help her up he felt sick and stormed out of the room.

"Hey!" Mark called after him.

"I can't do this!" Was all Mark heard as Aaron disappeared out of the room.

The sight of Nina laying there exposed made him feel sick to his stomach. He remembered when she belonged to him - well he thought she did - and then to see her displayed for everyone to have a piece of hit home, she didn't respect herself so why did he care so much for her. He thought about the cameras and what Tressa had said about Nina being a disgrace echoed through his mind causing him to ache some more.

He gathered himself together as best as he could and made his way to the hotel bar for one last drink before he went home. He was finished with Nina for good this time he couldn't cope with her a minute more. How could he love someone who broke him into a million pieces? He was happy for Mark to be her guardian, at least she had someone.

MARK.

"Stay there!" Mark commanded Frank as he finished tending to a terrified Nina. "I'll call the Police," Mark said digging in his pocket for his phone.

"No! Please no!" Nina begged because I chose to come here, I knew what I was letting myself in for."

Mark looked at her with pure dismay, "Why?"

"Because I had to know it was him for sure, he's been playing with my life since we first met and he made something so simple so complicated. I had put an end to it."

Mark didn't understand and was confused to how it would have ended if he hadn't turned up with Aaron.

Nina stood up clinging tightly on to Mark. He'd finally finished buttoning up her coat because she had nothing on underneath and they left the room leaving Frank in the corner.

"I'm sorry Mark," she whimpered.

"It's ok," he squeezed her shoulder letting her know it was over and she was now safe.

"It's not ok though," she cried, tears cascading down her cheeks, "where's Aaron?"

Mark didn't get how she could ask for him when he had bailed on them, "I think it's time you forgot about Aaron and I also think it's time you packed this rubbish in, you could have been killed," he cussed after her, "Promise me you will pack this in Nina, promise me."

Nina hid her face out of shame in Marks jacket and he felt her nod her head. That was enough for him. "It's going to be alright," he said kissing the top of her head as they walked out of the hotel to the car park where Nina's car was parked.

CHAPTER 42

Mark provided support to Nina as they made their way to Nina's car. Unbeknownst to them they had just missed Jordan entering the hotel lobby and aiming in the direction of the bar. She had decided to put on her glad rags after much deliberation with herself and become lost in whatever the night had to offer.

Jordan took a seat at the bar and caught the attention of the bartender who promptly made his way over to her to take her order. As she waited she spun around on her bar stool absorbing her surroundings, fine gentlemen in suits sat in small groups on comfy chairs, groups of classy women did the same and mature couples indulged in night caps. Then there was a loner sitting a couple of bar stools away from her drowning his sorrows in consecutive vodka shots.

Picking up her drink she clambered down off her stool and made her way towards him and lightly tapped his shoulder. He turned to face her and his hazel eyes cause her to smile softly as she climbed up on to the stool beside him. "Aaron what are you doing here?"

Aaron stared right past her into space.

"Aaron?" She made a second attempt at captivating his attention.

His eyes locked on hers and he began to laugh, "Jordan what are you doing here? Don't tell me, you're an escort to?"

Jordan had never encountered this kind of behaviour from Aaron before and began to feel a little uncomfortable, "No Aaron I'm not, what are you talking about?"

"I caught her," Aaron started to explain, "and…" He stopped himself mid-sentence. He downed one last shot of Vodka and wobbled to his feet and staggered towards the exit.

"Wait!" Jordan got up and went after him propping him up as best as she could, "Come on let me take you home," she offered leading him to her car and making sure he was in safely.

Jordan wasn't expecting this, she thought tonight would be about meeting new faces, maybe a tall, dark, handsome stranger who would sweep her off her feet and show her a good time.

Aaron muttered and mumbled drunken nonsense some of which Jordan managed to decipher, "Mark...cameras...Nina and Frank," then he rubbed his head and poured out his heart and soul about his undying love for Nina. "What did I do wrong?" He turned to face Jordan who was concentrating on the road.

Jordan safely pulled over to calm him down, he was in a terrible state and she was finding it difficult to get his address out of him. She went into her purse and dialled Alec's number.

"Hello," he answered straightaway.

"Alec, it's me Jordan, I'm with your Uncle and he's drunk, could you tell me his address so I can make sure he gets home safely?"

"Sure," Alec gave her the address and a couple of simple directions, "It's not hard to find."

"Thanks Alec.." Jordan was just about to hang up when she heard Alec say something more.

"Jordan...where's Mark?" He asked knowing it might be a touchy subject.

"I don't know, why do you ask?" She said confused.

"Because I'm babysitting Antoine for my Uncle so he could have a night out with Mark."

"Ok," Jordan listened.

"But he erm..."

"Go on," Jordan encouraged him.

"He left the flat in a bad mood so now I'm worried."

"Why? What happened?"

"I can't say Jordan, I'm sorry I shouldn't have even mentioned anything, please, just bring him home, I'll be here waiting," and with that Alec hung up the phone.

Jordan tapped her fingers on the steering wheel and looked at Aaron staring out of the car window at the night sky like a child. "Aaron?" She poked him, "Where's Mark?"

Aaron continued staring at the sky and without moving he replied, "With Nina, they left together."

Luckily Mark hadn't even began drinking before all hell had broke lose therefore he was fit enough to drive a fragile Nina home. He made sure she was seated comfortably in her car and was just about to start the engine when Nina touched his arm, "Mark I don't want to go home."

Mark saw the sadness present in her big, brown eyes and he couldn't fathom how she had reached this place in life. As he stared at her he remembered the bright, chirpy Nina, the Nina always laced in the latest fashions, Miss Independent, clever, intelligent and smart. Every man's dream, quirky, stunning and a hard worker. Why did she escort? How did it all begin? He couldn't turn his back on her she was family and he knew her well. He knew that tonight she didn't want to be alone with herself just like when they were kids and her Aunt had to work nights and her Brother went out with his mates. "It's ok you can stop at Moms, I'll set up the spare room for you, I'll even put your favourite blanket out for you just like old times," he smiled to try and cheer her up.

Nina did smile as they drove off taking comfort in the fact that whatever happened, Mark never judged her.

Jordan had taken a detour to Mark's Mothers house furious that after everything Nina and him were rubbing their relationship in everyone's face, even Aaron's.

Aaron still remained in another world, still staring out the window at the night sky as Jordan drove the desolate roads like a maniac, skimming across roundabouts and high flying amber lights.

As she pulled up outside Irene's house she saw Nina's Mini pull up at the same time. She turned off her headlights and the engine and sat still with Aaron and watched as Mark got out of the drivers seat and went around to the passenger side to help Nina out.

Jordan's heart ached. She hadn't laid her eyes on him since the night she bullied him and threw him out and now, here she was witnessing him doting over who was once her best friend, in her opinion the woman he had always truly loved.

Jordan watched as they giggled. She watched as Mark kissed Nina's forehead. She watched as Mark dug into his trouser pockets searching for his house key. She watched Nina trip up a stone on the garden path and fall over. She watched as Mark bent down to scoop her up into his arms and carry her to the door. She watched until she couldn't watch anymore and neither could Aaron who had quit pretending to be admiring the night sky a while ago.

Jordan darted out of the car in a wild rage. Aaron put his arm out to grab her, to tell her to forget it but she escaped his grasp so he jumped out the car to chase after her.

She ran at high speed towards Mark carrying Nina and pushed them over so they landed on the grass and started slapping them with no remorse.

Aaron had eventually caught up with Jordan, alcohol still partying in his system. He grabbed Jordan around her middle as she kicked and screamed and fought against his grip digging her nails into his hands until he couldn't tolerate anymore and he let her go.

Jordan freed herself and flew at Nina but Mark automatically rolled over to shield her.

Too much was occurring in front of Nina's eyes, it was all too much to bear. One minute they were walking up the path into the house and the next minute a crazy, wild Jordan was flying out of nowhere ready to attack with Aaron swaying in the background. Her pulse began to race and she tried to press herself into the ground in hope of it swallowing her up some time soon. She screamed but no sound came out, she tried to move but she felt paralysed. All she saw was Jordan's hand coming towards her face, "NOOOOO!"

"It's ok."

Nina heard voices as she opened her eyes to see Jordan, Mark and Aaron kneeling beside her. Jordan was gently stroking her face, "It's ok," she reassured her, "You passed out, I thought you were looking a bit peaky."

Nina tried to speak but found it difficult, she was confused. One minute she was present in a deep, dark world of hate and anger and now she was awake in a bright comforting embrace of the faces that meant everything to her.

Eventually they sat her up and Mark helped her take a few small sips from a bottle of water he had taken from his car. "The poor guy only asked you to marry him," Mark chuckled making light of the situation.

"Let's give them some space," Jordan ushered Mark away from Nina and Aaron to the car.

Aaron sat next to Nina on the ground and cradled her in his arms. "Do you know what happened?"

Nina shook her head embarrassed.

"You and Jordan were ready to leave for the airport to start a new life in America and I had to catch you before you left because I want to marry you. I want you to be my wife," he kissed her cheek. "I asked you and you passed out on me," he laughed. "I would say think about it but you have a flight to catch and you're already behind schedule."

Nina stared into his beautiful eyes as he explained to her in such a calm manner.

"I don't want to pressure you and if passing out is an indication of that then I'll let you go, but just so you know, I wasn't going to let you slip away without trying. I love you Nina."

Nina sat herself up feeling stronger and observed Mark and Jordan leaning against the car chatting and laughing. She felt uneasy, the thoughts, dreams or whatever it was she had just experienced was still very vivid, very vivid indeed. It all seemed and felt so real, tangible and troublesome. She stared into Aaron's welcoming eyes, "I'm sorry Aaron but I can't. I don't want to be the one responsible for hurting you." With that she kissed his lips one last time and stood up slowly and steadily.

Aaron helped her and hugged her tightly, "'Bye," he whispered in her ear before kissing her once more.

Mark and Jordan halted their conversation as they saw Aaron return to his car, he gave them a wave and drove off.

Jordan helped Nina into the backseat of the car with her.

"We better go and get some food pronto in order for you to be fit for your journey," Mark told them as he started the car.

Nina rested her head on Jordan's shoulder.

"It's going to be fine," Jordan rubbed her head confused as to why Nina had refused Aaron's proposal but secretly grateful because she was desperate to leave.

"Atlanta here we come!" The girls shouted from the back of the car as Mark drove on forcing back tears.

Lightning Source UK Ltd.
Milton Keynes UK
UKOW04f2309250315

248550UK00001B/197/P